MEET THE BIZARRE INHABITANTS OF THE FUTURE:

TARAWASSIE — Born of the crystal ship humans, raised on drugged dreams of oblivion, she escaped her narcotic existence to descend to the real world below, where she learned of her people's horrifying history, of the alien race that had usurped the planet, and of a strange cult of death.

MOON SHADOW — One of the primitive yet vital alien race, he became Tarawassie's guide through the real world, teaching her of the forgotten past and of the meaning of life and death.

MEGAN — In her youth, she had been chosen for an experiment that left her half human, half machine—a bionic woman created for space travel. But the project was deemed too expensive and when it was abandoned, Megan found herself a freak among her own people.

GRYF — Part of a new breed of tetraparentals (people with four biological parents, chosen to produce offspring of superior intelligence and ability), his life had been fully planned by the government. It was inconceivable that, after all the training and preparation, he would refuse duty. When he did, he was sent for punishment to Redsun's strictest prison.

Books by Robert Silverberg

The Best of Robert Silverberg
The Crystal Ship

Published by POCKET BOOKS

THE
CRYSTAL
SHIP

*Three Original Novellas
of Science Fiction*

---

by Vonda N. McIntyre

Marta Randall

Joan D. Vinge

*Edited and with an Introduction
by Robert Silverberg*

A KANGAROO BOOK
PUBLISHED BY POCKET BOOKS NEW YORK

THE CRYSTAL SHIP:
THREE ORIGINAL NOVELLAS OF SCIENCE FICTION

Thomas Nelson edition published 1976
POCKET BOOK edition published October, 1977

No character in this book is intended to represent any actual person; all
the incidents of the stories are entirely fictional in nature.

POCKET BOOK editions are published by
POCKET BOOKS,
a Simon & Schuster Division of
GULF & WESTERN CORPORATION
1230 Avenue of the Americas,
New York, N.Y. 10020.
Trademarks registered in the United States
and other countries.

ISBN: 0-671-81069-3.
Library of Congress Catalog Card Number: 76-26902.
This POCKET BOOK edition is published by arrangement with Thomas
Nelson, Inc. *The Crystal Ship* copyright, ©, 1976, by Joan D. Vinge.
Megan's World copyright, ©, 1976, by Marta Randall. *Screwtop* copy-
right, ©, 1976, by Vonda N. McIntyre. Introduction copyright, ©, 1976,
by Thomas Nelson, Inc., Publishers. All rights reserved. This book, or
portions thereof, may not be reproduced by any means without permission
of the original publisher: Thomas Nelson, Inc., 407 Seventh Avenue, S.
Nashville, Tennessee 37203.

Printed in the U.S.A.

ACKNOWLEDGMENT

The poem on p. 52, "Night Journey to the Spherical Man," is by
Russell Grattan; copyright, ©, 1969, The Vorpal Galleries, San Francisco.
Reprinted by permission of the author.

CONTENTS

Introduction

MOST SCIENCE FICTION has been written by men; most of
the science-fiction readership has been male. These are not
meant as inflammatory statements. The first can be confirmed by a quick examination of any bibliographical work
on science fiction or by a visit to the nearest bookstore.
The second has been amply demonstrated by question-
naires and other statistical sampling techniques. *Why*
science fiction should for so long have been a largely male
province is a fascinating problem for sociologists, but that
it has been is not a matter for debate.

However, there has always been a small but significant
female presence within the science-fiction world. One of
the earliest of science-fiction novels, *Frankenstein*, was
the work of a woman, Mary Shelley. In modern American
science fiction, C. L. Moore—*Catherine* Moore—was a
preeminent figure in the 1930s and 1940s; another woman,
Leigh Brackett, was a popular author of exhilarating space
adventures in the 1940s and 1950s; such women as Judith
Merril, Wilmar Shiras, Katherine MacLean, and Margaret
St. Clair made distinguished contributions to science fiction in the same period, and Andre Norton, who is actually *Alice Mary* Norton, won a wide following with her
long list of books for younger readers. Nevertheless,
though the work of these and other women writers was respected and admired within the science-fiction community,
they remained a minority in the territory dominated by
Messrs. Heinlein, Asimov, Bradbury, and Clarke.

More recently the statistical distributions have been
changing in science fiction. Not only are women for the
first time a significant proportion of the reading audience,

as can be seen by the attendance at any science-fiction convention, but the numbers and relative influence of female writers has increased radically. Ursula K. Le Guin, a writer who first emerged in the 1960s, is at present perhaps the most discussed and honored figure in science fiction, revered and besieged by readers as no woman ever has been in the past. Kate Wilhelm, Katherine MacLean, Joanna Russ, Anne McCaffrey, and Vonda McIntyre have, like Ms. Le Guin, been awarded Hugo or Nebula trophies; as recently as 1968, no woman had ever won either of science fiction's premier awards. And hosts of other, newer female writers keep appearing: Josephine Saxton, Suzy McKee Charnas, Lisa Tuttle, Katherine Kurtz, Grania Davis, Doris Piserchia, Pamela Sargent, and dozens more.

Which is all to the good. Men and women are different not merely in physical appearance; they receive different cultural training from earliest childhood, and their ways of interpreting experience, of reacting to human situations, of perceiving the universe, often differ in ways growing directly out of those differences in upbringing. If science fiction were written almost entirely by men, as it once was, we would lose the benefit of those differences in perspective; and a literature that bases its appeal on its infinite scope can hardly restrict itself to a view of the universe as seen only through the eyes of one segment of the human race. Diversity is vital, and diversity is what the influx of women writers has brought. Of course, it is important also that these writers be *good* writers. Unique perceptions and responses to experience are of little value if the literary talent is not there to express them. But there, I think, we have been lucky. Most of the women who have entered science fiction have been extraordinarily gifted. I don't think the percentage of literary talent is any higher, overall, in the female population than in the male; but perhaps in science fiction, so long a male-dominated preserve, so far the only women who succeeded in breaking in at all are those of superior attainment, the others having been discouraged at the outset by what has, until recently, seemed to be an almost impassable barrier.

At any rate, science fiction is no longer so exclusively unisexual, for which let us rejoice. Let us rejoice, particularly, in this collection of three long stories, never before published, by three of the most promising of the newer female science-fiction writers. These are not doctrinaire feminist stories, nor are they particularly concerned with what used to be thought of as the traditionally "female" themes of fiction—love, marriage, children. They are simply stories of people set on far planets in the remote future, stories written by human beings who bring to their work that special perception that is the inevitable consequence of having been raised as women in our society. To be female is, I think, neither better nor worse than to be male; but it is *different*, it is beyond doubt *different*, and the difference has value for us all.

—ROBERT SILVERBERG

THE CRYSTAL SHIP

Joan D. Vinge

Joan Vinge, like her two companions in this volume, is a young West Coast writer who made her professional debut in the 1970's—in her case, 1974, with a noteworthy novella called Tin Soldier. She is part Erie Indian, has a background in anthropology and archaeology, and lives in San Diego; her husband, Vernor Vinge, is also a writer, whose science-fiction stories have been appearing for the past four or five years. The story she offers here is in some senses almost a sequel to the Marta Randall novella which follows this story. It examines the impact of human being and alien on one another, not at the point of first contact but long afterward, when the damage has been done and the final reckoning is at hand.

THE CRYSTAL SHIP fell endlessly through orbit, tethered above the pinwheel-clouded world. Within its walls, among the many rooms, the dreamers sought oblivion in beauty. There were barely fifty of them now, none who remembered why their ancestors had come here, or even cared. But still they came, after five hundred years, as though it were a ritual.

Within the high-ceilinged torus hall, the dreamers gazed out over the bright crescent of their world or lay entranced in the liquid folds of lounge or chair. Ruby chitta syrup congealed along the clear rims of fallen cups, like dribbles of blood.

Chitta reddened Tarawassie's lips, while the stars danced on her fingertips, and she cast aside the false barriers of being and perception to become one with the limitless universe, formless, timeless, mindless. . . . Tarawassie dreamed, as she had always dreamed—as she always would have, if not for Andar's madness:

Colors fading from the sunset sky, petals crumbling to pastel, fragrance lost to all but memory. Soft barriers enclosed her; bonds of flesh, bars of bone, settled around her as Tarawassie fell back again, with sorrow, into the holding state.

"It is true! It's true—!" Sudden sound battered her, bursting inside her head in murky incandescence.

Her hands rose, not knowing what to cover; ears, eyes—A pale, burning face swelled into her sight, she was dragged up, shaking, shaken, through a tunnel of reverberating sound, "Look at youyouyou . . . you don't care . . .

animals; rotting, rotting . . . !" She cried out feebly, coming alive to struggle as the pain released her and thrust her back into the undulating couch.

The face, moving away from her, took on reality and form; she recognized Andar, his bright robe billowing like wind through a field of grasses as he shouted: "I know the truth! But *you* can't *see* it!" His hands caught, accosted, rejected others as he stumbled through the rooms. Instinctively she rose and followed his progress through the transparent halls; watched him fall over other inert forms as he made his way to the thing at the heart of all beauty—to the Star Well. "I love you, I hate you—" He was laughing, or sobbing. "Your living death! I'm the only one—the only one *alive*—and I can't stand you any more." He had reached the rim of the Well, knelt down, hanging over the cool, pulsing depths. "I know your secret"—to his own shadow-face—"and I'm ready, I'm ready . . . to pass the dragon, and enter the dark abyss. Accept me! There is a heaven, and it is death. . . ." Sobbing now, clearly, he toppled forward into the Well, embracing its shadowy ambiguity. Ripples of phosphorescence spread in the unwater, vibrant with aquamarine; he lay still. Tarawassie stared, struggling with reality.

And he lay still; he lay so still. The others who had seen and could comprehend came to gather around her, moving slowly, silently, wonderingly up through the rooms to stand at last at the Well's rim.

Andar's body lay below them, not quite drifting, not quite supported, somehow suspended. Shadow waves of blue-green lapped him gently, shifting his patterned robe, his long, fair hair, cupping his curled fingers. Tarawassie knew that her own hand would find nothing, capture nothing and yet be cooled, reaching down through that blue-greenness. The mystery of it had never disturbed her, she had never thought to wonder why. The stars seemed very large, very near, as though they lay sleeping in the silken depths.

"Andar . . . Andar?" Someone reached out instead of her, caught a motionless hand, tugged. No response. She watched Sabowyn draw Andar's body to the rim, turn him softly, still suspended.

"What's wrong?"

"What did he do?"

Hushed voices murmured questions, Sabowyn shook his

head. "I don't know. I think—I think he—died." His hand touched Andar's lips. Andar's mouth curved, fixed forever in a smile of joyous release. His eyes were open; unblinking, he gazed up through the dome crystal at the stars, and beyond them, lost in wonder. Tarawassie looked away from his face, avoiding the surge of unwanted emotion that it stirred in her. She looked down at her own face, mirrored dimly in the Well's illusive surface: eyes blue-green, melting into the unwater; black hair falling forward to merge with its phantom reflection.

"He *is* dead," Mirro said, laying her hand on his chest.

"How could he be dead? How could he die?"

"He said he wanted to die."

"He was insane."

"But how could he—?"

The voices wove a net of incredulity around her. Tarawassie leaned away from her image. "The Well . . . the Star Well. It granted his wish."

"Is it a Wishing Well?" Someone laughed, tentatively, behind her. "Is that what it is?"

"Poor Andar. He was crazy . . . he was always crazy. He wasn't happy."

"He must be happy now." Sabowyn stretched, gesturing. "Look. Look—his face seems so peaceful." He sighed, pushing his own hair away from his face, and sat back.

"But it never does anything to us. The Well, I mean."

"I don't know." Sabowyn shook his head. "It doesn't matter. Poor Andar, he's happy now. It doesn't matter, now."

"What'll we do with the body?"

"Send it down to the city. Somebody'll take care of it."

"Poor Andar."

"Poor Andar . . . poor Andar . . ." Their voices gave a benediction. "But he's happy, now."

Tarawassie shut her eyes, still crouching, her head moving from side to side as they pulled him up and bore him away. *Is he?*

"Tarawassie." Mirro's hands fell lightly on her shoulders. "I'm going to dream, now. Will you weave at the Loom?"

Tarawassie stood, aware of a painful stiffness in her joints. She shook her head; consciously, this time. "No. I can't. I have to go down to the city now."

"Why?"

"My mother is sick." She time. No one seemed to ren prised, or angry. "I have to se

"Oh." Mirro turned away, spiraling ramp. "I'll find someoɪ

Tarawassie followed the bear to the lowest level of the Crystal her formless shoes moved silently faces. She came to where they sɪ for the arrival of the ferry-raft. Sh ing down through the transparency, the appalling void below her feet world was a mottled bird's egg, blue and rust clouded with white, the colors half hidden now by night's eclipse. She could encompass it in the circle of her arms—she spent a moment lost in the sensations of the possibility.

"It's coming," someone said. She shifted her gaze, saw the brittle glance of sunlight from the far-tinier ovum of the closing ferry. She watched it rising to meet them, felt the faint tremor pass into her as its droplet-form was absorbed into the greater continuity of the Ship itself, into the docking slip.

A soft chime sounded; she turned with the rest as a lock opened in the wall behind them, pulsing green. She waited as they settled Andar into a seat in the ferry's close cabin, fastened straps across him. She moved forward finally, as they finished, to step inside.

"Are you going too?" Sabowyn asked.

She glanced back through the short passageway from the cabin, sat down in another seat, fixed her own restraining straps. "Yes. My mother is sick. I have to see my mother."

"Oh. Well, when you get there—you know—if you see anyone, tell him to take care of him?" Sabowyn looked down, his dark hair half obscuring his face.

"All right." She nodded.

Sabowyn brushed the silver plate set in the wall, and when the airlock had closed between them, the ferry became a separate entity, complete in itself, once more. Like a drop of rain it fell free from the tube of the docking slip, away from the Ship, beginning the long fall to earth. Tarawassie rose against the web of straps, her weight falling away too as they left the Ship behind. She looked up, pressing her head against the grayed, padded seat

rystal Ship retreat, become a whole
any-faceted berry seeded with light.

er eyes, drained by her chitta dream, feeling
Ship grow insignificant now above, as the
grew wide and important below her. She tried to
centrate on her duty there, while her mind struggled to
escape from the unaccustomed burden of reality, and
grief. Her mother was dying, and there was nothing that
she could do. Only see to her needs, try to ease a suffering
for which there was no comfort anyone could give—and
then flee, back up to the Crystal Ship, back into the dream
world where all griefs were forgotten.

She opened her eyes, blinking at the sudden unutterable
vastness of the world's blue misted rim, crowding the sky
now before them. A heaviness that was more than the
gradual return of weight settled her once more against the
seat; humming vibration transmitted to her skin, a mockery of anticipation. She turned her head slightly: Beside
her Andar gaped, unseeing, at the vision of a world in
majesty—transcending it, and all worlds. He smiled
fixedly, serenely.

"Andar." Awareness was stirring in her now; she turned
in her seat to stare at him. "Oh ..." She rubbed at her
face in sudden confusion; felt her hair, the golden circlet
that kept it back from her eyes, felt her fingers ... and his
own hanging hand, coldly translucent, like marble, as she
reached out. She did not know him well; she did not know
anyone well, any more than any of them knew her. But
she knew them all, the handful of people of the city and
the Crystal Ship, and loved them all as a family, for their
gentle ways and shared dreams. But Andar had never been
at peace, and his dreams had as often been weeping night-
mares as things of beauty.

Andar's placid gaze looked through her at the sky below. "You are happy, now." It was not a question, because
it had already been answered. "But why—?" knowing
that she would never have that answer, wondering if perhaps the answer was only in having an end to all questions.

But the Star Well ... She remembered her own voice:
"It granted his wish." It had never done anything to anyone, for anyone, in all the time that she had known of it.
And yet he had gone to it in his madness, tired of living,
tired of his pain. He had asked it to accept him, to give

him death—and it had answered him, she was certain. She was certain. He had died painlessly, joyfully, and he would suffer no more . . . no more. . . .

The clouds swept up to meet them, taking form; enfolded them and parted once more, showing her the concentricities of the city. The vibration grew against her as the city grew below, and at last they dropped through the slotted dome of the ferry shed to bump in semidarkness. The hatch slid open in the ferry's windowing side. She unstrapped and slipped out into the echoing gloom of the shed. It was empty, as usual; there was no one to tell about Andar's body. Other ferries, large and small, sat patiently in line, their transparency marred by films of dust. She did not notice the dust; she had never seen any of them in use.

Tight autumn gusts whipped the gaudy swirls of her robe, as she moved through the long shadows of the deserted streets to her mother's apartment. She walked quickly, slowly, quickly again, oblivious to the chill wind that plucked her shivering flesh. She would tell her mother about Andar . . . No, no, how could she? She watched image ripples glide along the darkly mirroring building walls, stumbled on the tree-levered, uneven pavement hidden by brown wind eddies of spade-shaped leaves. She reached the corner of her mother's street, skirted a small pile of rubble. Her steps slowed once more. The wind pushed at her back, insistent, until she stumbled into the dark building hallway and began to climb the stairs. Her mother had refused to move to a lower floor, or to a building where the others stayed now. Illness and age had made her stubborn; she had clung to the patterns of long familiarity, against the uncertain shape of the future. Now, she could no longer leave her bed. Old, doddering Zepher looked in on her occasionally when Tarawassie was gone. He was too old to bother with the journey up to the Crystal Ship, and he was the only other inhabitant, now, in all the six levels of the abandoned building.

"Tarawassie—is that you?" Her mother's voice came to her faintly; her mother had little to do now except lie and listen.

"Yes, Mother." Tarawassie followed the dark polished path her steps had worn through the dust to her mother's door, and went inside.

The air was always close and unpleasant here, even to

her own dim sense of smell. Her mother had complained about it; but she could not make the windows open. "Mother, how are you?" She took one long breath and held it, against the constriction in her chest.

"Happy, now. Happy to see my daughter." There was no reproach in her mother's voice; but a strange sorrow lay in her faded eyes as they touched on Tarawassie, and beneath it, understanding for the helpless anguish that kept her daughter away from her.

Tarawassie moved across the bare expanse of floor to the bedside; kneeling, she pressed her mother's burning hand to her cheek, feeling the roughness of the loose skin, feeling her mother smile. "Oh, Mother . . ." When tears would have started, to wet the fragile hand within her own, she pushed herself up and hid them in a fury of pillow settling. Her mother sighed, a thin, rasping sound, as Tarawassie smoothed her dust-gray hair.

"I'll heat some dinner." Tarawassie forced optimism into the words as she went to the cooler, pulled out the one half-filled dish of arbat stew she found inside. She frowned in fleeting concern. Tomorrow she must remember to go to the offering place for more food; she must— she *must* remember, this time.

She set the bowl in the small tabletop heater; the hood snapped shut, she saw the light go on. Light . . . She realized the room was growing dark, moved to rub a light globe, filling the space with soft silver, soft grays, that clothed the sharp nakedness of the room.

Tarawassie fed her mother one spoonful of heated stew, saw her choke convulsively, shaking her head. "No . . . no more, Tara. I can't eat." She lay unresisting as Tarawassie wiped off her face; tears spilled down into the hollows of her cheeks. She had eaten nothing for two days.

"Mother, let me bring you some chitta so that—so that—you can dream, again." Her voice trembled; she looked down. "Please try."

"No." Her mother turned away as if it were suddenly painful to look at her, gazing out the window at the twilight city. "It burns, inside me—it hurts too much. I'm past dreaming." Tears glittered as a tremor shook her, crystals in the globe light.

"Mother . . ." Tarawassie felt the words force their way out past the barrier of her denial, drawn to a greater need. "Mother, a strange thing happened today. Andar died.

He—he went to the Star Well, and he asked for death. And he died. There was no pain. He smiled. . . ."

Her mother's eyes moved back to her face, searching, demanding, "How did it happen?"

"I don't know. But I—but he looked so peaceful. When he'd never been at peace." She buried her face in her hands. "He said, 'There is a heaven, and it is—death.' "

Her mother touched her arm, trembling with the effort. "Yes, Tara. I would like to go to the Ship, and try. I'm so tired . . . so tired."

Tarawassie left the room, searched out old Zepher. With his help she carried her mother's wasted form, bundled in blankets, back through the darkening streets to the ferry shed. She saw, thankfully, that someone had found Andar's body and taken it away. She settled her mother across three seats, making her as comfortable as she could; her mother lay very quietly, the muscles twitching in her face. Tarawassie tapped a signal, and the ferry sealed and rose, drawn up on a cord of silent vibration, retracing her journey from the Crystal Ship. Her mother did not speak to her, gazing outward as Andar had, at something beyond vision.

Sabowyn, at her asking, carried her mother up through the rooms of the Crystal Ship to the lip of the waiting Well. Tarawassie followed him, their progress woven into the strands of stimulation that Mirro coaxed from the Loom. The Loom's catch-spell of light/music clogged her senses; she struggled to clear her mind of the fragments of past dreams that called her away from reality. She clung to the sight of her mother's pallid face, given lurid life by the warp of unreal colors. A spark of strange emotion broke from within to fill her mother's eyes as she looked down for the last time over the crescent world. Dimly Tarawassie became aware that others were being drawn to them, out of their own dreams, following them up through the flaming pavane of a funeral procession.

Tarawassie stood once more at the Star Well's rim, gazing down through phantom depths darkened at last by the endless depths of night, afraid to find her own reflection. Sabowyn knelt beside her, his own face expressionless, to settle her mother on the ledge.

Her mother stirred slightly, lifting her head. Tarawassie found her eyes, sank down to hold her close, crying suddenly, "Mama, I don't want you to go!" A weak hand reached to stroke the night blackness of her hair.

"I must ... I must, Tarawassie. Because you love me, you must help me. Tell me again, what did Andar say—"

"He said he was ready. He said, 'There is a heaven, and it is death.'"

"Yes," her mother whispered. "Yes! Let me go, Tarawassie ..." Her mother stiffened within her circling arms, casting her off, casting off life. Slowly Tarawassie released her, and let her slip down into the starlit dreamwater.

Her mother sighed, closing her eyes as though a great weariness had risen from her, and smiled. Blue-green seeped between her fingers. She lay still.

Tarawassie leaned forward, her hand closing over her mother's hand for the last time. Her tears dripped into the Well, fell soundlessly. She drew back again, into the world of color and noise, into the dream that she could share. She heard the murmured astonishment of the others who had surrounded her, grew aware of them again, as she grew aware that they were already beginning to separate and drift apart. Someone lifted her mother's body from the Well and carried it away. Tarawassie sat back on her heels, barely aware that she was weeping—for the loss of a touch, the comfort of an embrace, that she would never have again.

"She's happy; her wish was granted." Sabowyn still stood beside her. He put his hand on her shoulder. From somewhere he offered a silver cup filled with chitta. "Be happy, too, for an end to suffering."

Tarawassie took the cup gratefully, swallowed the ruby syrup, concentrating on the sensation of cold fire in her throat. He led her down the spiraling ramp to the dreaming place. Lying back on the yielding viscosity of a lounge, she fell desperately through the fragile membrane that separated reality from rapture.

Tarawassie woke, tears streaming over her face, not knowing whether she had just begun, or whether she had wept for hours. She raised her head. Room, stars, rainbow symphony, and figures slowly separated as she blinked away tears and confusion. ... There was no beauty! Her mind closed on the terror of disappointment, of disillusion, of colors mired in corruption, mindless noise ... no comfort, no vision, only ugliness! She had never dreamed like this! How could she endure——?

Sabowyn lay on the couch across from her, his eyes vacant. She tipped toward him across the low crescent of table, shaking him uselessly, as Andar had shaken her. Andar ... had all his dreams been like this? Dazed, she rose and followed his path to the Star Well's rim, to stand teetering, searching for his face, or her mother's face; but only finding her own, distorted by nothingness. She stepped onto the Well, breath held; coolness lapped her ankles. A sudden dizziness swept her, she swayed, like a reed in the water, in an unseen wind. And nothing happened.

She stood waiting, until she realized gradually that nothing would happen—realized with growing awareness what it was she had tried to do. Suddenly afraid of the taut, yielding surface that pressed her feet, afraid of falling through into the depth of stars, she stepped back onto the Well's rim.

She made her way back down the spiraling ramp, found Mirro alone, playing at the Loom. Tarawassie stepped into the room, forcing her way through the glaring web of Mirro's weaving. The closer she came to the Loom, the more profoundly its stimulation worked on her—the sensations of light and sound that were merely superficial, the truer harmonies that struck deeper resonances in the fiber of her nerves.

"Mirro," Tarawassie whispered above the faint shadings of sound. "How can the Star Well give death? What is it? Why is it here? And why—why couldn't I die too?"

"Do you want to die?" Mirro looked at her curiously; her face settled back into deep lines of habit. Her finger slid over the surface of the Loom below the shining threads. Colors glimmered in the transparent bar, flared up the strands, wove a filigree cloth of light.

Tarawassie shut her eyes against the hypnotic flow, against the memory of a failed dream. "I don't know. But ... I couldn't dream."

Mirro turned back to the Loom, her flame-dyed robe shimmering with the movement. "You were sad. But it passes. It always passes. You're young; you'll see."

"But the Star Well? You understand the Loom—can't you tell me about the Star Well?"

"I don't know about it." Mirro shrugged. "Nobody knows. It doesn't affect us; it doesn't matter. Don't worry."

"You can't. No one here knows."

"But I want to know. How can I learn——"

"What about in the city? What about the natives? Andar went out past the offering places, and he knew the answer." Tarawassie pulled at the sleeve of her own robe, fraying it.

Mirro shook her head; her hair rippled, silver and black. "Andar was mad. He shouldn't have gone. You shouldn't go; there's no point to it."

Tarawassie turned back through the barrier of sensation, went down to the lowest level where the ferry waited. She took up a cloak and a light globe from the scattering of castoffs on the floor. She looked back once, as she touched the ferry entrance, but there was no one to see her go.

Tarawassie set out through the brightening canyons of the city, going first to the offering place, where the natives left them food and bright cloth and trinkets—and chitta, in clay pots or sometimes plastic pitchers. The natives and other wild creatures had come to share the city with her own people, who had no use for, and no interest in, the miles of glass and stone. Her people kept now to their few dwelling places near the ferry shed, and were content.

A raised platform, that might once have held something else, was thinly littered with the dressed carcasses of small animals, bowls of dried autumn fruits, baskets of coarse grain. Something rose, flapping and ungainly, and flew away at the sight of her, uttering sullen cries. Vaguely disappointed to find nothing else, no creature she could question, she sat on the edge of the platform, shivering in the chill dawn air.

Hunger stirred in her at the sight of food, almost a nausea. She could not remember how long it had been since she had eaten last. The raw meat repulsed her; she ate the tasteless fruit. A pitcher of chitta waited too, drawing tiny gnats to destruction on the surface of its sticky syrup. Her hands quivered, her gaze drawn to it as the gnats were. She turned her face away. *Later*. She would come back later, when there was a need. . . .

The edge of the city was very close, here: between the stubby towers she could see the plain; the golden-gray sweep of ripened grass flowing beneath the wind, the umbrella trees flaming and heavy with fruit. The cloud-banked sky brightened, pink and yellow and subtle green merged to stain the dome of violet-blue, and stir her sluggish emotions.

Gazing into the morning, she almost missed the small flicker of movement at the perimeter of the square. A figure hesitated, bolted back into the deeper shadows as she stood and called out, "Wait!" She ran across the square, calling again, but finding only a street half blocked by shrubbery, empty of life. She heard a noise, far off, of something dislodged clattering down; the settling quiet oppressed her as the echoes died away. For a moment she stood, breathless with the abruptness of her movements, and uncertain about everything else. But someone had been here, and someone could give her an answer. How else could Andar have learned the Star Well's secret, out in the city's heart? Still uncertain, she entered the street.

Through the long day she probed the quiet, twisting city streets. Sometimes sounds reached her, distant and distorted; sometimes her mind filled with the awareness of a watcher—or only her own imagination? She never knew. She called, and echoes answered, or the scuttling of tiny scaled things, a flurry of wings in the trees above her head. A lattice of heavy beams and finer filaments cast shadow-netting down across her path, to end abruptly in vine-draped fangs above a mound of dust and twisted metal. Falls of stone masonry treacherous with burnished windowpane blocked her way.

Strangely reluctant, she did not try to enter one of the empty buildings until after midday. At last, her heart beating wildly, she passed through an arching, empty doorway into the darkness of the interior. Her light globe blossomed feebly, showing her a wall patterned with mosaic tiles, portrayals of human life—and twin embers gleaming. A snuffling growl, and the high yelping of a cub, sent her fleeing again into the sunlight. Tantalized and terrified, she did not try to enter another building.

As the shadows lengthened once more, irritability grew in her. She realized at last that she could not remember why she had come here, and what she had wanted to find. Her body ached with unaccustomed exertion, her stomach ached with hunger ... hunger ... craving hunger. ...

She knew that the craving was for chitta. It had been too long, the residue of euphoria that filled the waking hours between her dreams was dissipating, leaving her to face the emotions she had never wanted to know. She needed chitta, she *needed* it—

She started back along the street, hurrying now, her new goal clear in her mind, until she began to see that she could never retrace her wandering journey out from the square. Struggling with her rising fear, she saw that she would have to climb, to reach a height that would let her find a familiar landmark to guide her home.

She chose a spiraling ramp that circled upward to support the airy lattice hung with vines that arched above the street. She wondered fleetingly at its purpose—whether it had ever been intended for human feet, whether it had ever had any purpose at all. But that didn't matter; only chitta mattered . . . only chitta. She put one foot carefully onto the ramp, clung with her hands. The incline was sharp, but her moccasins held to the time-marred surface. She did not look down. The path narrowed, and faint cracklings reached her ears as every step settled.

There was a tearing sound. Her foot came down on open air. She tumbled forward, and heard her own voice screaming into blackness.

Tarawassie opened her eyes, blinking away dust, wiped crusted dirt from her lips, her nose. She licked her lips, tasting salt, not recognizing the taste of blood. Around her, under her, lay a pile of dust and something sharp, which dug into her side as she lay. She drew her hands in close, cautiously, to push herself up; one wrist flashed sharp warning up her arm. Collapsing abruptly, she raised her face instead, blinked her eyes clear again.

The watcher shifted, squatting beyond her reach, and met her eyes apprehensively. The watcher was not human. His eyes were gray, with pupils long and set obliquely in an iris without white. His face was sharp to the point of being a muzzle. . . . *His* face? She classified the sex instinctively, by standards that were not entirely apt. A native? Her astonishment drove all else from her mind—her discomfort, the incongruity of her own presence here. She sat up frantically, before she lost her nerve to pain. Startled, the watcher leaped up, bounding backward, in one lithe movement.

"No, wait!" She flung out her hand, her voice breaking.

The native stopped, indecisive; silvery fur ridged his scalp, along his shoulders. He lifted one foot, rubbed it nervously against the ankle of the other leg; his feet were covered by softly wadded leather shoes like her own.

She let her arm drop and sagged forward, aching, drained. She held his eyes, wanting to speak again, not knowing what to say, remembering that the natives were very shy—and very stupid.

The native moved slowly back toward her, something in his eyes that perhaps was concern. He crouched down again, still out of reach, cocking his head and snapping his whiplike tail across his shins. The tail was half-naked at the tip, and gray, like the palms of his hands folded in his lap; the rest of his body was silvered with clinging fur. He wore a kind of loincloth wrapped around his hips, a formless, sleeveless jerkin of faded red cloth, strings of beads. A leather bag was belted at his waist, along with a steel knife. Her eyes caught on the knife; she looked away at his hands. His hands were abnormally slender; she realized that he had only three fingers on each, instead of four.

Abruptly he lifted one of the hands, pointing at her; the tip of a retractable claw showed ivory. He made a series of sounds, somewhere between a chirp and a bark, and sat back again, watching her expectantly. She made no response. He repeated the string of sounds, more slowly, waited again.

She shook her head, not understanding what he wanted. Her eyes left him, searched the darkened walls. Only the tips of the towers, like gilded nails, were dipped in sunlight, but the fingertips of light were reversed. Had she lain there all night? She shuddered. But there was a more subtle wrongness about these brightening canyons.... Why were they empty? Bones ... there were bones in the street. Dark eyes of shattered pane gazing down at her, piles of rubble raising new walls from old, arches that crumbled to dust.... This wasn't her city, not the city she remembered. *It wasn't like this yesterday!*

She covered her mouth with her hands, holding back the cries of madness.

"What ... wrong?" the native asked.

He leaned toward her, stretching his neck, as though he were trying to touch her through a cage. The words were halting, misshapen, slurred—but she understood them. His eyes were too-human with tension and concern. "Are you bad?"

" 'Bad'?" She lowered her hands; laughed—unexpectedly, shakily. " 'Bad'?"

His face brightened at her response. "Bad . . . here?" The tip of his tail swept down his crouchng form. "Or bad . . . here?" The tail tapped his head; he drooped into a perfect image of despair.

Tarawassie sank back down in the dust. "Bad . . . both, I think." Her voice trembled. "How . . . how did you learn to speak?" It did not occur to her to ask how he had learned to speak her language; it did not occur to her that there could be another one.

"Not learn." His silvery head moved from side to side. "Know. Always know." The silver rippled as his forehead wrinkled, as though forming the words—or the very act of speech itself—was a difficult task for him. "I human; all humans know."

"You're not a human!" she shrieked.

She pushed herself up, her muscles wrenching with stiffness and her skin raw with scratches. She made her way to the closest window's dark reflection. She stood very still for a long while, gazing at the scarecrow figure swaddled in dusty, ancient cloth, the gaunt misery of the bloody face— the incomprehension in the hollowed eyes of blue-green, all that remained of the dream Tarawassie she had always known.

And then, gracelessly, she collapsed against the pane and slid down, to lie still in the dust.

Tarawassie opened her eyes again in semidarkness, lying on her side on a pile of rags. But dusty sunlight came through the break in the crumbled wall, and light flickered strangely at her back, warming her like the sun. She looked about. The native crouched beside a small fire, his silver concentration highlighted by gold; he rubbed her light globe methodically with his hands. His tail looped out independently and caught up a stick to push into the fire. A coppery pot hung from a makeshift hook above the flames. She became aware of fragrance—the smell of food cooking, infinitely more appealing and appetizing than anything she could remember.

"I'm hungry!" she cried.

The native looked up, startled. He set down the globe, dropping forward onto his knees. "I hear you!" His head bobbed, his eyes shining with more than reflected light.

He produced a cup of fine ceramic ware, dipped it into the pot and held it out to her, full. She studied the delicate vining of fantasy flowers on its polyhedral surface as she swallowed mouthfuls of thick, steaming soup. And she savored the sweet tang of herbs, the richness of the meat. Feeding herself had become a tedious duty long ago, and food a tasteless, textureless, unappealing thing choked down to stop weakness. She had never known hunger like this, never known the satisfaction of fulfilling it. The sickness, the weariness, the discomfort lifted; her mind cleared. . . . She remembered the sight of her own starved body, the reflection of a terrible truth. Because it was true, she was certain of it now. The self and the reality that she had always known had been a dream, a dream. But not a fantasy. She remembered her mother's death, the Star Well. Were this ruined world and her own wretchedness what her mother had seen without chitta? And was this what Andar had seen?

A bark of elation came from the native. Looking up again she saw the light globe brightening in his hands at last. He glanced up at her, making a peculiar chittering noise. "You want more?"

"Yes." She held out the cup. "It's good." He dipped it into the pot, passed it back. He picked up the globe again, stroking it now, almost worshipful. She realized how long it had taken him to bring light from it. She sipped her stew. "Does it always take you that long?"

He looked up again, the smile fading, and nodded. "Always hard, for me. But sunball last long time, better than torch."

"Did you bring me here?"

He nodded again. "I bring. I wait for humans come out into city, to show them. . . ." He stood up, tensing at some memory. Stringy muscles slid under his silver skin as he shifted his weight. He might be stronger than he looked. "You see more—natives, when you come?"

"No." She wondered why it mattered. "Only one, yesterday, who ran away. I—I came out into the city to . . . find someone to talk to, to learn about my people," knowing suddenly that she would have to have answers to more than the secret of the Star Well, before she could return again to the Crystal Ship. Her hands knotted together in her lap.

"Yes . . . ?" The native squatted down again, his eagerness breaking through his unease. She thought of the two children she knew; his impulsive openness struck her as childish. "Me, too—I know about Star People! One with yellow fur, he come here too. He throw things, hurt me. Not let me come in." His tail lashed, remembering fear and frustration.

"Come in where?" Andar—had he seen Andar?

"Building, over there." His tail jerked vaguely at the doorway. "Star People leave much good stuff. But door not let me in. Door let Yellow Fur in; *he* not let me in." His face turned hopeful. "You let me in?"

"Yes, if you'll take me there!"

He sat down suddenly, chittering. She realized all at once that he was laughing. "My friend, my friend! ... I show you all I know!" He hugged his knees; his eyes came back to her, the dilated pupils making them almost black in the half-light. "Other Star People never come here now; no one come but me."

"Why do you call us 'Star People'?"

"Because you come here from Fixed Star, up in sky." He looked as though it were the most obvious thing in the world; she supposed that maybe it was, after all. She had seen the Crystal Ship in the night sky, been hypnotized by the beauty of it—a constant jewel that only the moon out-shone, midway up the sky among the wheeling constellations. She wondered how it would look to her now, if she found it among the stars tonight.

"Real People"—the native's tail tapped his chest, as though his body were something separate from his mind—"they always live here, on world, from Real Time long ago. They say, when Star People come, Real Time end, for-ever. I say, Real Time come *with* Star People"—his hands reached out to caress the light globe—"but nobody hear me. Nobody let me *show* them. ..." He slumped forward, his bitterness rattling the beads against his chest.

"I'll let you show me." He straightened up as she spoke; she felt her own shoulders lift, with a sudden insight. "I think—somehow we lost our Real Time, too." She raised a hand coated with grit. "That, maybe, we found a dream—and lost ourselves."

The native looked at her strangely, and scratched his back with his tail.

"What's your name? What do they—call you?"

"Moon Shadow." His open hand struck his chest; his

face took on a perverse look of pride. "Moon Shadow Starman."

"Starman?" She frowned. "You mean—you said before that you were a human. But you don't—you don't *look* human. . . ." It sounded stupid, but he didn't seem to be offended.

"Not here"—he gestured down at his body—"here"—he tapped his head. "I last of Starman kith. Long, long time past, we show with Star People; they part of us, part of me. I last one be both Real and Starman."

"Oh." She smiled hesitantly. "I'm Tarawassie," she said.

"Human names not have reason. What it"—he grimaced, concentrating—"what it—mean?"

"It doesn't mean anything. It's my name." She smiled again. "Does it have to mean something?"

"All Real People have kith name. And birth name, tell of signs when they born. . . . When I come from pouch, Night Beast swallowing moon. People make much noise, Night Beast spit it out; but I come out while moon gone. They say"—he plucked at his beads, broke a string, so that they tumbled over his bony knees—"they say, I be strange—Moon-Shadow child. I be last of Starman kith, bad kith, born with evil spirit. Always, when show me things, they think I be strange . . . and so it come true." He picked up the scattered beads, dropped them into the bag at his waist. Tarawassie recognized strange bits of wire and glass, shiny flecks of etched metal.

"How are you—strange?"

"Starman ancestor-spirits guide me. But Real People say Star People have evil spirits, not Real spirits. They say only Real People show real way do things, no good learn anything else. They try make me stop, not learn about this, my city. But they live in Star-People city too! They give food and chitta, so Star People let us stay. They crazy ones, not me!"

Tarawassie thought of the offering place in the square, remembered that she had always known the natives brought the food that kept humans alive . . . and that she had never wondered why they should. She remembered the native who had run away. "Why are your people afraid of us? Aren't we 'real,' too?" *But we aren't even real to ourselves.*

Moon Shadow pondered, his fur settling. "But we only Real People. Star People like—like spirits. Much in sky—

have much magic. Star People make Real Time change.
My people not remember all of why—too long ago—but
remember to fear spirit-people, give them much
chitta. . . ."

"Chitta?" she burst out. "You give us chitta! Of course
. . . of course!" She made a small noise that was not really
a laugh, that hurt her throat. "But where everyone is
blind—who misses the day, who notices the darkness?"

"I call you Star Woman," Moon Shadow said, out of his
own thoughts. "It be true calling—like Moon Shadow."

Tarawassie nodded absently.

He smiled, showing white, sharp teeth. "Moon Shadow,
Star Woman—we be friends. I show you my secrets.
Now?" He leaned forward, strangely intent. "I show you
something now?"

"Yes. Can we go to where you saw Andar . . . Yellow
Fur?" She sat up on her knees, hoping that it wasn't far.

He drew back, looking down, as though she had refused
him.

"But I want you to show me—?" She frowned, puzzled.
"Can't you show me the place?"

His tail flicked impotently. "Can only show what I
learn already; not know secrets of new place yet! I show
you others, then we go there; then you understand stuff
good, like me."

Tarawassie shook her head, patience lost in the rush of
her newly freed emotions. "What are you talking about?
You mean you want to tell me what you've already
learned, first? Is that it?"

"Not tell!" His own eagerness butted against the wall of
incomprehension between them. "Show—I *show* you. Here
. . ." He reached out at last to catch her hand, pulling her
forward.

She started to get to her feet, but he pulled her down
again, his hands locked around her wrist. "Aren't we going—? Let go of me!" She jerked back with all her
strength, breaking his hold, as he forced her hand against
the silver fur of his stomach. "What are you doing?"

Moon Shadow winced. "Not hurt you! Just *show* you—
just show you. . . . Please, Star Woman." He rocked slowly
on his knees, his hands clenched, his gray eyes yearning.
"Nobody let me show them, nobody be my friend. . . ."

"Show me *what*?" Her face burned with unfamiliar in-
dignation. "Why do I have to touch you?"

He stopped rocking. "You not have pouch. You not know!"

"How would I know? I don't know anything!" She brought her hands down hard on the dusty floor. The pain of her injured wrist shocked her free from the hold of emotions she couldn't handle. "I'm sorry."

Moon Shadow nodded. "It passes. . . . I see. I try—tell you." He sighed. "With Real People, little one grow in pouch of mother, not come out long time, till strong. In pouch, mother show little one many things. After little one born, father show, kith-friends show. Man have pouch too"—he patted his stomach, searching her face for understanding—"can't carry, but can *show* little ones, *show* friends." His fingers twisted, claws protruding, as if he could wring clarity out of the air. "Put hand in pouch— and what friend know, you know, right now. Not tell—see, with friend's eyes. Friend *show.* . . ." As if he hoped by repeating it often enough, loudly enough, he could make her feel the meaning. He spread his hands, waiting.

Tarawassie sat back, sifting the words in her mind. "I see that it's more than just telling. But—but it's not like anything I know. We can't touch someone and read minds. How could I read yours, anyway? I'm not even a native. Can't you just—tell me?"

"Can't tell, Star Woman." He grinned forlornly. "No have enough words, no have way." His shoulders rose in something like a shrug. "Talk too hard. But *can* show you. I Starman because that be so." He held out his hand.

She half raised her own. But she drew back again, afraid, unsure. "Not yet. I'm not—ready, yet. Will you show—take me to the place we talked about, now? Then . . . I'll see."

His hand dropped; he nodded dispiritedly. "I take you. I keep my promise." A slight emphasis on *my*. "Anyway"—he straightened—"I get inside place! We go now, yes." His tail swept up the light globe, tossed it into his hands. He stood, kicking dirt onto the fire, smothering it.

Tarawassie got up, bent like an old woman, another kind of fire burning her pulled muscles.

"Not far." He smiled encouragingly—not wanting her to refuse him again, she supposed. His tail twitched toward the bright entrance. "Walk do you good."

She pressed her uninjured hand against her spine.
"Several kinds of good, I hope."

"Here. Yellow Fur press here." Moon Shadow pressed
his own palms flat against two incised ivory panels set at
chest height in the high dark doors. Nothing happened.
"Hurry, Star Woman. My people angry if see us here."

Tarawassie limped forward under the portico, shuffling
through dry leaves. She stood staring up at the height of
the entrance for a long moment, made dizzy by it. "Were
they giants?" she whispered, frightened, shivering with the
cold and anticipation.

"No," Moon Shadow said impatiently, rubbing his arms,
rumpling the fur. "They like you—just like you. We go in
now?" He looked back down the street.

"They weren't like us." She looked down. "No, never
like us. . . ." Slowly, as though in a ritual, she raised her
hands and placed them on the seals. The heavy doors
parted, like water flowing, with a faintly metallic groan.
The long afternoon light threw their distorted shadows
ahead of them into the interior. Tarawassie stood swaying,
indecisive. Moon Shadow stopped beside her, abruptly subdued. She took the light globe from his hands, holding it
before her like a talisman. In the rectangle of double light,
their tall shadows paled, were transformed.

"Spirit-people," Moon Shadow murmured.

"Our spirits." Tarawassie breathed in, held it, without
realizing. "Maybe we are giants, after all. . . ."

They crossed the threshold together, and as though in
welcome, incandescence flickered around them, filling the
vast darkness with artificial light. They froze, dumbfound-
ed, gazing up and up, their eyes climbing the walls of the
vault in which they stood. Somewhere, among the hidden
secrets of this place, Andar had found the truth that had
made him crazy and set him free. And set her mother
free. And now she had to know for herself. . . .

"No good!" Moon Shadow's bitten-off voice leaped from
surface to surface, raining echoes down on their heads.
"No good stuff here, no real things!"

. . . things . . . things . . . things . . .

Tarawassie covered her ears against the echoes. "What
do you mean? This is where Andar came to learn, isn't
it?"

"But all word stuff here. No good. Not understand

words, only things." He pointed at the light globe. "Things work—I make them work. But words. . . ." He mimed throwing something down viciously. "Words! I no good at words. . . ." It ended feebly; he turned his back on her, hiding his face. "Always, ancestors tell me this be good place, important place—now I know it only words." He spoke something that she didn't understand, that sounded ugly. "You not need me, Star Woman. I go now."

"Wait, Moon Shadow—" He stopped, facing away, as she called. "Don't leave me alone. . . . I mean, I don't understand this place. I need you to help me learn how—how this place works."

He shrugged, but his voice brightened. "I find you word boxes. I work them good." He turned. "But you never find right words here, in long time. Too many—too many words." He gazed up past floor upon floor.

"Andar found something, somehow. He didn't have forever."

"Maybe he leave it; maybe not. We look, though. . . ." Moon Shadow moved away, peering down at the floor. "Here! I see—Yellow Fur walk much in here . . . go many times . . . this way . . . to lift box. We go up." His tail gestured at her to follow.

She followed, looking down, barely able to detect a pattern of ivory-on-ivory smudging in the floor's pale film of dust. She entered the lift with Moon Shadow, standing back to watch him touch the symbols on the wall with a flourish, one after another.

They rose, wrapped in a quiet vibration, to the second level. Moon Shadow peered out at the floor, shook his head. They rose past two more levels before he nodded, slipping out onto the ivory tiles of the mezzanine. He led, tracking, along half its circumference. Tarawassie looked out, and up, and down past the low, latticed fence, trying to imagine what ancient mysteries lay captive in this place.

She heard a barked exclamation, saw Moon Shadow disappear down one of the side corridors. She went after him, found a double width of floor between the ceiling-high banks of tiny compartments. The opening was crowded with tables and smooth seats. The tables were cluttered with mechanisms she didn't recognize, and strewn with oval disks no longer than a thumb. Some of the countless compartments along the walls gaped crookedly open, as though they had been forced.

"This where Yellow Fur come. Maybe this be what you want. Many words here." His hand swept the table.

"Where? How——?" Tarawassie felt the blind resentment rise up in her again, at her helplessness, at the fact that a dim-witted native should know more about her people's secrets than she did.

"In show boxes." Moon Shadow picked up a disk, tossed it to her. "Put in show box, egg talk, or make vision . . . or make only words. Egg have— Not work if you pull it open!"

Tarawassie stopped prying, irritated.

"Magic get out, only dust inside. . . . Green egg talk, black one show picture, red one only make words." Most of the disks on the table were red. "Show box not show like Real People—not remember good after, forget too much."

Her hand closed over the red disk. "What's the difference between 'making words' and 'talking'? It's the same thing, isn't it?" She opened her hand again, looking down.

Moon Shadow shook his head. "This show box only show words. . . ." He reached out, did something to one of the odd constructs on the table. A dark square plate suddenly filled with light, patterning over with fine green symbols.

"That isn't 'words.' "

He nodded, facing her with pride and exasperation. "Draw word pictures, tell eyes story. I see"—his finger stretched, the claw tracking—" 'and it . . . death.' " He paused, scratching his ear.

Tarawassie flung the red disk away. "No, it's not fair!" She clung to the table. "I want an *answer*."

Moon Shadow came back to her side. She felt his cool gray palms close over her shoulders, forcing her rigid body down into a seat. "Peace, Star Woman. It still bad with you. We go now. Tomorrow, next day——"

"I don't want to wait! I want an answer *now*! I've wasted my whole life already." She leaned forward on her elbows on the hard tabletop, her hands clutching at the limp tangle of her hair.

"Then day more not matter." Moon Shadow sat down on the next seat, awkwardly, as though he seldom bothered. "What Yellow Fur know that so important? Why you come here? What make you come?"

"He knew about the Star Well." She raised her head.

"It's in the Crystal Ship. It made him die, or let him die. And it—let my mother die. She was sick and suffering and she just—died. I let her die, I let her go. But it wouldn't take me. I want to know how it passes judgment—and I want to know why nobody knows that!"

"And you want know if spirit of mother find home."

She met the gray eyes, startled. "Yes."

"You have chitta ceremony, after?"

"After she—died?" Tarawassie nodded. "I drank chitta. . . ."

"And you not dream good."

"H-how did you know that?"

"I know. I see why you come. . . ." Moon Shadow shifted on the chair, uncomfortable. "Happen sometimes with Real People, too! One die; kith have chitta ceremony, open selves to spirit—spirit of dead friend come among them, come into all who show with him when alive, become part of them forever. But sometimes kith-friend grieve much, and shut spirit out. Friend have no peace, spirit have no home. Grieving one must go out alone, search—search heart. When understand all, and—accept all, then spirit enter him. Spirit find rest, he find peace, all kith be glad, whole, again."

"How do you accept losing the one person that mattered to you—that you loved? How can you ever be glad again, knowing all the things you didn't do and couldn't do and should have done for her? I only let her die. And I never told her—I never even told h-her—" Her voice failed, as she sank into the waters of grief.

"Only body die; spirit part of us—part of us." The clumsy voice reached out to touch her, like a comforting hand. "Ancestors live forever, become part of friends, of kith. With chitta, feel this; feel beauty of spirit when friend come into us."

There is a heaven, and it is death. Tarawassie rubbed her eyes, making her hands wet, making the scratches burn. *But that's not what Andar meant.* "We don't believe that—that chitta shows you the spirits of the dead."

"Not believe?" Barely audible.

"No. They're only dreams, they don't mean anything."

"Maybe death not same for Star People, Real People . . . ?" Moon Shadow searched his own reflection on the tabletop. "But all people die. And my ancestors, they be human spirits. . . . But I be last Starman, and nobody show with me." Moon Shadow glanced up, glanced down again; she heard him sigh. "We go now, Star Woman, before somebody come. You rest. Tomorrow we find answers."

Tarawassie stood, accepting the support of his sturdy, fragile arm, and wondered whether there was any question that led to an answer, instead of to another question.

As they returned to Moon Shadow's camp, Tarawassie had searched the wedge of sky for the Crystal Ship's bright star point, but darkening clouds had closed down like a lid above the city. The wind was bitter; it drove her into her cloak, buffeted and oppressed by her isolation from everything she knew.

Now pale winking flurries of snow materialized in the shelter's entrance, as the wind gusted through the blackness beyond. The snow puddled, gleaming, as it found the floor, but Tarawassie huddled close to the fire, warming her hands on a cup of thick, hot soup. Moon Shadow's tail flipped sticks into the flames as he swallowed his own meal; his fur stood out from his body, insulating him against the cold.

"How—how did you learn to understand the word pictures we saw, Moon Shadow? How could"—she guarded the tone carefully—"you ever imagine what they meant?"

She heard his soft chitter of satisfaction through the crackling of the fire. "Always know, because I Starman."

"You mean, you didn't learn it somehow, somewhere? There isn't a place where I can learn it?"

He shook his head stupidly.

"Why didn't you tell me that? How am I ever going to—?"

"I show you." He looked up, his pupils dilated, disconcerting her. His hand quivered on his knee. "I show you, Star Woman, if you want?"

She nodded, desperate with frustration and fatigue. "Yes, then! Show me." Wearily she put out her hand. He took it hesitantly, drew it toward him locked in his own. "It won't hurt?"

He shook his head. "Not hurt you. Not hurt my friend."

Resolutely she did not pull back, felt her fingers brush the rough cloth of his faded jerkin, the gray-silver fur of his stomach; his fur was the consistency of clouds, the sleekness of water. Startled, vaguely embarrassed, she shut her eyes as her firmly guided hand entered the close, warm pouch in his flesh, where—some part of her tried perversely to laugh—where his navel should have been.

For a long moment she felt nothing more than clinging, formless warmth. And then, gradually, as though her fingers rested against a charged surface, a tingling grew, intensifying. Like numbness, it ate its way along the nerve paths of her arm. She tried to withdraw her hand, but Moon Shadow's grip pinned her arm. "Wait"—a plea, his face, his eyes, closed in concentration—"I see . . . you see."

The electric tingling grew more intense, verging on pain, as it spread through her shoulder, up her face. But sensation burst through into her mind, her fear and her anticipation were lost together in a storm of radiance brightening to blackness. . . . And beyond it, her eyes patterned from within with a blazing static of incoherent imagery. Paralyzed, she crouched stone-still, caught in a timeless dream of someone else's making, fed from the spring of an alien perception.

Tarawassie sat blinking, blinking—slowly realizing that she had clear vision once more. The fire-bright center, the rim of shadowed darkness, took form before her, and Moon Shadow, silver and gold, sprawled on an elbow, staring.

"Moon Shadow?" She made her voice reach out to him, with no strength left in her to raise a hand.

He glanced up, his eyes vacant, shook his head to clear them. "You"—he shook his head again—"you see words, now? I show you. . . ."

Images crackled and spat behind her own eyes, making them water. "I don't know—what I see. Everything is going around and around—things that don't belong in my mind!" She pressed her hands flat along the sides of her head, forced her concentration to fix on her own reality. "It didn't work!"

He nodded woodenly, pushing himself up. "It fight me. I feel—you come into me, not wanted. Is bad thing." He gestured at his head. "Wrong to feel that, never feel it with Real People—never." He grimaced, teeth flashing. "But ancestors—ancestors say it *right*!" He stared into the fire, his pupils shrinking to oblique slits.

Tarawassie massaged her arm. It felt hot and swollen;

tiny points of redness, like pinpricks, marked her hand.
"How can it be right if it didn't work?" She lay down
abruptly on the pile of rags, breathing in the smell of dust
and smoke, and wrapped her cloak around her. She saw
the golden-edged crest of fur rise with his irritation, settle
again. With a grunt of weariness, or disgust, he curled into
a knot at the fire's edge, shutting her out.

Shivering with the chill, her mind and body aching with
bruises and defeat, she welcomed sleep, which was a kind
of death.

There were many dreams, but unlike any she had
known before. In vivid detail, they sorted and aligned a
disorder beyond her comprehension—not disturbing her
sleep, but instead guiding her unconscious through to a
deeper peace.

She woke at a sudden noise, filled with a feeling of
wholeness and well-being. Searching for the sound, she
saw Moon Shadow duck his head as he entered the building, silhouetted against a leaden glare—and further along
the wall, a sealed doorway, marked by a sign, "EXIT."

Moon Shadow came on toward her, toward the fire, his
hands clutching two small kirvat carcasses, and a peculiar
snarl of three thongs and three round stones looped in the
hook of his tail. She saw his breath frosting as he neared;
saw, as the firelight illuminated his face, the disillusion-
ment that thinned his lipless mouth. He dropped the two
small animal carcasses by the fire and crouched down,
pulling the knife from his belt.

"Moon Shadow." She sat up, remembering everything,
suddenly—new to her—ashamed. "Moon Shadow, look at
that word! *Exit!* I know what it means. I can—read!"
Hoping that would mean more to him than any apology.
"You did show me!"

His head came around, his eyes searching her face, anger forgotten. "Yes? Yes? Is true, Star Woman? I show
you good?"

"Yes!" She nodded, laughter rose to her lips from deep
inside her. "It's all come into place, I can understand everything. . . ." She felt fragments of stranger new memories
eddying at the perimeter of her consciousness.

"Maybe"—Moon Shadow hesitated, struggling with
some emotion she didn't understand—"maybe now I share
what you see. I not understand words good. But your

mind come into mine, like Star People long ago. Maybe you show me what you—read. And I show you all they know."

"Together we can find all the answers! And then . . ." She stopped, frowning. "And then . . ."

"We go soon to word place." Moon Shadow nodded eagerly. He turned back to dressing the carcasses, and she did not watch him with the dead.

Tarawassie went first to the reader that already held a tape, in the cramped alcove of the deserted library, where Andar had hoarded his truths. Moon Shadow hung at her shoulder, guiding her hands at the reader's row of buttons, reciting instructions as though he had learned them by rote from some unknown teacher. She rejoiced in her new-found cleverness, as she began to identify sounds with symbols, one after another; and then whole words, an entire sentence. The ultimate cleverness of the one who had first created symbols shaped like sounds, to preserve a thought across miles of distance or millennia of time, filled her with courage and hope.

And yet a small part of her mind rebelled against the clumsy, insufficient tedium of words and symbols. So pointless, so wasteful, so unnecessary, when a person could simply *show*— And startled by the obviousness of that truth, she recognized it as not her own, but a pocket of stubborn, mind-closing resistance that belonged to Moon Shadow, to whom too many words were only a confusion of the essential. For Moon Shadow, for the natives, only the barest, most obvious patterns of daily life needed words. For them any thought or feeling or piece of knowledge more intimate or complex would be shown and shared directly, mind to mind. And the very attitude of the donor was transmitted as well, fixing an entire matrix of attitude-idea firmly into the mind of the receiver.

Her own mind had a matrix of alien experience, to let her separate her own beliefs from his—and yet, even so, she almost hadn't known. To grow up in a group where absorbing pieces of another's mind was something that began even before birth—how would you ever know yourself from the attitudes that formed you? From your parents, your neighbors? From your ancestors?

Moon Shadow looked down at her, as if he felt her eyes on him; smiled questioningly, not needing words.

And taking one sentence at a time, each time a little more easily, she began to read.

Who can worship death, and live? A credo, and an epitaph. *There is a heaven, and it is death. . . .*

Tarawassie pushed herself away from the reader plate, away from the table's edge, with the stiff motion of one transfixed by a terrible vision. Death's awful beauty had seeped through her eyes, hidden in the plain geometries of the printed words. . . . The reek of death had filled her being in that afternoon, and she had been answered. . . .

Moon Shadow had spent the first part of the day in nervous trips to the building's entrance—keeping watch, he had said, in case his people sent someone to search for him. But now he lay stretched on the floor, napping, having lost patience with, and finally interest in, her tortuous study. She did not wake him, wondering how she would— how she could—show him this truth: That her people had committed suicide—as individuals, as a group, as a world. They had worshiped death, not as a means to an end, but as an end in itself. They had died—died by means she could not even comprehend—died by their own hands, in an ecstasy of necrophilia. And their world had died with them, leaving its bones scattered over the earth to weather and decay and be eaten by time, leaving the handful of living to linger here, like the final flesh on the crumbling skeleton of the city. And she was alive . . . alone . . . among the living dead. *But why—?*

A hand brushed her shoulder; she started.

"What wrong, Star Woman?" The first words Moon Shadow had spoken to her he repeated now, and this time she could read the expression on his face. And reading the incomprehension on her own, he said softly, "I—hear you."

She turned her face away. "Everything is wrong. The more I search, the more I find answers—the more I wish I'd never started. And yet, the more I want to *know*. Why did this happen to me? I was happy!"

"What you find in words? It be bad thing? You try show me, and . . . I share bad with you." He stood expectantly, rubbing one foot against the other, as though it were a gift, an offer he was not used to making.

"I can't. I can't show you something so ugly about— about us."

"About Star People?"

She nodded. "You don't want to know—nobody should!"

He fumbled for words: "You show me, hurt go out of you ... hurt shared. I know. I need, but nobody show with me. ..." He toyed with a tape disk. "Need—*need* show, with somebody!" His fingers tightened, the disk shot away across the polished surface.

Startled, she was caught by a sudden memory of her childhood—as bright, as unreachable now as the starry depths of a Well in the sky. Her mother's arms, the muted rainbow of her mother's robe, the dreamy murmur of her mother's voice hushing the tears of a lost sorrow: "Don't cry, don't cry. Shared hands, shared hearts, will make a burden light, little Tara. ..." Tarawassie nodded silently, and put out her hand.

This time, because she was not afraid of pain, pain was almost nonexistent in the tingling intrusion that rose through her nerves. And this time, it was as though the dinning static in her brain sucked a part of her back across the bridge of living electricity that bound them, sucked away the fragmented images. Struggling against the dazzling mental noise, she recalled the malignant death ecstasy that had reached out of the past to destroy her future, her people's world. And carrying her crippled memory picture, her confusion and isolation passed through into Moon Shadow's awareness ... were shared ... were eased by his acceptance.

But then, as though the images had tripped some switch deep inside his mind, Moon Shadow's memory began to fill her own mind with a responding image. And suddenly she *was* Moon Shadow, in a swift, disorienting transition. Saw herself through alien eyes, saw herself as an alien, felt silver fur ridging on her scalp in startled disbelief. ... But as she drowned in alien sensation, she found that memory was not Moon Shadow's alone, and she was sucked down, as he lost control, into another mind—a human mind, preserved within the matrix of Moon Shadow's memory and rising to the present from the depths of generations past:

Her name (not Tarawassie, who was Tarawassie?) was Shemadans. *Shemadans.* She repeated it again, to stabilize herself, her heart beating too fast. She felt the cord from the sack of medical supplies cutting into her shoulder (Tarawassie grimaced), painfully real. She had come into the city only for supplies, but now she was returning to the camp with an infinitely heavier burden—the realization of their worst fears: the sabotage of the transporter. She forced herself to slow down, keeping to the shadowy edges of the crowded street. (Tarawassie stared wildly, her panic feeding on the impossible mass of humanity). A fine powder of snow dusted the ground beneath her boots. Tarawassie/Shemadans glanced up at the airy, vine-hung snow screens, realized with a shock that they no longer functioned, that the vine leaves were graying with frost. . . .

Someone's hands closed over her arms; she almost screamed her terror. But the rough face gazed through her, vacant; the stranger steadied himself and moved on. Tarawassie/Shemadans drew a shuddering breath. So hard, so hard to keep believing that she was a cultural historian, and not a frightened outcast. . . .

She realized gratefully that no one near her had noticed her sudden panic; all of them were strangers, now— strangers to reality. They drifted past her, oblivious to her, oblivious to the cold, the day, the world—Death Cultists, wrapped in a blanket of chitta dreams, thinking they dreamed of death. A sweetly repulsive stench reached her, as she passed the narrow space between two buildings; desperately she did not look to the side. . . . Because dreaming became an obsession with them, and if they were stopped from dreaming—*who could worship death, and live?* They had all gone insane! No part of her mind denied that, now. And it had happened so quickly. . . . How much longer could this city, or this colony, go on, before their autumn madness became the final winter for which there would never be a spring? *What will we do, if our world dies? We can't leave our kith-friends! Oh, Basilione, Basilione. . . .* She hurried on, the sack of supplies banging clumsily against her leg. She rounded the last corner, saw the snowtrack still sitting where she had left it. *What will become of us all, now that they've destroyed the transporter?*

Sprawled across the orange hood of the snowtrack, a bright, unidentifiable thing, a pile of crimson-spattered rags. . . . *A suicide? Oh, no. No!* Shemadans stopped, screaming it within the sheltering walls of her mind, witnessing in microcosm the death of a world. . . .

"No . . . no . . . *no* . . ." Tarawassie came back into herself again, with the cries of someone else's horror still constricting her throat. "Moon Shadow!" She pressed her aching hand to her mouth, swallowed the bitter aftertaste of fear. "What—what happened? Who was it? It wasn't you!"

Moon Shadow shook his head. She saw the aftereffects of shared terror fading from his face as her eyes came into focus. "You call—call ancestor spirit, call Shemadans"— he struggled with the word—"when you show. Memory come to memory."

"She was a *human*. . . ." Tarawassie began to see at last how literally true his claim of a Starman—a human—kith must be. She had asked without knowing, and her question had been answered—by a vision from her own past (the memory of the living streets took her breath away once more), which had somehow become a part of his. How had it happened? How long ago? And what had happened to Shemadans? Suddenly she wanted desperately to know, to find out more about this new part of herself, this new world opening up to her.

Because she knew now that all Shemadans had feared had come to pass; knew that the people, their world, had died—because of chitta. Tarawassie saw it so clearly now, in the anguished parallax of Shemadans' perspective and her own. And she wondered numbly how this last handful of her people had managed to survive for so long, in this imitation of death—this imitation of life.

Moon Shadow touched her arm, breaking her out of her reverie. "We go soon? Stay here too long, dark come. My people see light, come, punish me. . . ." He hesitated, looking down. "I show with you, share bad thing. I make it less. I be your kith-friend—?"

"Yes." She nodded, still unsure of whether the answer she found in the showing had made her anguish less or only increased it, but knowing somehow that it was very important for her to thank him for the sharing. "Yes, thank you . . . my friend." She found a smile. And now that one question had been answered, she knew that she had found the spring of real knowledge, and that she could never leave it until she had drunk her fill. "Moon Shadow"—she put out her hand again, forgetting his warning—"show me what happened to your ancestors, what happened to Shemadans?"

He took her hand. This time she felt no surprise, as her mind and Moon Shadow's focused her question, her need to know, and let it sink into the deeper levels of her/his awareness, into images fragmented by transmission error and incompletion through the years, but which still rose to let him see through ancestral eyes whenever some need, or some sight of this ancient city, called them up to guide him. . . .

For a fleeting instant she was changed again. Still possessing thin gray hands, a shining silver belly, but not Moon Shadow's, Tarawassie looked down into a human face, a man's face contorted with pain. She crouched below the charred flap of a burned-out tent, needing all her strength to absorb that terrible pain, as she tried to bring him comfort. . . .

And again. She became a human man—a *man*, this time, her name/his name Basilione (Shemadans—where was Shemadans? Where was she, Tarawassie?). . . .

Basilione turned slightly, lowering his hand, looking away from the procession of snow vehicles still working its way toward their camp along the river valley. *Shemadans*. . . . He reassured himself that she stood beside him, a shapeless bulk in her heavy clothing, only her chill-reddened face showing below her hood. She looked back from the river to him as he turned, as if their movements were one. Her face gentled as she met his smile. She reached out as he reached out; they drew each other close, the motion drawing their kith-friends closer around them, all of them together, as it should be.

But not all of them. . . . He had sent a part of the kith away—the vulnerable part, the *native* part (her/his mind protested against the need for a distinction, now). Because that was not simply a group of men approaching below, he was certain; it was a mob. He turned further, looking back through the dozen tense and anxious faces of their friends. The high whine of the approaching snow vehicles reached him constantly now. Across the snowdrifted tundra, past their own ordered, deserted camp, he could see the squalid, inadequate shelters of the main native village, where this group of wretched survivors of the human encroachment existed on lichens and grubs. All of the natives had fled at the first sign of trouble.

Tarawassie/Basilione's gaze moved mechanically across the too-familiar landscape left by retreating glaciation—a gouged cliff face, the rubble of a moraine, the powder-fine, sterile dust that lay beneath the snow, which one day would sweep south to settle into rich farmlands. . . . But here below the rim of the glacial lake this land was as barren as a moon, and the Real People huddled on the edge of extinction, and hated his own.

God, was it nine years since he had come through the transporter from the Homeworld? Only nine years, since he had come here to verify that the natives were subhuman, and believed, himself, that they were an evolutionary dead end, no better than animals? Shame flickered in him. But no, no need to feel ashamed now. That had been someone else, a different man. . . .

A sharp thrust of memory showed him his home, Homeworld, the man he had once been. Spring—and he had crossed the ancient quad of the university campus, with the scent of the flowering silth trees heavy in the air, to enter a lecture hall where the students had standing room only, bcause their world had standing room only. A world where he and his wife had been afraid of closeness, even between themselves, because then closeness had meant a crowd and nothing more.

He held his wife closer now, feeling the deeper closeness of spirit and mind that they shared with each other and with their friends—because of showing. Nothing could separate them now, not the ostracism of the Real People, not the anger of the human men below. If they could only make someone *see*—make both sides realize what kept their kith together in the face of hardship and persecution, what had made them glad to stay, the things they had come to know together—things neither people could achieve apart. . . .

Shemadans stiffened against him; he heard someone mutter uneasily and a child sneeze in the cold wind. The four snowtracks had stopped, fifty meters below them. He kept count as the vigilantes climbed down . . . fifteen . . . eighteen . . . twenty-four of them; watched them point, and begin to move upslope toward the camp on foot. He squinted into the wind, beginning to make out details—the set, vengeful faces, the glint of light on weapons, the parkas, patterned with the ebony fur stripped from a butchered native elder, the silvery-white of a murdered child. He set his teeth against a cry of grief that rose out of memories not wholly his own. Shemadans moaned softly, setting one foot against the other ankle, as though she would flee if she could. Behind her Pamello bit off a curse: "Butchers . . ."

"No!" at himself, most of all. "We can handle this, if we don't lose control of ourselves! We knew they might come. They've got a good reason to be angry, this time— and afraid." *Good reason.* He remembered the kith meeting, three weeks before, when Shemadans had returned with the news of the transporter and the further deterioration of the city.

And these humans had come the four hundred kilometers from the city in snowtracks, not the flyers of the Colony Police, who had harassed the camp in the past. Things were falling apart faster now, goaded by fear. These men were not even quasi-official any more; this time they were out for blood.

"What do you want here?" he demanded.

The colonists stopped five meters below him on the slope. He saw the ugly projectile weapons clearly now, trained on his people, on him. "Stand where you are. You know what we want. We want your 'friends' "—their leader made an obscenity of that deepest honor—"kangaroo-lover! Where are they?"

He had seen that man before, or maybe only too many others like him, too many faces made faceless by blind bigotry. . . . "They've gone where you won't find them." His eyes swept the faceless mob.

"We'll find 'em." The leader signaled, sending a party to search their tents and the native camp beyond. "And when we do, you can watch what we do to them for destroying our world."

"We know what the Cultists did to the transporter." Basilione spoke quietly, evenly, with an effort. "We know they've cut off contact, that nobody else can come through to us now. But these natives aren't to blame for that!"

"Then who the hell is to blame? It's their chitta that's destroyin' our people, drivin' us all crazy! They planned it that way, to take our world!"

"*We* took *their* world." He had to include himself consciously in humanity. "Do you really think a bunch of—of 'kangaroos' could plan a revenge like that? It was our own fault, for letting the drug get out of hand!"

And yet, he remembered that Shemadans had said it was a kind of revenge, a kind of ironic justice. How many countless times throughout human history had "primitive" groups like the Real People been decimated and demoralized by the vices of a superior technology? And this time, this *once*, it had gone the other way.... "Can't you see that everything we've done here was wrong? We've got to change if we want to salvage something, our lives, from this disaster. We've got to work together, we've got to work with the natives. . . ."

His voice ran on, stumbling, fumbling over clumsy words, words that could never capture the essence of what it meant to see through the eyes of another being, to let them absorb a part of yourself in return, and to know that part of you would live forever.... If he could only *show* them how his own ingrained human selfishness had been altered by the presence of other viewpoints, other minds; how much all the humans in Camp Crackpot had grown less preoccupied with self, more tolerant of themselves and others—more concerned with the stability that had always seemed to elude humanity.

And the Real People had been changed by showing, as well. For their species, the stability of the showing ritual had evolved into an overspecialization that perpetuated mediocrity, that rejected change or innovation. Showing with humans had infected the Starman (he took a perverse pride in the native epithet) kith-friends with the humans' attitude that change was right. And any human could imprint the secrets of technology on a Real One's mind, directly, permanently, giving him instinctive knowledge of things that evolution's trap would have denied them forever.

And all that they learned could be taught, instantly, almost painlessly, to another human. "What could uniting our peoples bring to either one of us except good? There's never been a complementary union of alien cultures before, but we could have one now! Together we can—"

"Shut up!" the leader of the mob bellowed, raising his gun. "You're as bad as those goddamn chitta zombies—worse! We don't have to listen to this kind of filth from you. We don't have to take it from a bunch of animal-loving queers! Take apart the camp, bust it up, burn it!

Smash everything! The main camp, too—don't leave anything! This's how they want it—let 'em all freeze here together." He raised his arm, sweeping the mob outward.

As though time had suddenly turned inside out, Tarawassie/Basilione saw the mob begin to spread like water, saw Pamello's little girl pick up a smooth round stone, lift it, hurl it—saw it strike a man full in the face. Blood spurted red against the leaden sky, as he heard Shemadans scream, "No!" But it was too late, too late. Living a nightmare, he saw the guns turning, training, but he could not move, and it was too late, too late even to run. . . .

Tarawassie came to herself, sitting hunched over her knees, sobbing with pain. Slowly she straightened, drawing her hands away from her breast. She stared at them for a long moment, stared at her faded robe. But there was no blood, no pain, no need to cough out her life, here in this abandoned library. . . .

A soft, heartbroken ululation filtered through to her as her dry sobbing eased. Moon Shadow sat back in his chair, eyes shut, hands against his own chest.

"Moon Shadow," barely a whisper, "what happened to us? What happened? Did we—did *they*—all die? All of them?"

His head moved listlessly in negation. "They me. They me. I all that still is them. . . ." He took a deep breath, opening his eyes.

"But they were murdered. They *died!*" And somehow it was so real, happening inside *her*, that she had believed— She sat forward, her hands twined before her on the tabletop, as the fog of images and loss began to lift, giving her a clearer objective view of all that she had seen. And she saw, suddenly, the true significance of the word *native*. "Moon Shadow, do you—hate me? The mob, they must have been my ancestors. And all the humans—what they did to your people. . . ." The memories-within-memories of atrocity rose, as freshly vivid as though she had seen them done, after—after five hundred *years*. She could not comprehend the span of time. "Am I like them?" She remembered her own feelings about the natives, her mouth tightening.

Moon Shadow shook his head, not meeting her eyes.

"You not like them, Star Woman. You like *my* ancestors. You like—you like me."

Basilione had not been ashamed, because the bigot had been another man.... "Yes," she nodded, "and—I think *you* are more like *me* than anyone I know." She laughed, very softly, as the full implication of it struck her. "Now ... but I still don't know what I am."

"You my friend." Moon Shadow's hand touched his chest. He smiled. "My kith-friend."

A clear, rising pleasure filled her like a light, as she grasped at the deeper meaning of the word. "And anyway"—shadows formed again behind her eyes—"what was done, was done long ago—to your people, to mine. Your chitta brought the humans to ruin, in the end. Your people are their inheritors. All that was theirs has been left to you, to let you prove how wrong they were in passing judgment on you."

"Maybe." Moon Shadow twitched his shoulders; his beads rattled. "Or maybe they prove right, prove we never change. We live here long time, inside human city, but nobody want magic, nobody use! Still say already know best way, not need new way. . . ."

"But if the Real People really were as—as primitive as the ones Basilione knew of, haven't they changed . . . ?"

"Little things! Stupid things. Not big things. Not enough."

Tarawassie shook her head, rubbing her hands together, rubbing her arms. "But—but the memories that you have, Moon Shadow. Couldn't they still change your people, through you?"

"My people not *let* me change them!" He shook his own head, in denial. He stood up, his foot rubbing his ankle in a strangely familiar gesture. "We go now, before they come."

"Moon Shadow, wait." She caught at his wrist as he rose. "Show me one more thing; please? I still need to find the answer to the first question I—I ever asked myself." She reached out, her mind shaping an image of the Star Well. "Somehow, someone in your mind must have known about the Crystal Ship, about the Star Well. . . ."

Reluctantly Moon Shadow dropped into his seat again, surrendering, like a sinner torn between dread and ecstasy. She saw him close his eyes as her numbed hand slipped again into the warm folds of his pouch, felt gratification fill him and become her own as the current joined them once more.

Shemadans sank wearily, cross-legged, into her place in the circle of expectant friends. (Tarawassie looked out through her eyes in disbelief, at the dark, worried face of Basilione, the faces of a dozen other humans interspersed with native faces—all alive, still alive?) Shemadans looked out across the double ring of faces, watched the gray tent wall heave in the frigid gusts of the night wind beyond. She ordered the thoughts that had been hers alone for the four long days of her return from the city. She began to speak, even as she showed to Hunter's Luck on her left; thinking that in a group this large, there was still a place and a time for the use of words. . . .

"The news is very bad, this time. The snow screens have failed, the city is falling apart, there aren't enough people left who care to do anything about it. Sixty percent must be using the drug now, I saw them everywhere. They drift like zombies, they barely look to their own needs, and they ignore everything else. . . . And if they're deprived of chitta, they—they kill themselves! It's true, I saw it myself. The others have become obsessed with the deaths. It fascinates them. . . . And there isn't enough chitta for them all any more." The awareness that she was not alone with the memory flowed back into her from Hunter's Luck, bringing her comfort. . . .

(And Tarawassie understood, finally, that all this had happened before the ultimate confrontation. Shemadans, Basilione, all the rest had never died, would never die; they continued to experience life—through the bodies of their descendants. They *were* Moon Shadow. And they would be a part of her now, for as long as she lived.)

Shemadans pushed back the hood of her jacket, refocusing bleakly on the present. "But that isn't the worst." Tarawassie/Shemadans watched their faces, the colors of flesh, the colors of fur blending into one continuity for her. "The Cultists have sabotaged the transporter." She braced against the rush of cries and questions, the stricken faces. "But wait! Wait—they dismantled only the receiver, not the transmitter. We can still leave—if we still want to." *The humans can.* She looked down.

"But no one can come to us? No one from the Home-world?" Basilione asked.

She nodded. "The damage was irreparable. The Cultists wanted to make sure no one could come through to stop them. If people want to leave, they don't care. They're glad—glad to see them go. . . ." She pictured them in her mind, clustering like flies in the transporter station, drawn by their morbid fancies to gaze at the corpse of one who had passed through, adrift in azure lines of force among the stars (The transporter? Tarawassie grasped frantically at the shred of image—the Star Well, *the Star Well?*—but Shemadans' mind shifted like dunes of snow). . . . "They aren't violent toward anyone but themselves. But the undrugged ones are panicking now, and between the two of them—"

"This colony is doomed, between the zombies, and the mobs." Basilione nodded. "It's not as if we didn't see this coming. . . ."

"Help come," someone said. "Come from Homeworld, when afraid-humans pass through, tell all. Humans come again, in starship."

"But that takes forty years, at least," someone else said.

"If anybody ever comes at all. . . . What's going to happen to the Homeworld now? They'll fall apart, if they can't bleed off colonists to this world."

"What happen *here*, now?" Tarawassie/Shemadans turned her head to look at Beautiful Sky, whose life Basilione had saved, who had been the first Real One ever to show with a human. "Angry ones, they maybe blame Real People. This—blame us too. Where we go, what we do, then?"

"We may not have to worry," Shemadans said softly. "The humans may all kill themselves, kill each other. And all the Real People will have to do is wait a little longer, and this will be their world again." And the tragedy of it sickened her, but she couldn't deny its justice.

She pictured the transporter and the fragile threads that had tied this world so tenuously to reality, to sanity; pictured one of them already broken—*and the dark abyss* (Andar, what had Andar said? *Please*, Tarawassie cried silently, reciting in her mind: *'To pass the dragon, and enter the dark abyss.'* . . . *Please, show me, show me now!*). . . . And obediently, Shemadans' mind slipped deeper into memory, found the poem:

Who will dissolve? Who coagulate?
Who to pass the dragon and enter
the   dark
abyss?
Silently   without   motion
he enters   the ocean.

The poem by Grattan, the painter-poet who had captured, for Shemadans, the mystical experience of a rite of passage, to animate the cold substance of her knowledge about the transporter's function. . . .

And Tarawassie absorbed all that Shemadans knew about the Star Well: A transporter station (the Ship, the Crystal Ship!) had been sent to this world from another, which was one of many worlds already bound together by Star Wells. For forty years a ship had journeyed across distances unimaginable to her, to deposit crucial materials to found a colony and to establish a gateway here at journey's end. The gateway was the Star Well, fixed in the transparent heart of the dismantled starship still circling endlessly above their world, a gateway that let humanity cross the chasm between the stars in scarcely more time than it took to cross a threshold.

But those who chose to cross paid the supreme price, for the threshold between the worlds was Death's. The body must be cast off, before the spirit—the essence?—of each traveler could pass through the darkness and be reborn in the light of another sun. By some process Shemadans/Tarawassie could not even imagine, the Star Well's mechanism captured the pattern, the precious thing that made each man or woman a unique being, and transmitted it, leaving the husk of flesh behind, recreating the identical being, in an identical body, at its destination.

But who would dissolve, who coagulate? Each person who chose to journey must comprehend, and accept, the fact of their own self-destruction. And that was the reason, Tarawassie realized, that the Well had never accepted any human she knew, before her mother and Andar. Only Andar had known the truth. Only her mother and Andar had been fully ready to pass the dragon and enter the dark abyss—as all humans must once have been, accepting death without qualm, thoughtlessly, as a transition, never seeing their bodies drift lifeless behind them, only aware of their arrival, their renewal. . . .

"But that means," Pamello was saying (Shemadans' mind returned to the present, Tarawassie's to the past), "that through the rest of our lives, at least, things are probably going to go on getting harder and harder for us. Even if the colonists leave us alone, we won't have access to the equipment, the supplies. The question is, can *we* survive this now?"

Shemadans shook her head. "The question is, can we bear to leave our kith-friends now? No one is being forced to stay here. But no one who leaves this world can ever return. I know that, for my own part, this is my home now. My place—our place"—she glanced at Basilione—"is here in the kith, whatever comes." He smiled, his fingers squeezed hers on the hide mat between them.

"No one ever said any of us wanted to leave," Pamello said, a little gruffly. Lines of worry eased between his pale eyes. The other humans, one by one, shook their heads around the circle. "Only that now Camp Crackpot is not going to be such a luxury resort. . . ."

Laughter spread around the circle, and Tarawassie/Shemadans understood the differing ironies and sorrows of human and Real One that lay beneath it. She looked down at her hand and Basilione's, both of them cracked and calloused, aged by unaccustomed hardship. *Unaccustomed?* She smiled again, wistfully. *Surely not, after nine long years.* She looked up again, to see in her mind's eye Hunter's Luck repairing an infrared heater, Basilione bringing down an arctic springer buck with only three round stones knotted together by thongs. *We have changed, all of us. We can learn to live with the future, if we have to.*

In the corner of this tent—where they had shared so many sparse meals, sitting down cross-legged or crouching on the insulated floor—she saw the children now, sitting together in a showing/sharing session of their own. They would live to see a better future, when this time of hardship had passed—and through them her own spirit, and those of all the kith, would continue, would multiply, would see their hopes realized, and have their belief remembered. In time the fear and suspicion of the Real People would fade, the Starman kith would be able to reach them at last. And if help came from the Homeworld, they might already have begun to build a new colony, the *right* way....

"But it didn't happen that way...." Tarawassie clung to the fading glow of hope and pride, fighting the sense of desolation that filled her return to the present. "The humans were killed, and—and the Real People must never have listened to your ancestors. What happened, where is your kith now?"

"They all here...." he said softly, not looking at her; it took her a moment to realize that he was speaking directly to her. "I last—last Starman...." Seeing her incomprehension, he leaned forward, knocked a tape disk clattering. "I show you rest."

She offered her red-pricked hand; she barely noticed the discomfort now, locked into a deeper sense of realization, a different awareness. And this time, as she slid again into a silver body, a shared mind, she felt what it was to be the last of a kith.

A mosaic of minds, of images, of years, patterned within her/Moon Shadow's mind this time, as he relived his past again.... In the long, grueling winter after the village and their camp had been burned, their friends slaughtered, their Star People possessions destroyed, the thirty-odd members of the shattered Starman kith had tried to rejoin the main band of the Real People. They had tried to help them rebuild, recover, adapt—only to find themselves all the more unwelcome for it. And without the idea stimulus they had received from the humans of the kith, they found themselves unable to create new tools, new innovations, to replace all they had lost. Where once they had been feared for the magic they controlled, now, when they were powerless and friendless, they were scorned and mocked instead, held on the fringes of society.

As time passed and the Star People disappeared from the land, the Real People had dared to migrate back again into better lands and finally to enter the very cities of the decimated humans. But even in the city—especially in the city—the Starman kith was kept at bay, and few Real Ones would willingly show with them, or mate with them. Attrition grew as discontented descendents of the kith abandoned their outlaw beliefs, by choice or otherwise; as they left to join other roving bands, or were sucked away into the mass of the whole. And as the numbers of the parent kith shrank, inbreeding made their ancestral memories more and more aberrant. There were not enough friends to show with, to share with; there was not enough diffusion of memory to produce the integrated whole acceptable to their people, who came to regard the Starman kith more and more as fey, possessed by evil spirits, creatures to be shunned.

Until at last he, Moon Shadow, was born, the only child of the last Starman kith-woman. Haunted by the voices of the past, driven by the strange whims of ancestral spirits too strong for him to control, he had been hounded into this solitary, half-fugitive existence by the censure of his father's unyielding kith. His mother was gone; her spirit lived only in him now. But he had refused to submit to or join his father's kith. And so he was spied upon and abused for his searching of the ruins, by the ones who still feared the Star People, their memory, and particularly their power. There would be no kith-friend to hold the chitta, calling for him, when his body died; no one to absorb his spirit and all of the ancestors who survived now in his mind alone.

He would be lost, abandoned, bringing evil dreams in the night to the unwilling souls that refused him shelter. All of his kith would end with him. He would die as no one in his memory had ever died; he would be forgotten forever, accursed, a part of no one's soul. . . .

Tarawassie clung to his sleek and calloused hand, understanding now why he had pressed so desperately to be her friend. *A kind of immortality.* . . . She sat back. But even knowing that they were valued by one another, she knew that they would both always feel isolated, alienated, lost, because they had no purpose here, no reason for existing in an alien world. "There's only death, here!" Her voice caught; she saw in her mind Shemadans' memory of the Star Well, tying this world of madness to one which had been sane. . . . "What if my mother is still alive? The Star Well worked; it accepted her. Maybe she was—recreated, on our Homeworld, without her sickness, alive and well. Or maybe the people who could make a Star Well could cure her, and she's waiting for me, on a beautiful world, but she can't tell me how to come to her, she can't *reach* me." She remembered her mother's body and

Andar's, drifting lifeless in the Well. "And I know, but I can't go. Because I'm afraid to die!"

"Maybe Star Well not work, maybe she die.... Nobody come here, long time. Maybe Star People all gone now; all gone everywhere...." As though he didn't know whether it was a good thing or a bad one. A kind of possessiveness came into his voice. "You stay...."

"They can't be. They can't be." She shook her head, not hearing him, knowing too well what Shemadans and the rest had known—that the sabotaging of the Star Well might have meant the Homeworld's collapse. "They just gave up; they didn't want to send anyone more to this world, to go crazy."

"Maybe they come back now, if Mother go to them."

"Are you afraid of that? Afraid that it will happen again? The mob, the persecution...."

He nodded; his tail traced obscure patterns in the pale dust on the floor behind him.

"But Moon Shadow—the way we can show together, it's something the humans can't do at all, something they'd value if someone could only make them understand. Shemadans, Basilione, all your ancestors, believed that—that it could protect you and defend you; it could make you as important to the humans as—as they are to themselves. You could become transmitters of all knowledge...." Shemadans' belief in the future, Basilione's vision, filled her, became her. "I can go to the Homeworld! I *can*. I want to go through the Well, I want to find my mother, and see—everything. I want to see a real human world. And if I go, I can make them want to come back here and find your people. I'll show them how special you are. They'll come, I know they will. And I'll come back on the ship—the Starman kith will live, we won't be forgotten...."

"I not die?" Moon Shadow stood up, his sharp face twitching with emotion. "Yes, yes, you go—you come back!" He caught her hand, dragging her up from her seat. "Our peoples be one. My people learn all Star People know. ... And I not die forever! Come, come, Star Woman, we go now to Crystal Ship"—chittering laughter—"while *I* believe!"

But I'm Tarawassie! Her own doubts, her unanswered fears, stirred again, denying the strangers in her mind. But Moon Shadow pulled her toward the lift, and back into the rush of his own bright emotion.

They went out through the high, heavy doors of the library entrance, into the chill autumn twilight.

And stepping out of the shadows into the glow of Tarawassie's light globe, five natives met them there. Tarawassie froze as the cold light glanced from spearpoints leveling toward her. She heard Moon Shadow's barked curse.

"So, evil one. Still you disobey your people!" The tallest of the natives, silvery-gray like Moon Shadow, confronted him; his eyes gleamed with triumph. Tarawassie realized that she understood him, even though he used the native speech. "This time we make you sorry enough. Drop spear!"

But she realized that the others were holding back, hesitant behind the shield of their spears, their eyes on her, fearful. As though he sensed it too, Moon Shadow kept his grip on his own sharpened metal tube, shaking his head. "Not so, brother! I be under protection of Star People. You not touch me, or you be sorry ones." He stood at her side, glancing from face to face, as though he dared them to approach. Surreptitiously he touched Tarawassie's hand, reassuring, seeking reassurance. Her fingers closed for a moment over his, giving what answer she could. "Leave us!" He dropped his own spearpoint, returning the challenge.

Two of the others backed up slightly, but Moon Shadow's—brother?—stood his ground. "Not let you go, evil one. Swift Springer judge you, and this spirit-woman, this time."

And Moon Shadow nodded, suddenly smiling; his teeth glistened. "Yes, then! This time, he not deny me. . . . I go to village with you."

His brother met his smile, his fur ridging slightly. "You not have choice."

They went ringed by spears through the windy, crumbling, blue-shadowed streets. Tarawassie gazed upward, her breath frosting the deepening blue-violet of the sky's dome, where one star shone, canted down from the zenith before her. The star that was not a star, but held the thread that spanned the darkness to all the stars. . . . She lifted her hand to it, in a promise, and an appeal; her hand dropped away again, tightened into a fist at her side. She looked down past her feet, picking a path through the half-seen rubble. "Moon Shadow," she murmured, keeping her voice steady. "What are they going to do to us? Who are they? You said, 'brother.'. . ."

He spoke in human, keeping his own voice low. "Is half-brother—father's son. Others be kith-friends." His voice roughened: "They take us Swift Springer. They not hurt you, Star Woman. See how they not touch you—fear you."

"Who is Swift Springer?"

"Shaman—show with all kiths, show very clear. Swift Springer know all; all people show with him, many many seasons past. He say, 'This thing Real, that thing not belong.' He say I full evil spirits. . . . But even he give you honor. You command him, he not punish me this time. Instead, he listen to me, make them all see what we do, see future!" He looked up at her, a kind of desperate determination burning in him. "Maybe this be good thing, not bad . . . kith-friend."

"Kith-friend," she nodded, uncertain. "I hope so. . . ."

The final undulation of the street turned them out onto a wide open space, like the square where the natives left their offerings. This one lay at the hub of six streets, fronted on six sides by reflection—building walls, a sheen of blue-black now, with deeper, purer pupils of blackness, framed in fractures of snowflake symmetry.

In the center of the open space a fire leaped and fell back, held in a palm of stone. Life's darting pulse mocked her, reflecting in the dark, abandoned eyes of this valley of mirrors. Her senses vibrated with glare, with heat, with the tart, acrid smoke smell of burning sapwood. And as though she had always known, she knew now that a spirit fire had burned there once, had been a sign to the Real People that they should settle here forever. When the spirit fire had died, they had created their own eternal flame, for it was a holy sign.

Tarawassie brushed the rim of stone as they passed, blackening her fingers with soot. Beneath the charcoal patina she could make out a faint tracery of color on the polished surface. And within the stained-glass golds and blues of the flames, silhouetted in soot, she saw a form of obscure grace. As she wondered what purpose it could have served, for a startled second she glimpsed a second vision, of the stranger beauty that human eyes had seen, when they had gazed upon "spirit fire," and she knew that its only purpose had been beauty.

Caught between the future and the past, she went on with Moon Shadow and the guards through the gathering darkness, to the base of a building that faced along the perimeter. And she saw at last that this place was not deserted, abandoned to the ritual fire. Two natives watched them from a doorway—two women, in sagging knee-length kilts suspendered by chains of glittering metal and beads.

The women stood shifting, indecisive, looking from her to Moon Shadow with silent awe. Behind them more fires burned, subdued, small family cooking fires within a great hall. She could see other figures inside, now, slender shadow-forms, and wondered how many of these buildings had been reclaimed by the world's new order. A child appeared abruptly between the women in the doorway; its downy fur showed silvery-white. Like a drop of liquid starlight, it climbed its mother's leg; drawn up by her hands, it disappeared, impossibly, into her pouch. Tarawassie's mind filled with a sense image of soft warmth, security, pleasure—the tender communication of a mother's thoughts. Her hands against her distended stomach, the woman turned and slipped back through the doorway.

The other woman stayed where she was beneath the sheltering overhang, her iron-gray fur brightening, ridging on her scalp as Moon Shadow's brother approached her.

"Swift Springer." He pointed at the ground between them.

She nodded, slipped quickly, wordlessly, through into the warm interior. Moon Shadow's tail twitched, his light spear rapped out a soft challenge at his side. Tarawassie pulled her cloak closer around her.

The long moments passed; her face began to ache with the cold. "What are we——" She broke off as a new body filled the doorway; more natives clustered in the background, blotting out the light. A man in a knee-length sleeveless robe, stooped and shuffling, emerged into the cool light of Tarawassie's alien globe. He leaned on a staff; his unruffled fur stayed midnight black, even here. Moon Shadow's crest rose.

Swift Springer stopped, faintly smiling, "What now, Shadowman?" His glance shifted slightly to focus on Tarawassie. His pupils widened, narrowed; he shook his head as though he thought his eyes betrayed him.

"I am real." Tarawassie spoke in her own language, knowing instinctively that she could not manage the clipped sounds of the native speech. She moved forward into stronger light, brushing back her hair; stood straighter, aware of the creature the old native saw, which was not herself—trying to become the mystery that even she did not quite comprehend. She reached out to brush Moon Shadow's pouch with her hand, pointed at Swift Springer.

This time the old native's crest did rise. His ageless face rumpled with emotion. She knew the desire to refuse, to deny, to castigate Moon Shadow that burned in his eyes as they touched on him. But Swift Springer could not refuse or deny his fear, his awe, of the half-remembered ancestors she represented.

"You honor Star Woman." It was almost a command. Moon Shadow met Swift Springer's gaze with stubborn pride. "Call old ones; I show you all, this time. I show all; my right!"

Swift Springer shook his head. "You show me, I choose. You think bad thoughts; no one here want twisted mind. I choose, if they see."

Tarawassie took a deep breath. "Call them all. They have a right to choose for themselves whether they want to know this. I want him to show them all!" She brought her palm up against her chest, as she had seen Moon Shadow do, trusting in the tone to make her meaning clear.

Swift Springer bristled, straightening, his fur ridged. She withdrew her cloak, unsure of asserting herself, expecting failure.

"Coward, Swift Springer!" Moon Shadow brought the spearbutt down with a *clack* on the pavement, his voice reaching out past Swift Springer to the dark cluster of watchers at the door. "Springer's-dung, you fear your power come to me. Not fear I show them evil!"

Swift Springer shook his head again, violently, jarring his brittle frame. "We see, Shadowman, who give his kith most honor tonight!" Mockery edged the words; he turned abruptly to push through the cluster of onlookers. Tarawassie heard his speech—sharp, chattering, unintelligible barks echoing in the great hall. A gangly silver child squeezed out through the crowd at the door, and darted past them away into the night.

"It happens . . . it happens!" Moon Shadow murmured, almost disbelieving. "Old ones, young ones, all come; I show them all. This time I show them change—I show them change be right." His gray eyes found her, he smiled. "What we do tonight be shown forever!"

"A kind of immortality," Tarawassie whispered, glancing up into the moonless sky, at one star brighter than all others. "A kind you can be sure of."

Moon Shadow nodded, his elation shining; she realized his brother and the guards had retreated. He motioned her back across the plaza toward the fire.

Tarawassie waited, holding the light globe and spear clutched against her, warming her back at the blaze. The minutes passed, and a crowd of natives gathered, watching her watch them. From the crowd a handful of men and women came forward, led by Swift Springer, to stand between her and Moon Shadow. They chittered sharply, privately, among themselves. Most of them, she saw, had body fur grayed to black—elders. And also, ones who saw most clearly, Moon Shadow's memory told her—ones who could pick the most details from another's showing, and could pass the image they absorbed to others, intact, for the spreading of important news.

Moon Shadow did not look at her, trusting in her presence, lost in the attention of his own people and the obsession of his need to show. She felt the eyes of the others brush her from time to time, heard their halting inquiries. At last she saw the chosen group begin to form a chain, each one carefully placing a hand into the pouch of the next, until Swift Springer reached out, as though he approached something unclean, to make contact with Moon Shadow.

A muttering passed through the crowd. Moon Shadow closed his eyes, his face enraptured.

The crowd fell silent. Tarawassie hugged the light globe to her, feeling the barest trace of warmth, feeling the heat of the fire at her back and the cold air burning inside her head—imagining the heated tingling that passed along their arms. The flames snapped and spat beside her, like the electric dissonance of an alien presence in her mind, like the charge of hostility that flowed between old hatreds. She tried to picture what might fill the minds of Swift Springer and the other receivers now—a bright, tantalizing scatter of human magics, the secret power of the

Star Well, herself swept away like a spirit to another world, bearing the secret of the Real People, the possibility of a future when Real People would prove the value of their gifts and share equality with the Star People and have for the showing all the secret magic. . . .

"Evil—!" Swift Springer broke away from Moon Shadow, the weakest link in a chain of hope. "Evil spirits come into me, from evil mind!" The others, who had been linked through him, stood dumbly, as though they had been stunned, watching as he struck at Moon Shadow with his staff. "Evil!"

Moon Shadow staggered but did not cry out, a strange, shattered expression growing on his face.

"This evil one *show* to Star People, give them power over him. He show us lies, hide truth, much evil! I show, all see, this evil. . . ."

Tarawassie leaned forward anxiously, not understanding. Her hands tightened around the spear as Moon Shadow began to back up, step by step, prodded by Swift Springer's staff.

"You not force me!" Half denial, half plea. Moon Shadow moved his head from side to side impotently.

Swift Springer gestured with his tail. Two men broke from the crowd to seize Moon Shadow, pinning him between their arms, their tails wrapping his legs, holding him immobile.

"Moon Shadow!" Tarawassie called out, but he did not hear or see her now, his teeth showing bright with a snarl of fear, his hackles rising. His eyes were only for Swift Springer, moving forward again. One man seized Moon Shadow's hand, forced it into Swift Springer's pouch; Swift Springer placed his own hand in Moon Shadow's. The elders re-formed their chain, the nearest slipped his hand also into Moon Shadow's pouch.

Moon Shadow stiffened, with an anguish she could not comprehend. A high, thin wail, born of no physical pain, broke from him, continued, starting a susurration among the crowd. Why did he let them do this? What was happening? Should she——? "Stop it! Stop it!" Her voice beat ineffectually at Swift Springer. She forced herself forward, bracing the spear.

But even as she did, the chain separated again. Moon Shadow wavered, his cry fading away as his eyes came open. The two men who held him released him then; he sank down to hands and knees, as if all strength, all resistance, all pride had been drained out of him in one swift incomprehensible assault. Swift Springer looked away from him to her, the virulent satisfaction still plain as his eyes met hers. He pointed with his staff. "Stop!"

She stopped, but letting the spear's tip droop toward him. "What have you done?" She spoke as evenly as she could. They stood like fencers. The elders ringed them in; she felt the eyes that had touched on her with a kind of reverence branding her now with fear and suspicion, cold like the wind.

Swift Springer raised his voice to the crowd. "I give you truth! This one"—his staff whacked Moon Shadow—"and this one"—he brandished it threateningly at her, still not daring to strike her—"want us be swallowed by Star People again, like beforetime! We show you truth!" The elders moved past them at his sign, into the crowd. "Chitta save us, give chitta Star People, they die, forever! Give chitta this one now—watch her die. . . ." His staff struck the spear like lightning, jarred it clattering from her deadened hands.

She caught the light globe to her, feeling herself as they saw her now, shorn of her ancestral spirits—a wild-haired, ragged scarecrow-woman, powerless against the avenging they would claim for their ancestors'—their own—suffering. She saw Moon Shadow rise up on his knees, her own fear and despair magnified in the mirror of his face. "Go!" She could barely understand the words, "Star Woman, run!"

She was already turning, to break past the edge of the crowd. She fled blindly back across the plaza, plunged into the dark mouth of a street entrance and kept running.

Followed at last only by the memory of fear, she struggled on through the narrow canyons of night, stumbling, falling, half-mad with the jagged overlay of one world on another, memories of a city of life and noise that illuminated the broken silences of the dark and empty ruins. But finally no need, no vision, was strong enough to goad her frozen feet beyond a walk. She halted, pain twisting beneath her ribs, and raised her eyes to the battered symmetry of the skyline. The climbing moon, like a tiny silver face, peered down at her past the shadow towers, filling the dark windows with ghost lights like her own, as her mind filled them with the specters of the past. Something slithered through a puddle of liquid moonglow by her foot, disturbing a clutch of bones. Her half-cry of fright beat back at her, layering echoes, draining away into stifled silence. As though she alone were left living . . .

But as the realization grew in her that she was lost, in body, in spirit, moonlight touched the unmistakable form of the broken building where Moon Shadow kept his camp, a silver hand pointing the way to shelter. She moved on, pushing her aching legs, pushing all thought, all fear, all sorrow down, gratefully reaching out for the one concreteness left in this world of night.

She found the broken wall in the pooled shadows and slipped through into the empty interior. But no one tended the burned out fire; no one sat waiting or lay stretched on the heap of rags—he had not come. Tarawassie dropped to her knees on his bedding; sank back, her mouth trembling. Would he ever come? Had he died, too? Had they seen his secrets, good and evil, and then killed him—as another mob had killed—as they would have killed her too, for both the good and the evil, for showing them the truth?

But the reason didn't matter, had no meaning. . . . He was gone! And she had no power to call home his soul. She had no power of immortality, no power over anyone's soul, not even her own. Only a terrible emptiness left within her. Moon Shadow, her mother, both were beyond tears, regret, loss, and pain—and she was left behind with all those things. And there were so many things done or left undone—and no way she could change them now. All her opportunities to do or undo were lost . . . lost. . . .

Grief caught her by the throat and shook her with the fruitlessness of her waking dreams, which had been no more true or clearly seen than the dreams that chitta showed her. Why had she believed that the Star Well held the answer to everything—to anything? How could she have expected it to accept her, with her mind so full of unknown quantities, doubts, and fear? How could she have pretended to believe that they wouldn't matter? She was just learning what it meant to be alive—did she want to die so soon?

Because how could she *know* that there was a whole civilization waiting beyond the passage for her? Whether it was one she would want to spend her new life in, whether it would accept her—whether it had gone to dust like her own? Her mother was dead, had been dying, and it was only grief that made her believe, or need to believe, that some miracle, somewhere, had let her live. No one had come here in five hundred years to seek her people out— no one would ever come now. If her mother's spirit had found a home, it was nowhere the living could follow. . . . Or had she only been dissipated in darkness, lost among the spectral silences of frozen gas and dust. And did she care—did she even know?

"I don't *want* that! I don't want that!" Tarawassie jerked upright, sitting back on her knees, in the rebounding echoes of her own tormented cry. "I don't want her to be gone!" she threw the echoes back. "I don't want to know the truth about it, and I don't want to waste my *life*." She pressed her fists together in the lap of her ragged robe. "And I don't have to. There's no reason to go, no reason to try. I don't have to!"

A shuffling reached her, the clink of dislodged rubble, as the echoes fled. She twisted like a startled animal, pulled back into the present, squinting through the fingers of light that probed like a betrayer's hand into the dark haven of her lair.

She bit off another cry, knowing too well that her voice had played betrayer already.

Abruptly a figure blocked the light—a native. A voice called, a hoarse bark of sound, not demanding, but strangely familiar.

Tarawassie climbed stiffly to her feet, not quite breathing. "Moon Shadow? Moon Shadow?"

He came forward into the dim interior, moving awkwardly, like a cripple. She struggled to fix her vision on his silver-haloed face. He reached her where she stood beside the fire ring, hesitated a moment, gazing through her. His face quivered, confusion and something darker clouded his eyes. But then they came back to her; he lifted his hands and settled them on her shoulders, squeezing gently, in a gesture of reunion. She raised her own hands, pressed them down over his. A rueful smile split his face; the weight of his hands drew her down with him as he sank wearily onto the pad of rags. She lowered her own protesting body slowly, carefully, to keep him from falling. Splotches of darkness matted his rumpled fur.

"Moon Shadow . . ." She drew one of his hands down in her own, seeing the congealed blood trapped between fingers where a claw had been torn away. She opened her own battered hands. "Were they mad? Or were we . . . ? How could they hurt you?" Her hands folded close again over the thin three-fingered one. "How? Why?"

He shrugged slightly, as though it hurt. A low, mournful singsong came from him, like a dirge.

She glanced up, filled with a premonition. "What is it? What's wrong? What did they do?"

Moon Shadow shook his head, avoiding her eyes; he spread his hands in a gesture of emptiness, of incomprehension.

"You can't understand me?" Her voice rose. "What happened, what did they do to you?" She stopped. "Then, how can we——" Remembering she put out her hand. As it slipped into his pouch, he jerked loose, his body rebelling against her touch. Her hand tightened on itself, empty. She pulled back in turn, wounded by surprise and dismay.

Moon Shadow reached out to catch her fist, smoothing the fingers, drawing it back toward him, his eyes filled with apology, his face set in frustration. He slid her hand into his pouch; she felt his own hands twitch with some emotion she couldn't read. And then, as though in explanation, he let the memory pass into her of what had been done to him at Swift Springer's will:

She/he endured again his humiliation, held helplessly, like a criminal, while Swift Springer extracted his guilty secret and inflicted punishment together. She lived the indignity of an intrusion—the forced revelation of a memory not given freely, that was also a kind of perversion, committed in full view of all his people, permitted by them, as though he were less than nothing.

The singsong dirge filled his throat again. Tears brimmed in her own eyes, slipped out and down, unheeded this time as someone else grieved within her. She watched through his eyes as Swift Springer turned against her, and she/Moon Shadow could do no more to help her/Star Woman than tell her to run away. . . .

And then she/he crouched, without the strength to rise, watching the fresh, evil truths of the humans' brutality that had been torn from him spreading like ripples over water through the crowd, knowing that the promise, the hopes, all the possibilities of a new life that had been in him too would not be carried with them, but would sink

like a stone into the depths of oblivion, lost ... lost. ...
He began to moan.

Swift Springer began to speak again, with all the halting
eloquence he could muster. He heard himself, Moon
Shadow, called a committer of perversions with the Star
People, a madman who preferred the madness of his
bastard ancestors to the proven truths of the Real People.
One who would have them all lose their Reality, be
destroyed again by the evil of the Star People, as they had
almost been swallowed by the Star People before, as this
one, Moon Shadow, had been swallowed by the Night
Beast. ...

Moon Shadow struggled to his feet again, found his
voice, denouncing Swift Springer in one final half-formed
defiance, crying that here, in the place made holy by the
eternal fire, he had not been heard fully, or judged
fairly. ...

Swift Springer's staff came down across her/his shoulders
to knock him sprawling, and the Real People, infected and
inflamed by the transfer of his own memories of human
atrocity, had closed around him then, and passed judgment.

"*No!*" Tarawassie broke contact, screaming her horror,
his horror, as she felt the hatred of a hundred strange
minds forced into his own, exploding him, shattering him;
an overload of image burning out the circuits of his brain,
stripping him of his identity, his ancestors, his Reality. ...

Moon Shadow swayed and collapsed against her. She
slipped her arm free, supporting his narrow back, stroked
the warm, matted fur with fierce tenderness. She whim-
pered helplessly, with the knowledge of why he had been
afraid of her touch, any touch. ... But how could it have
happened? He had been in *control* of the showing, in control of Swift Springer, with her presence—until Swift
Springer had broken the showing bond and turned on him.
And then he had surrendered, losing control, losing his
confidence, forgetting even his goal. How could it happen,
what had made it happen to him? Why? Why?

Moon Shadow stirred, raised his head from her shoulder, keening softly. Tarawassie drew a ragged breath at
what she found in his eyes, and another as it began to
fade. He nodded at last, sighing, and met her eyes again.
Gently she reached out to place her hand in his pouch,

picturing in her mind the crucial instant, trying to convey her own failure to understand *why.* . . .

Moon Shadow made a small exclamation—at what, she wasn't sure. Her mind began to fill with memories of Swift Springer—Swift Springer the shaman, the clear-seer, the eldest among the old ones who absorbed all knowledge, who passed judgment on the validity and the fitness of what was shown. Swift Springer, who embodied the absolute in attitude and behavior in the mind of every Real One—even in Moon Shadow's own mind. Even knowing that his ancestral belief was right, still he believed in the omniscient judgment of Swift Springer. She saw again Swift Springer's denunciation of him, felt his own belief turning against him, to make him falter. And Swift Springer had known that he would have to falter, and that had been enough. The static system that he had hoped to transform had defeated him instead, because he himself had always been a part of it. . . .

Tarawassie broke contact again, lurching with the sudden giddiness of fatigue. Leaning to catch Moon Shadow's supply sack, she dragged it close so that they could reach the store of dried meat and fruit. They ate silently, despondently, not wasting strength on useless words. Words might be useless forever now.

But Moon Shadow took her hand again—the other hand this time, not stiff and tingling—letting her touch him now with no hesitation. Her head echoed with the plans for her passage through the Star Well, and a sense of urgency, demanding. . . . Demanding to know, she realized, whether she would still try, and urgent with the need for her to agree.

She shook her head, clearing it, denying. She could not, she would not—she let all of the unanswerable questions, all of her doubts and fears, flow patternless back into his mind in response. There was no reason, and no need. . . .

A burst of anger-sounds startled her ears; she opened her eyes to the anger on his face. Insistently, he pictured her plan again, her longing, her curiosity, her mother's face. And his mind groped, fumbled, forced out a disoriented, fragmentary vision of the Starman kith together, sharing their secrets and their unique talents. He was the last, the last Starman, and his people had destroyed his ancestors. If she never brought her people back—never returned to realize their hope—then he had suffered for nothing! Only she could save his ancestors or make him real again. If she never brought her people back, never returned to him, he would die too, he would die forever. She was his kith-friend, his only friend, and she had promised ... promised. ...

Again she let her doubts make an answer, picturing her people gone, as his ancestors had feared. Nothing would be gained. ...

The image of her passing through battered again at the back of her eyes, clouded with starbursts of brightness by his vehemence; she was his only hope, the only hope of his kith, the only hope of all. ...

"But I'm afraid!" She broke away from him. "I'm afraid, for me. No one else has to do this—not you, not them, not anyone but me. Damn you! Damn our people—there's never going to be anything between them, they're too afraid, too selfish! I'm selfish too. I have to be certain, I have to be sure, or I won't be able to pass through—I have to be sure that it's all there is, the best thing for *me*. ..." She plucked at a rag beside her ankle, not looking up at his face, watching his hands rub distractedly across the fur of his stomach. She lifted her eyes finally to the desolate incomprehension on his face, that could only answer her unspoken question with another.

Moon Shadow sank back on one elbow, and then down onto his side with a sound like a grunt. His eyes held her for a moment longer, the oblique pupils wide and black; and then, as though he had kept them open for as long as he could, the lids fell shut. He sighed, without comfort.

Slowly she stretched out beside him, easing her own stiffened limbs down onto the narrow pad of rags. The faint radiance of his body heat joined with her own in the space between them, soothing her, soothing them both, with no fire to warm them. She breathed in the subtle, dusty, alien scent of his body, letting the tension of enduring release her, letting go.

Moon Shadow's breathing fell away into the unobtrusive rhythms of sleep. Yet her own mind resisted her body's demand, searching the depths of her being, weighing, measuring, assessing. ... If she did not try to enter the Star Well, or if she failed to pass through, what was left to her? To live here in the ruins with Moon Shadow forever, picking through the secrets of the past, forever reminded of death and loss. And they could not communicate forever about the past. They had proved the bond that showing could have been between their peoples—but how could they communicate the future, or even the present now? Would his crippled mind even be able to re-create her speech again?

But she could not go back to life as she had always known it, lost in dreams among the dying—to a living death in a crystal coffin. Was it better? Was it worse? Was it better to hoard this meaningless, futureless, living death, only because it was a thing she could be sure of? Or better to gather her life in her hands and fling it into the unknown, where all happiness and fulfillment might reward her—or nothing might, nothing at all . . . ?

She opened her eyes abruptly, to stare at Moon Shadow's sleeping face. His fears, his own awareness of death made bright static against her denial, telling her that she *must* try, for his sake/her own sake—in order to live, to live forever. But she was only Tarawassie! Tarawassie, not Moon Shadow, not Shemadans or Basilione or the savior of anyone's aspirations—Tarawassie. And it was her body that would drift lifeless in the blue-green limbo of the Star Well, her soul that might never be reclaimed. It would be so easy, so much easier, if she could have shared enough to truly believe as he did, or to trust, as Shemadans had, in the Star Well. If she could *know* that someone waited to recapture her disembodied soul, as she gazed down through the transparent mysteries of the Well. . . . *To pass the dragon, and enter the dark abyss.* . . . So easy, if she could be certain. But was anyone ever certain, really certain, of anything? Was it possible ever to know the future?

She had experienced so little, and she wanted to experience so much—and no amount of measuring or assessing would answer the question of whether she was willing to accept the terms of the gamble, willing to gamble her very life, in order to live. Only her heart could tell her, only her heart—and the Star Well would hear the answer. . . .

A thin drift of snow lay in the entrance of the building with the coming of a new dawn; the flakes sifted down like the pale dust of ages. Moon Shadow moved haltingly, as though he sometimes forgot his purpose; he struck a stone against his knife blade, finally sparking a fire to warm their aching bones.

He glanced at her often, his eyes searching her expression as they ate, huddled before the flames. But she kept her thoughts hidden, assembling images, putting her house in order. At last she reached out to him, showing him an image of the Crystal Ship, promising nothing, except that she would go that far.

He nodded, but the sudden joy in his eyes dimmed, was transformed into a deeper emotion which had more of sharing and an understanding of her fear. She felt again how great a part of him, within her, would share in her success or her failure.

They went out, then, and through the twisting maze of streets, on a final journey to an uncertain end. The snow wrapped them in a purity of whiteness, clinging to her lashes and hair, to her ragged cloak, to Moon Shadow's stained fur, anesthetizing, disguising. For a moment Tarawassie recoiled from the sight she would present, the wretched, wasted thing that would greet new life if she passed through the Well. . . . But she remembered that this body was no more than a vessel for the pattern, the code, the essence that would be transmitted, poured forth into the universe—a vessel that would be re-created in perfection, surely, without the superficial scars and wounds of life's careless handling. She saw her mother waiting for her, well and strong—clung to that vision, to keep from seeing the endless, dark abyss.

They reached the snow-capped dome of the ferry shed at last. She entered slowly, feeling like a stranger, Moon Shadow trailing behind. She heard the irregular pattern of his new hesitation as he walked, saw around her the signs of decay, the unnatural gapings in the domed vault of the shed. No one else was waiting. But a ferry was down. She was glad, not wanting to be given time to hesitate, to vacillate.

She stopped by the opening in the ferry's transparent hull. Moon Shadow stopped beside her, his eyes fixed on it with total incomprehension. She pointed up through the dome at the opaque sky above, getting no more response. Reached out then and showed him a memory of this tiny jewel-facet rising, to rejoin the Crystal Ship where the Star Well waited. He stepped back, his crest rising at the vision of flight, fearful incredulity in his eyes and no human words to express his awe. For half a second delight began to brighten where fear had been, but abruptly his gaze blanked, wandered.

Pain wrenched her. No, she couldn't—she couldn't leave him behind like this, not like this. . . . Somehow there must be a way for them to go on together, for him to explore this final secret with her. She gestured at him to come with her into the ferry.

He shook his head, the fear not fading, but underlain now by a kind of defiant resolution. He touched his chest. "I not forget. I wait till you come. I never forget!" He squatted down, told her with gestures that he would wait for her—whatever happened, he would wait for her return.

She nodded, accepting, remembering that Shemadans had known that the Star Well had never been intended to serve the Real People. Realizing that this was meant to be her journey alone, depending on her decision, her courage, her strength, that this separation was to be a partial payment she must make, a test of resolution.

Moon Shadow rose again and placed his hands on her shoulders, squeezing gently, glancing away and down, as her eyes would have touched him. He spoke very softly, a short, chirping phrase: "My friend . . . my friend . . ."

She lifted her own hands again to cover his, drew him to her, and for a long moment held him close in her arms. "Yes, my friend . . . my friend . . . my friend! Good-bye . . ." She broke away, before her resolution failed, and entered the ferry. She watched his strange silver face through the glass, with its rainbow play of emotions, watched its astonishment as the ferry began to rise, watched it abruptly blotted out as she left the ferry shed, and the world, behind. And she felt a part of herself being torn away, and remaining, the part of him within her alive in her mind forever. And she knew that she had been wrong to think that they would lose one another forever, even in this parting. . . . The clouds closed around her in a shroud of gray.

Tarawassie stepped through the passageway from the ferry, her feet on crystal, her head among the stars. Somewhere there was music, of a kind, playing—loud and toneless, out of tune. Wall surfaces filmed with murky bleeding color. She stood still in the heedless clutter of the waiting area, covering her ears, blinking back her disbelief. It wasn't, not—the Loom? Not Mirro, at the Loom! This bleating, bleeding stridency was not the gossamer cloth with warp of light and woof of music! But what else could it be? She shut her eyes then, too, but could not close out the deeper violations in the fibers of her nerves. *You knew what it would be like, you knew, you knew—from the moment you saw your own reflection. Go on! Go on. Face reality. . . .*

She went on through the corridors, almost running now, to the room where Mirro had always played: Where she wove still, snared inside the web of distorted sensation that she could not tell from beauty. Tarawassie stood shuddering in the doorway, wanting to scream at her, wanting to tear her loose from the abused console that had never been meant for music, and make her stop, stop. . . . But she knew she would achieve nothing, against chitta, and nothing would ever be gained. . . .

She went on, trailed by the wraiths of her reflection, through the hallways to the main dreaming place. The dreamers lay as she had lain so often, or wandered aimlessly, wondering at the stars. A few looked up as she entered, without interest or surprise. Faded robes hung like sackcloth on their emaciated bodies. Faces she had known for years were the masks stripped from the faces of strangers, empty-eyed and gaping. The smell of chitta, and of human stagnation and filth, choked her, nauseated her. . . . Someone stumbled against her. She turned to find Sabowyn, recognized only after long, agonizing seconds. He caught her to him, steadying himself, smiling at her inanely. "You were gone. . . ."

"Sabowyn . . ." She worked her hands loose to seize him, shake him. "Listen to me. You can't drink chitta any more, you've got to stop! You're dying, dying, because of chitta! Please, *please*, listen to me!" Suddenly, too vividly, she remembered Andar's madness.

"Let me kiss you, Tarawassie . . . I'm going to dream now, but I want to kiss you. . . ." His hand stroked her hair awkwardly, as though he couldn't remember why he did it, his beard scraped her cheek. She pushed him away, her face twisting with despair, saw him fall onto a couch, still smiling through his confusion.

She found the spiraling ramp beyond the room and did not stop until she reached the Star Well's rim. She knelt beside it, gazing down at the endless pattern of stars that moved imperceptibly below the azure lines of force. She passed her hand through the cool, reassuring blue-green mist, searched her own eyes of deeper blue and green, reflecting. And behind them, below them, she found the face of her mother, and Andar's face—smiling, at peace. And locked into the essence of her being was a part of one other, to be carried with her always, whatever came to pass. One who carried within him a part of her own essence, wherever she herself might be. A kind of immortality, an eternal flame. . . . Slowly she rose and stepped onto the rim.

Silently, without motion, she entered the ocean.

Epilog

And Moon Shadow received the body of Tarawassie, which came down in a crystal tear from the Crystal Ship, where the Star Well lay. He bore the body away, and where it lies no one knows, for that was the custom of the kiths, to keep a body safe from evil spirits. He held the chitta ceremony, to call the spirit of his kith-friend back to him from the far silences, in case it had found no truer home. But whether he dreamed, or what he dreamed, was never shown.

Then, as he had promised, he waited for her return. He waited for thirty years, scorned and shunned among the Real People of the ruined city. But in that time she never came. And after thirty years he died, and there was no one among his own people who would hold the chitta calling or give his spirit rest, for he was the last Starman.

So is shown the legend of Tarawassie and Moon Shadow.

MEGAN'S WORLD

Marta Randall

Marta Randall is a young Northern Californian whose science-fiction stories have been appearing with increasing frequency since 1973, in New Worlds, New Dimensions, and other publications. Although she has already had two novels published, this is her first venture into the difficult and demanding novella form—a sensitive, rich exploration of the collisions and conflicts that will arise when explorers from Earth encounter fragile alien societies on the worlds of other solar systems.

One

THE SHUTTLE BROKE away from the mother ship and
drifted until she was well past the blast range before her
donkey-engines opened and she slid down toward the
shrouded planet below. Padric Angelo gripped the re-
straints of the webbing and leaned forward, trying to see
around the pilot's seat.

"Calm down, Angelo. You'll get there soon enough."

Padric turned toward the stocky ethnologist. "It's my
first out-planet," he explained, willing in his excitement to
talk even to Jes Abrams, who had spent most of the trip
out deliberately antagonizing him. "I mean, Non-Fed
planet. And I've never met aliens before."

"With luck, you won't meet them this time. That's my
field, not yours. You stick to your monkey wrenches and
leave the natives to me."

"I wasn't intending to interfere," Padric snapped.

"Good. There's nothing that makes my job harder than
a wet-ear prying around the natives."

Padric held his tongue and bristled, aware that the pilot
and the two technicians were listening intently.

"Among other things," Abrams continued smugly, "you
haven't got the training."

"Among *what* other things?" Padric demanded, then
flushed as Abrams gave him a knowing look. He slumped
into the webbing and scowled at his boot tips, and eventually the two technicians began a conversation of their own,
while Abrams pulled out a tape and began reading. Padric
forced himself to breathe deeply and evenly, until the knot
of anger in his stomach loosened.

How much, he wondered, did Abrams actually know?

Some things were, of course, obvious—that at twenty-three Padric was rather old to be a cadet engineer; that his acceptance on the mining ship *Starborne* had been requested by Harvey Jakowski, one of the big-time company managers; that Padric had not worked out of the Federation before; that this was, in fact, his first job. But these were all results, not reasons, and he gnawed on his lip, glanced at the ethnologist webbed in beside him, and wondered just how much had leaked.

That Jakowski had arranged the job just to get Padric off-planet, and away from Jakowski's pretty daughter? That Padric had met Myrim Jakowski at a kittlebum encampment while she was slumming and he was trying to outgrow the crisis of his latest failure to make a niche for himself? What about all the reasons for his series of failures? Padric followed the reasons in back of the reasons, and considered them bitterly as the shuttle angled into the atmosphere. Some things, he decided, were insurmountable, and the reasons for his reasons fell into that category.

For Padric's background was unsavory. His mother had been a theoretical plasma physicist who dabbled in atomic biology, doped too much, and committed suicide when discovered as the source of a highly potent pleasure drug of her own invention. His father, a stochastic technician of some repute, found himself in financial difficulties after his wife's death and the accompanying cessation of profits from her drug. He began using his talents illegally, predicting for profit the results of political elections, was caught with a two-mill payoff, and died in prison. Padric's one sibling, a sister much older than he, was chosen for her intelligence and education to be the subject of an experiment in human-mechanical interface and, although she had volunteered enthusiastically and of her own free will, when the experiments were scrapped she deliberately stole four mills' worth of her employer's property and a company space yacht and disappeared. Padric, understandably enough, had problems adjusting himself to his world, and had already been through three complete reintegrations, two partial wipes, and one reconstruct. He knew all too well that he came from a family of brilliant failures, and now hoped to be the first brilliant success. He tried to overcome his background. He attempted to do his best.

Unfortunately, he didn't always succeed. His parents and sister had been respected and well known in their fields, and their fates had touched the public imagination in such a way that, at least on Padric's home planet, "to do an Angelo" meant to be highly intelligent and absolutely untrustworthy—Padric found no way of fighting against the automatic assumption that he would follow in his family's footsteps, and no matter how well he did at something, each achievement of his was viewed as indicating a correspondingly greater untrustworthiness. Even off-planet, where the family reputation was not such common knowledge as to inspire slang, his background had always been far too accessible to anyone interested in him, and the distrust dogged him to such an extent that finally he became secretive and devious. This behavior was accepted as proof that the family genes were making themselves known, and the more suspected he was of deviousness, the more deviously suspicious he became. His second reintegration took care of many of his antisocial aspects, but the bitterness remained.

Abrams, oblivious to Padric's brooding, continued to peruse his tape. Padric slowly levered himself up, leaned forward, and peered over the pilot's shoulder again. Startlingly close ahead lay the range of mountains they had chosen, and soon they would be settling down in the tiny, rich valley that their instruments had picked as the most likely place on the planet to make a large strike.

"How much longer?" he asked the pilot.

"Hour or so. We've got to find the right valley, then find a good place to put it down."

Padric sat back and Abrams tucked his tape into his pouch and opened his mouth.

"Listen, Abrams," Padric said quickly. "I don't give a damn about your natives one way or another. You get your job done, and I'll do mine."

Abrams elevated his thin eyebrows. "Really? You should care about the natives, you know. I'm not pleased that we'll be setting down near that city of theirs, not at all. But if that's the place the instruments picked, then that's where we'll be. You have to remember what the main thrust of this voyage is, you know. It's not meant as a pleasure trip for curious engineers." Abrams spoke in his most measured, oily, and annoying tones, as though to a preadolescent, and Padric clenched his fists in a fury. "You have to know how to handle the natives. It's very important if we're to make a large strike quickly and get

out without trouble. And you know how important that
is." Abrams tapped his pouch with one stubby finger. "I've
got the specs here, on tape, the first reports from the orbi-
tals, and I've been over them very carefully. Type Seven-
B's down there, superstitious, greedy, backward. Typical.
First we take the land, and if they object, we try to buy it,
and if that won't do, we announce that we're gods from
the skies and that should do it."

"And you need training to come up with malarkey like
that?" Padric asked.

One of the technicians giggled, but Abrams snapped his
mouth closed, glared at the young engineer, turned con-
temptuously away and stared again at his tape. Padric's
small triumph deflated quickly. Abrams, after all,
outranked him and was not likely to forget Padric's comment.

"Valley's ahead," the pilot called suddenly. "Looks open
and smooth—landing should be easy as trips."

This time, even Abrams leaned forward to look.

The valley looked calm and inviting in the late-after-
noon sunlight, and Padric held back his impatience as the
pilot initiated the necessary atmospheric double-checks.
The procedures passed quickly, though, and as soon as the
hatch split, Padric scrambled down the landing beam and
stood on the alien earth.

The first thing he noticed was the startling clearness of
the thin mountain air, which seemed to make things appear much closer than they really were. The air was heady
and laced with the sweet scent of alien flowers, and Padric
briefly forgot about Abrams and his problems as he took
one deep breath after another, clearing his lungs after
months of ship's-air. The sky was a light, translucent blue
undisturbed by clouds, and even the green of the valley
grasses and the browns and whites of the towering peaks
seemed to partake of this slightly insubstantial quality. It
was only after Padric had spent a full minute staring at
the land that he realized the colors were all wrong, the
browns slightly too much to the umber, the grass too much
to the blue, and the white even whiter than he thought
possible. The grasslike plants on which he stood were not
bladed, like the Terran-base grasses of the Federation
planets, but tall and snaky, and deltoid in cross-section.
They were interspersed with tiny orange flowers, each fac-

ing the declining sun, and when he leaned forward to inspect the blooms more closely, he found them to be the
origin of the sweet scent in the air.

"Pretty, isn't it?"

He turned to the technician, a young brown woman
with the traditional webbing of radiation scars across her
face.

"Yes," he replied. "It's like stumbling into Eden."

"Well, don't get too fond of it. It's not going to look
like this at all when we're finished with it."

Padric looked out over the valley. He knew the specifications of the mining equipment, of course, knew what it
was supposed to do and how it was supposed to do it; but
now, for the first time, he actually imagined the great
machines in action. They would start there, probably,
where the stream slid out of the mountain, and would follow the course of the stream down the length of the valley
to where the mountains shouldered close, with just the
smallest pass between them. First the silent lasers would
slice a deep, V-shaped trench in and around the stream
bed, into which the bulk of the silver machine would fit;
then the lasers would slice the ground in layers to either
side, and the traction beams would suck earth, rocks, trees,
and flowers into the wide side-slits of the machine, where
they would be processed, anything of mineral value extracted, and the remains dumped behind as the machine extended its V-shaped track and moved farther down the
valley. Padric translated specifications and textbook
knowledge into a vision of a sleek gray omnivore, gulping
greenery and loveliness and leaving desolation in its wake.

"No," he said, shaking his head. "They can't rip it up,
not a place like this. It would be a crime."

She shrugged. "If we don't make a strike this time, the
whole company goes down the tubes, and it's out for me
and out for you, too. Anyway, it's not *your* valley."

"But what if someone objects?"

"Over one small tuck in the mountains? Not likely.
Besides, that's Abrams' worry, not ours."

A shout came from the direction of the shuttle, and the
technician ran over to help the pilot unload the probes and
meters that would determine the landing site for the
mother ship. Abrams, on the far side of the shuttle, was
busy beaming a report to the ship's computer far overhead.

Two technicians, one pilot, Abrams, and me, Padric thought. That's all it takes to run the whole show, plow up Eden, and take the leavings home. Not even that, really—Abrams could run the whole show with the ship and that little box of controls he keeps strapped to his waist. And maybe, someday, I'll be the one wearing that box. Padric pulled his scopes from his pouch and, mounting a small hummock, began a sweep of the valley floor. Eden can wait, he decided. There's a job to be done.

Something anomalous flashed by the field of the scopes, and he backtracked slowly, trying to find it again. Something white and hard, not snow—when he found it in the scopes, he shouted, then fumbled for the comset on his waist and beamed an open channel.

"Abrams, there's a building at the far west end of the valley. Looks like some sort of temple to me."

"Don't assume out of your field," Abrams snapped. "Where is it?"

Padric quickly figured coordinates, repeated them to the ethnologist, and began walking toward the temple. Abrams soon caught up with him. Out of curiosity, the pilot and technicians followed.

The building was unmistakably a temple. Its flat roof rested on stocky rectangular pillars of stone, its floor was paved with the same material, and in its exact center stood an altar of the same white rock. The altar supported a huge stone mask, intricately carved with geometrical figures; slightly snouted, with triangular, tufted ears, and slitted pupils clearly indicated in the slanting eyes. The mask, magnificent beyond its carving, was imbued with such tension, such a sense of age and dignity that it seemed to leap from stone to life, and the feline eyes fastened on the Terrans and observed them with a brooding calm.

Abrams took a deep breath, cleared his throat, and said pedantically, "Primitive carving is often startling in its rude appearance of power."

Padric, though, was so lost in the presence of the mask that he ignored Abrams' unctuous announcement and, when two tall, feline figures appeared on either side of the mask, he was not even terribly surprised. Abrams immediately pulled his analog-translator from his pouch and aimed it at the aliens. They froze and stared at the machine.

"Hello," Abrams said loudly in Standard, and the word echoed coldly in the temple. The aliens said nothing.

"Hello, we come in peace," Abrams said, and again they remained silent. But they took a step forward, their spears lowered, and another, until even Abrams finally began the step-by-step retreat from the temple. He continued talking into the machine, until both Terrans and aliens stood on the blue-green grasses.

Then, as though the power of the mask ended precisely at the temple's edge, one of the aliens lifted a hand and began speaking in a strong, melodic voice. Abrams pointed the analog-translator at him and waited impatiently as it ingested the new language. Finally a tiny amber light glowed on the machine's front, and its flat, metallic voice translated the alien's words.

"Tayteklosh welcomes you to High Valley," the machine reported. "He has seen your descent from the skies, and wishes that his people may know of your power and your exploits. The city and the people of Apantha await your coming."

"Well," said Abrams. "That's more like it. If we've already got the approval of the local god, all we need now is to make it good with local rulers, and we're home free."

"They haven't put their spears away," Padric said. "And you might remember that we haven't got our weapons with us."

"Nonsense. There's nothing to be afraid of, Angelo. They obviously know that we're superior to them already. Now I just have to cement it. Besides," he added, "I always have this," and he patted his control box, then raised the translator to his mouth. The gesture half completed, he stopped and stared before him. Padric, following his glance, saw that they were surrounded by tall felines armed with spears, and despite his sudden fear, he grinned at Abrams.

"Convinced of our superiority, eh?" he said.

"One more comment and I'll have you 'martialed," the ethnologist snapped. But the aliens remained impassive to Abrams' translated threats and pleas, and by evening they were herding the Terrans out of the valley and down a long, rocky trail leading, Padric assumed, to the city below.

Two

FAR BELOW THE sacred valley, sunlight spills over Apantha the Mountain and slides through the gray stone avenues of Apantha the City. The Taebish are still asleep, and the quiet is unbroken save for the sounds of small, birdlike flyers. The buildings are thick, square, and multileveled—the sunlight does not yet penetrate the deeply recessed windows, which do appear as gaping black rectangles in the bright gray stone. The streets alone in the city are curved, banked high in the centers and slanting sharply into gutters which run with clear water. Bridges of stone slant across the gutters to the entrances of buildings, and tall, yellow-green trees are allowed to grow on the sides of these bridges; their pale roots shoot down from the rock into the water below, and there they float, long filaments of silver that stir gently in the slight current. The roots siphon wastes from the gutters of the city, the trees flourish thereon, and the water leaving Apantha the City is as clean after its journey through the stone streets as it was emerging from the mountain above.

In the center of the city rises a tall, artificial hill surrounded by a high stone wall. On the eastern side of the hill lies the palace of the king, a massive square of stone whose outer simplicity of line hides the maze of rooms and passageways within. Narrow rectangular windows stripe the face of the palace—the topmost windows are twice as wide as those lower down, and admit the sunlight readily. These topmost windows open into the private chambers of Agin King, and here the early-rising servants walk with special care, so that the royal slumber be not broken. The valet crouches outside the bedroom door, his tufted ears cocked for the sound of movement within, and his short tail lies still. He moves his hand toward the servants, and they obediently step more quietly around the antechamber as they prepare for the royal breakfast. An adviser sticks his head in the far doorway and begins a loud-voiced question, and the valet peremptorily waves him to silence and away, then listens carefully at the bedroom doorway. The king, however, is not easily wakened. He lies in his cushioned chamber, heavy draperies pulled against the advent of light, and his long, heavily furred limbs twitch slightly as he dreams.

The western side of the hill holds the temple of the god Tayteklosh, and the dwellings of his servants and priests. Outwardly, the temple is identical to the palace of the king, but within the public rooms are larger and more airy than the royal throne- and council-chambers, and the dwelling quarters are, correspondingly, smaller and more mazelike. The topmost rooms are those of Han-Tor, brother to Agin King and high priest of the god, and here, too, the servants move quietly. But not for fear of waking their master.

Han-Tor stood ceremoniously, hiding his impatience, as the Witness crossed the bedchamber toward him. The old man took his time, walking slowly and carefully with stubby tail erect for balance, so as not to disturb the small bundle he carried in his arms. Han-Tor strove to look aloof and serene, although the night spent alternately running to and from his brother's palace and pacing the antechamber floor outside this bedroom while attendants scurried officiously through the hangings did little to increase his calm. A high priest, though, more than any other, must understand the value of ritual, the uses of time, and Han-Tor watched the old man stretch his moment of importance to the hilt, his progress across the room seeming interminable. Eventually, though, he halted before the high priest and an attendant opened the bundle in the Witness's arms. Han-Tor looked down at the newborn kitling.

"Your wife is delivered of sons," the Witness intoned. The surrounding dignitaries shuffled with approval. "Here is your eldest. His name is Taeg. He is known by the marking of white in the shape of a wing on the right center side of his brow."

"He is welcome," Han-Tor replied, and the Witness then made his long way back across the room. The attendants parted before him, and at last Han-Tor saw Kiv-An, nestled in the cushions of the birthing bed, the second kitling curled against her side. The Witness, with a low bow, placed Taeg next to his mother. The second son was, of course, not displayed. There followed another eternity of ritual before the dignitaries filed from the room to continue their ceremonies in the sanctuaries of the temple. The high priest, too, left the room and retreated to his private chapel. When he was sure the corridor was empty, though, Han-Tor gathered his robes around him and crept back to his wife's chambers.

Kiv-An raised her head as Han-Tor closed the door-hanging and advanced toward the bed. He knelt and nuzzled the dappled fur of her neck.

"How are you?" he asked softly.

Her laughter was a low rumble deep in her throat. "They were right, you know," she said. "It was as easy as popping seeds. Aren't they fine sons?"

"And important ones." He touched his eldest lightly. "Until the king my brother has sons, this one is next in succession. Taeg King-to-be. But this one—" His hand rested beside the second son, and when his wife nodded, he lifted the kitling in his arms. "This one is important because he is ours."

"They both are," she said.

"Yes, of course. But Taeg will be taken to the palace, hand-reared by the keepers of kings—he'll disappear from our lives, either forever, or until Agin marries and has sons. But this one, this one. Have they named him?"

"No."

Han-Tor grimaced. "Second birthling. Tag-along. Not important enough to be named in ceremony. The second is always useless."

"Not so," she replied. "You were given a ceremony name."

"I am a king's son. I was given a name to make sure it was known that I was second, so there would be no confusion. This one, this Taeg, and my brother Agin, were named by inclusion. I was named by exclusion." He paused. "There shall be no 'Tor' in my son's name."

"Bitterness will not change things—"

"Bitterness! Do you know what my royal brother was doing last night? No, of course not. My royal brother Agin King left a deputation from the fishers to flick their tails all night, and will, if he pleases, maybe, grant them audience this morning. We need the fishers, Kiv-An; we need their produce and we need their good will. River Margave ties the entire kingdom together, and if the fishers decide not to cooperate with our messengers, we'll eventually lose the entire eastern lands, because we simply won't be able to communicate with them. And the fishers are touchy folk, still not reconciled to being under our rule—any raw-brained novice knows this! So my royal brother ignores them, and makes no provision for their keeping, and why? Because my royal idiot brother the king has decided that he needs a new robe, and spends the evening wrapped in yardage and purring while his kingdom falls apart. The Westerners couldn't have created more danger if they'd done it deliberately, and I'm almost convinced that they did plan the entire thing. Except that my brother doesn't need help destroying us; he can do it well enough on his own."

"Han——"

"I wish," he whispered fiercely, "I wish I could snap back twenty years and stick my hands in my mother's womb, and turn the order around. Three minutes, Kiv, three stupid minutes, and my brother the brainless mediocrity would not be king!"

She snatched the kitling from his arms and held both sons to her. "No! That's treason, Han, and if you're killed for treason, you'll be killed alone. I won't have my sons dead because of your resentment."

Her neck ruff was half extended, and her golden eyes gleamed. He caught his breath, and extended his hand to her, palm up. After a moment she placed her hand on his.

"I'm sorry, Kiv," he said. "I've been worried, and up all night—I haven't lost my senses. I had the fishers taken to the guest rooms here, and I'm to join them in a bit. I think I'll offer them temple-space for their god. They've never taken much to our mountain gods, and it might be a good idea to give them a chapel, maybe talk to them about that manifestation they claim they've got living on the river. The last time they spoke of it, Agin so obviously didn't believe them that they picked up on it. Yes, I will give them a sanctuary here."

"And Tayteklosh?" Kiv-An made a quick sign of reverence.

"Oh, I've had the portents read. He allows it."

"Are you sure, Han?"

"I'm the high priest. Who would know better than I?"

"Han——"

"No, don't get superstitious. The old man and I get along pretty well. He broods about his loss of place and I about my lack of one."

She shook her head, then glanced quickly at him. "Are you going to give the fishers space in High Valley?"

"I don't know. Temple space is easily given, though. It should content them."

"And if it doesn't?"

He looked troubled. "I don't know. Perhaps I *would* give them High Valley space. They're important, Kiv."

"And how would our people take to that? An alien god in the home of Tayteklosh?"

"If Tayteklosh tells them that he wishes it, they will accept."

"Will they?"

"Ah, Kiv. You're the daughter of a high priest and I'm the son of a king, and we both have distorted views of the way things are. But I think that mine are a bit less colored than yours, especially where the old man in High Valley is concerned. People get the god that best serves them, Kiv, and the god itself has little to do with it. A century back, Tayteklosh was the god we picked—a warrior god, strong and vengeful and demanding, a god who lived on human hearts and human blood. And he served us well; he sent us ravening up the mountains and into this city; he set us on the throne, and he set the Apanthese below us, and we flourished to the borders of the western lands, and to the sea on the east. But we have changed, Kiv. We're an urban folk now, and Tayteklosh has faded, bit by bit, giving up first the hearts and next the blood, until now he receives our respect and our obeisance, but not our lives. We are recently and rapidly civilized, Kiv, and our god has not yet caught up with us."

Half smiling, he glanced at her, but her face was set and stern, her back rigid. "You must find special favor with the god," she said curtly, "that he does not strike you down."

"I didn't say that I don't believe——" he protested.

"You didn't? But you would sign away his houses easily enough."

"Temple space, yes. The temple is a place for us to worship, not for him to live."

"And High Valley?"

"I don't know."

"But you will, if it serves your purposes."

He shook his head. "I don't think so, Kiv. Not about High Valley. If the god sits——"

"Yes?"

"If Tayteklosh sits anywhere any more, he sits in High Valley. There, does that content you?"

She looked at him dubiously, but he rose before she had a chance to speak. "You'd better rest," he said. "You've worked harder than I this night." He crossed to the doorway and paused with his hand on the hanging.

"Call him Ko-Te," the high priest said.

" 'Wanted one'?" His wife considered this a moment, then nodded. Han-Tor peered through the curtains, opened them, and slipped into the corridor outside.

Agin King stirs in his sleep, and his dappled fur mats against the embroidered cushions of his bed. He opens his eyes and lies without moving, staring at the bars of sunlight on the floor of his chamber. Bolts of cloth lie tumbled on the floor, their bright colors muddied by shadow. Agin twitches his triangular, tufted ears, and tries to pin down what it was that woke him so early, what problem bothered his sleep. Something to do with the night before, certainly. What?

The king turns over on his stomach and pushes his blunt snout into the pillows. The fishers, yes, some delegation. He should have taken care of them, he should have seen them. His advisers and his brother have warned him that the fisherfolk are important to the growth and progress of his kingdom. But the new fabrics were so tempting, the colors startling and deep. And he does need a new robe. Fabrics from the kingdom on the far west side of the mountains, woven with craft and delicacy. Agin King thinks sleepily of the good things coming from the west— the wines and fabrics and delicate fruits, the beautiful carving and bright jewels. He would not keep a western delegation waiting, no. But the east is peasant territory— rough, full of fish and nets and woven reed baskets, shallow boats and staple foods—and the music from the east is base, unpleasant stuff. Let Han-Tor worry about the east. Han-Tor always worries well about the peasantry. Han-Tor has undoubtedly taken care of last night's fisherfolk, and no harm done.

The king flips over on his side and curls his legs to his belly, but his eyes refuse to close. Korvan wants a morning audience, he remembers, and Korvan distrusts Han-Tor and counsels Agin against his brother. Korvan also distrusts, among many other things, the ambassador from the western kingdom, and the delegation of fisherfolk, and water from anything other than his own well. Dreary Korvan, always full of plots and suspicions, as though his extensive landholdings were not enough for him, and he had to fill his time and his mind with illusions instead. How could Han-Tor be a threat? No. Han-Tor is, after all, high priest to the god, and Tayteklosh would see to it that his servant was content. The king makes a clumsy sign of reverence as he thinks the god's name. The king's brother is respected, wealthy, and well placed—what more could Han-Tor want? And the ambassador from the west is a creature of culture and taste, far above Korvan's crude delights, while the fishers are base and boring, nothing more. Korvan is clumsy and dreary. Korvan is imagining things.

Agin King nuzzles further into his cushions, closes his eyes, and goes back to sleep.

Three

BY THE TIME Padric and his companions reached the city, they were too tired and too hungry to view the thick stone walls and clear-running, root-laced gutters with anything other than weariness. Their captors had kept them moving at a brutal pace, giving them only the briefest of pauses when they could no longer walk, and their silence, which had begun by unnerving the Terrans, soon began to exasperate them and, finally, left them with a dull terror so muted by exhaustion that Padric soon ceased to think about it altogether. Instead, he concentrated on the almost ritualistic movements of his captors as they led him down the steep, rocky path; their snouted faces remained, in all circumstances, fixed in solemnity, their furred arms, brown and white and gray and dappled, moved to the same rhythm, the same beat that controlled the swinging of their short, pocketed kilts and the dipping heads of their spears. As night had fallen, the aliens produced and lighted sputtering torches, and shadows had danced and jiggled and mocked the Terrans down the steep flank of the mountains. Halfway through the night march, Padric's increasing weariness had left him, for a few moments, tossed up on a shoal of sudden lucidity, and he connected with great clarity the solemn temple in the valley, the cadenced pacing of his guards, the stupefying mask of the god, and Padric's own ultimate fate in a line of perfect symbol and reality which, on the verge of explaining everything, was washed away by a tide of bitterness as the moment passed. Soon thereafter, this bitterness with which he viewed his present captivity as yet another example of the malice of the universe gave way to numbed terror, and so Padric entered Apantha the City, stumbling in the same daze as his four fellow Terrans.

A few early-rising citizens stopped and stared as the Terrans and their escort moved swiftly through the stone streets, but they kept silent and well back along the sides of the buildings, and Padric paid them little heed. He was, by now, convinced that he would be marched into eternity, ever enveloped in silence broken only by the stumbling of his own feet. He barely noticed the thick wall ahead, or the stone arch through which they penetrated the wall, and the square buildings also made no impression on him. Eventually, they were led into a small, cushioned chamber and allowed to sink gratefully to the padded floor. Within moments, though, the silent guards roused them and led them down a corridor.

The room into which they were finally marched, and in which their long journey ended, was instantly recognizable as the stone temple of the valley, although its ambience of power was unmistakably worldly rather than spiritual. At the far end of the window-pierced room rose a throne, carved with strange symbols, its back and seat covered with a deep red cloth. Seated on the throne and staring over the heads of the assemblage toward the Terrans was a thin, dappled feline robed in brightly patterned golden cloth, and bearing no sign of rank save for a brilliant stone suspended over his golden eyes. The eyes rounded slightly as he stared, and he turned to the robed figure beside him. As he did so, one of the guards cleared a way through the felines to the throne, and the Terrans were led to stand before the ruler.

"Stand up straight," Abrams whispered harshly. "Look important. They've got to be impressed."

Abrams drew himself up rigidly, back almost arched with the effort to seem imposing. Padric pulled his own shoulders back, but could find no energy to devote to looking superior, and didn't try.

The consultation on the dais, involving ruler, robed figure, guard, and some dignitary of the court, finally ended. The guard pointed at Abrams' translator, while the robed figure moved forward and threw back the cowl of his robe, revealing a face as dappled as that of the monarch. Abrams raised the translator, and the robed figure leaned forward and carefully spoke to the machine. After a moment, the flat mechanical voice translated his words.

"Know that you are in the presence of Agin King of this north kingdom, and in the presence of the high priest of Tayteklosh, whose valley and whose temple you have desecrated. What have you to say in your defense?"

Abrams looked outraged. "We came in peace," he said. "We have traveled between the suns to visit with Tayteklosh, and to accept the hospitality of his home. We have only just heard the rumbling of your god on this small and distant planet, and have come to pay him a brotherly visit. We are," Abrams added after a pause, "very powerful."

The machine translated this, and suddenly there was a rising murmur of voices in the big room. The citizens of the city stirred—there were tense movements of their flattened snouts and large, slitted eyes, their long-fingered, fur-covered hands.

To the side of the dais, one step above the citizens but one step below the king and high priest, stood a feline of slightly different stature, more bluntly built, and of a solid golden color, draped in robes almost as resplendent as those of the king. This dignitary leaned toward the translator. "You will, we trust, pardon our inquiries," he said. "However, can you prove your divinity?"

The room silenced instantly, and Abrams said with great confidence, "We have this machine, which enables us to understand each other. Have you ever conceived of anything like it? Is this not miracle enough?"

"A god has no need of translating machines," the priest said. "A god knows all languages perfectly and simultaneously."

"We came from the skies," Abrams said, and the golden feline on the step smiled.

"Yes, the priest of the valley told us that you descended from the clouds in a metal ship. It would, it seems to me, be very easy to *descend* in such a ship."

Padric choked on laughter which verged on the hysterical, and Abrams, frowning terrifically, pinched him harshly on the arm. But the aliens on the dais did not seem to notice. The priest was leaning toward the golden feline, while the king watched them with a touch of uneasiness.

"Does the ambassador know, perhaps, of such happenings as these in his country?"

"No. These people are as strange to me as they appear to be to you."

The translator failed to duplicate the intonations, as always, but it seemed to Padric as though some courtly animosity passed between the two.

"Perhaps, then, the ambassador would consent to leave these religious matters to me?" the priest said, and the ambassador waved a languid hand. The king scowled but remained silent.

"You will comprehend our difficulty," the priest said to Abrams. "You are, true, strange and impressive, and have displayed attributes which we associate with divinity. But the advent of a god, or gods, is a serious matter, deserving of deep thought and discussion."

"Discussion?" Abrams echoed. "What discussion? What more do we need to do to convince you? Shall we produce miracles?"

"I fail to understand," the priest replied. "What do you think you can do?"

"Anything," the ethnologist said with confidence.

The aliens huddled in whispered consultation again, and Padric said to Abrams, "Don't you think maybe we'd better find out more about their religion first? I mean, maybe their gods aren't supposed to be omnipotent, or all that."

"You shut up," Abrams whispered fiercely. "Stay out of this, or I'll have you tried for insubordination!"

Padric shrugged and turned back to the dais, where yet another figure had joined the discussion. Gray-furred, with a plain cloak and a woven band crossing the forehead, this new figure seemed more base than the others, tougher, more dangerous. Abrams swung the translator in her direction.

". . . by our river," she was saying. "And has often mentioned the distant suns, and the peoples thereon. There is no resemblance between them, but perhaps she could help."

"And do you believe that she, too, descended from the skies?" the adviser asked.

"Until now, I was not sure."

"Does she claim divinity?" This from the priest.

"Most stubbornly not."

"Then, Tebye-Mother, what would you counsel?"

"That we send for her and bring her here," the gray one said to the priest. "As an interpreter, as someone who might understand these people."

"And if she can not? Would she have wasted her trip?"

Tebye-Mother considered briefly, then said, "Let us send one of these here, with a guard, on the journey. If she finds it familiar, or even comprehensible, she can then come back with them to Apantha. If she does not, then we have only inconvenienced a few of our own people, and one of these manifestations here."

Without hesitation, Abrams stepped forward, dragging Padric with him.

"We find that this idea has merit," the priest announced. "We appoint this one to go." He nodded at Padric with approval.

"Well, Han? What happened?"

"Much, and more noise, and little resolution. I sometimes feel as though I stand in the midst of leashed flyers, and they insist on tangling their ropes."

"New gods?"

"I doubt it. But I cannot be sure. And the ambassador gratuitously insults them in our behalf, while Agin sits damn near purring, and Korvan smirks. All three combine to insult Tebye of the fishers. She's sensible and calm, but won't remain so always. And those foreigners, the new ones, have all the inconsistencies of gods and none of the presence. And ugly, Kiv, you wouldn't believe how ugly. Their skins bear no fur, their ears are round and fleshy, their eyes have white in them, they have flat faces with their noses plastered on as though someone remembered that they needed them at the last moment. Gods more fit for the tribes across the sea, perhaps, than for us. Gargoyle-gods. Fah. More wine."

"There. Tebye-Mother has left?"

"Yes, taking the young foreigner with her, but leaving that hothead Krispeh behind. She insisted on staying, and I couldn't very well deny her."

"She's the one you were thinking to marry to your brother?"

"And a good thing it would have been, politically. Turned our faces to the east. But they took one look at each other and fled, and I really can't blame either of them. She's a troublemaker, political, seems to believe all sorts of nonsense about us. As though she had lived a century back, when we conquered the river. And Agin——can you see my brother marrying a fisher who deliberately provokes those aspects of her culture that he finds most repulsive? Unless I can dig up another marriageable fisher woman, someone with some breeding and sense, he'll marry to the west, in the wrong direction. Which is just what the ambassador wants him to do. It's a pity Tebye-Mother is too old. It's a pity your sister died."

"But it didn't affect our marriage."

"No, of course not. You can't expect the king to marry second-litter, or second-birthling, can you? No, you were safe for me. For which, mind you, I am duly grateful."

"You flatter me."

"Indeed. Of course. Yes."

Four

THE HUT AND its adjacent lands lie beside the bank of a great, sluggish river, and in that particular girdle of semijungle, semiforest that circles the foot of the mountains. Here, the heavy moisture of the rain forest below is lightened by the cooler, fresher air from the peaks and, in the early light of dawn, this mingled air gives the clearing the limpid quality of a cool, clean-running stream. Winged things move silently above the hut and its gardens, and as they bank to return to the forest, the slanting sunlight catches and polishes the jewel-tones of their stretched, membranous wings, and silvers their small, furred bodies. A high, harsh cry rings from the surrounding forest, and in answer a magenta flyer releases a flurry of crystal notes as it slides between the branches of a tree.

Megan raises her gray head and watches the flyer disappear into the forest before returning to the preparation of her breakfast. She closes the fire door on the small, baked-clay stove, rises, and slaps her hands against her thighs, leaving dark streaks on the tan-colored fabric of her suit. Her dull gray fingernails tap sharply against the side of the kettle as she lifts it and sets it atop the stove.

The orange sun clears the topmost branches of the forest, and rows of gray-stalked plants shiver as their heliotropic red flowers turn to face the sunlight. The other plants in the garden respond less dramatically to the light, but the accumulated movements create a thin, gentle rustling of leaf on branch, bough on stem, flower on fruit. As the plants rearrange themselves to sunlight and settle down, the small burble of the spring can be heard again.

Megan pauses with plate in hand to watch her garden complete its morning turning. The day is already warm, and her abbreviated suit leaves her legs, arms, and shoulders bare. Sunlight glances off the rows of dials and meters implanted in her upper arms and shoulders. The sockets in her armpits, behind her knees, and at the nape of her neck and small of her back have long since sealed over, but the meters continue to function, indicating that her pulse and respiration are, for her, normal; the gravity is .01 over Terra Standard; the sunlight is a bit poorer in the ultraviolet; her digestive system functions at .02 over peak; the implanted assists are not engaged, and, this morning, she is 58:197/09-22-16 Terran years old.

She is thin and immensely tall; has gray hair; a second and transparent set of eyelids set above liquid crystal irises that shift color with changes in temperature and pulse in time to her heartbeat. Her bones are formed of high-impact, stress-resistant biosteel alloy, and her bluntly shaped finger- and toe-nails are of a dull gray metal.

Her skin is faintly lavender and occasionally glows in the dark. Tiny wrinkles make the skin around her eyes seem almost purple. Her forehead is unusually high and bulges slightly above gray eyebrows. Her mouth is large, with well-curved lips—a fine and lovely mouth, a completely normal Terran mouth. Her nose is aquiline and has three nostrils. Her inner organs, interspersed with the smooth packets of the assists, are strange beyond imagining.

Twelve kilometers down the large river lies a village of Taebish. They do not think Megan unduly odd. They think all Terrans look like that.

She lifts her toasted cheese from the grill and sits to breakfast, and a slight breeze from the river lifts her hair, exposing the transducer connections set high above her temples. The connectors had provided a snug fit for the couplings in the drive helmet, had shunted pulses to her brain that enabled her to see and smell and touch and taste things that no Terran in the worlds had ever sensed before. That no Terran would ever see again, for the experiments didn't work, the ship-and-pilot coupling was deemed too expensive to pay for itself, too complicated to be easily used. Her long metamorphosis was, they had decided, useless, and they dismantled the starship and dismantled as much of Megan as was feasible.

Much time has passed, though, and here on this distant planet Megan rarely thinks of her altered looks, or her altered body. It has been twelve years since she landed her stolen yacht on the banks of the great river, twelve years since she established her life among the Taebish. She has to a great extent convinced herself that she is, indeed, the norm of her species. And here, of course, she is.

She finished her gardening chores by noon and, after a quick lunch, she sat in the dense shade of the partially enclosed porch, carefully sorting through a box of seeds she had recently acquired from the gatherer folk a few miles inland. The dark seeds would become long, snaky vines bearing a tender-skinned fruit of which she was fond; the smaller, pink-white seeds grew into tall grasses whose thick, pliant trunks were useful for construction. The third pile of seeds glimmered faintly in the shade, their rich brown coats smooth and soft. These supposedly, came from a still more distant tribe, one nearer the coast, and would grow to become tall, flowering trees whose clusters of orange blossoms would attract flyers. Or so she had been told.

As she bagged each heap, the silence was broken by a great deal of splashing and shouting from the river, and she looked up to see a slim canoe nose into the bank and a number of Taebish leap out and haul the canoe up to dry land. She could make out the form of Tebye-Mother against the bright sheen of the river, and she frowned in surprise. The gray-furred Taebish walked rapidly toward the hut, followed by three others who, between them, carried an inert form to the edge of the clearing and laid it down in the shade.

"You are welcome to my house," Megan called, rising from her stool.

"We thank you. How have your days been?"

"My days have been well. How was your journey?"

"The journey was smooth. How is your house?"

"My house stands well. How are your people?"

"My people prosper," Tebye-Mother said with a gasp as she climbed the last step and squatted in the shade. She smiled at Megan as the Terran crouched beside her, and with great amusement the two continued the ritual greeting until all possible traditional questions were exhausted and they could touch their palms together and relax.

"You're home early, Tebye," Megan said. "Your people will be glad."

"Not yet," the Taebish said. "We're far from finished with the mountain folk."

"Oh?"

"Let me have some of your good kerah-juice, and I'll tell you about it."

Megan brought a large stoppered pot from the coolness below the house, and after pouring a cup of the fermented juice for Tebye-Mother, she carried the pot down to the edge of the garden. The other Taebish came and helped themselves and thanked her with ritual gravity. She left the pot with them and returned to the porch.

"So what happened this time?"

"Ah, you know those high-nosed folk up there. We got into the city at evening twelve days ago, after three days of hauling and portage and carrying the gift packs up those forsaken trails of theirs, and they showed us to the usual room and left us there for hours. Of course, we were hungry and tired and dirty, and of course Krispeh was all set to leave and burn Apantha behind us, city, mountain, and all. I got her calmed down just before the high priest came in. He's a cagey one, Megan. Brighter than his brother, perhaps bright enough to be a fisher—I get the feeling he'll be trustworthy for about two more years, and then having to live around that incompetent king will drive him crooked." The old woman drank from the cup and shook her head. "Maybe only one year, I don't know. Anyway, he put us up in the temple for the night, and there was some talk the next morning during the audience with the king about finding room for Hatama in their temple up there, if we want it."

"Why?" Megan asked with surprise. "I thought they were strict with their religion, and the last thing they'd want is a female fisher god in their temple."

"As I said, the priest's a cagey one. He's not content with Apantha's rule over us. He wants to bind us more firmly to the city, be able to count on our alliance and continued good will, our river traffic, all of that. If he manages an alliance, a symbolic marriage, between Hatama and Tayteklosh, he'll have created a bond which neither side will be willing to break. And there'll be benefits for us, too, of course, over and above the protection Apantha can give us. I think I just might do it, Megan. Hatama may not appreciate it much, but a god's got to make sacrifices sometimes." Tebye-Mother grinned.

"And Krispeh, how did she take this?"

"Loudly, as usual. She thinks that they merely want to bind Hatama to an Apanthese marriage, with Tayteklosh uppermost, rather than a fisher marriage where she, of course, would rule. Then, according to Krispeh, they subvert our under-language, take our ceremonies away from us, change our traditions, and turn us into river-dwelling Apanthese. Horrors."

"You don't find this upsetting?"

"I find it positively sickening," Tebye-Mother said calmly. "But it's not going to happen that way. We're stronger than they are. We're older than they are, and our god is a real one, not some outmoded blood-and-thunder hiding out in the hills. And that's the next thing that happened."

Megan refilled the cups and waited patiently for Tebye to continue.

"So, in the midst of all of this, in comes one of the High Valley priests with some speech about demons from the skies landing in the valley and desecrating the temple, and then they brought in the demons themselves. Sorry-looking bunch, with a lot of bluster to them. Agin seemed impressed, though. They started making threats, something about sky ships and fires and what-all else, and I thought perhaps you might know something about them. And they came from the sky, like you did. I took a chance and brought one along. Thought you might take a look at him and tell me if he's familiar. If he is, perhaps you'll come back to Apantha with us and straighten things out a bit, since you'd be closest to a middle-one in this business." Tebye-Mother rose and stretched. "I brought along the one I thought was more sensible than the rest, but I was wrong about that. He seems convinced that we're going to eat him or something, and he's spent the entire trip gibbering. Want to see him?"

"Wait!" Megan too rose. "Krispeh, didn't she try to skin him alive? How about the others—how do they feel? What do you think? You haven't told me that yet."

Tebye-Mother glanced at her curiously. "I, and the others, are very sensibly waiting for more information. And Krispeh stayed in Apantha. She slipped away from us before we left and I couldn't find her. I think she's got something on her mind about the 'demons' and I don't like it much. If it weren't for that, I'd stop at the village for a day or so, but I don't trust her alone up there, and the trip's taken long enough as it is—it's getting toward winter, and the trip back up's going to be harder yet. I want to start as soon as you've seen this specimen demon I've brought."

Megan rose, stuck her fists into the belt-pouches of her suit, and paced the veranda while Tebye-Mother watched her. The transparent lids snicked up and down rapidly, and her eyes pulsed into violet.

The last thing she wanted was the advent of Terrans, and that's what these demons of High Valley had to be— no other race that she knew of had space flight yet. So, Terrans—bringing with them the reminders of her differences, of what had been done to her and with her. Terrans to gape and ridicule. The Taebish had accepted her calmly, seemed to view her as a natural creature, odd but not a freak. Yet how would they feel about her once they had an opportunity to compare her with unchanged Terrans? She felt a wave of bitterness, and turned to Tebye-Mother.

"No," she said. "No, I don't want to see any of them. Take this one away, I'm busy."

"They say their ship is heavily armed," Tebye-Mother said. "They seem capable of great violence. And it's High Valley that they want—if they take it, we'll be drafted to fight Apantha's religious war. And we'll lose."

"It's a bluff."

"I don't think so."

Tebye-Mother waited patiently, and Megan sighed. The Taebish had been good to her, had accepted her with a minimum of fuss, had helped her establish a good life by the riverbank, and had asked no favors in return. And Terrans were completely capable of unloading their firepower on this world, of cindering the Taebish. To let her own selfish fears stand in the way would be a crime.

Besides, she realized, she didn't have to admit that she was of the same race as the Terrans. The very differences that had in the past worked against her could, in this instance, work in her favor. She could simply tell the

Taebish that while she recognized the Terrans as Terrans, she herself was from a different planet, of a different race, and that while they might be representative samples of their people, she was a representative sample of her own. Surely, twelve years had served to bury the memory of her deeds and herself back in the Federation, and of the thousands of separate worlds that comprised the Federation, her story had centered on but one—how likely was it that someone from that one, unimportant planet would be among the crew of this present Terran venture? No, her deception would work, her true identity remain hidden, and with some slight caution, she should have nothing to fear.

"All right," Megan said, shrugging.

Tebye-Mother led her through the garden and to the forest edge where the Taebish had set their burden. They stood back at the old one's shout, and Megan saw, rising from the duff, a rangy, uncertain, staggering, undoubtedly Terran form. It reeled for a moment, then glanced in her direction, glanced again, took three uneven steps forward to meet her and collapsed in her arms. She stood holding the man in amazement as sobs racked his body.

"Thank God," he gasped. "I thought they were going to kill me. I thought there was going to be nothing but—oh, thank the Lord."

She pulled his face around so that she could see it. And as he took in the alienness of her features, her eyes widened and shifted rapidly through the spectrum, while all thoughts of deception evaporated.

"I'll be damned," she said in Standard. "It's my little brother, Paddy."

She was even more surprised when Padric gave a groan of despair and anguish, and passed out.

Five

PADRIC ROSE SLOWLY on his elbow and peered around the dark camp. In the dim light of the fire, he could see the sleeping forms of the Taebish where they had sprawled, exhausted after the long climb up the flank of the mountains. But Megan, who had climbed the entire day without the least sign of fatigue, was nowhere in sight. Cautiously, he pushed his way from the sleeping sack, sealed his jacket against the cold night air, and went to seek his sister.

He found her seated atop a large boulder, elbows on

knees and feet dangling over an immense drop; the exposed areas of her skin gave off a slight lavender glow. Silently she made room for him on the rock. He shivered as he sat, but the cold didn't seem to bother her at all.

"Megan, I'm sorry I acted the way I did, back there by the river. I guess I didn't expect to see you."

"Oh?"

"Well, you've got to admit it was pretty farfetched that we'd meet each other here."

"And that I'd look like this."

Padric shifted about uncomfortably. "Well, yes," he admitted. "But, well, I'd been under a lot of strain. I thought they were going to kill me."

"The Taebish are very polite," she said. " If they're going to kill you, they always let you know first, and give you a chance to get away."

"And how were they going to let *me* know? I haven't got a translator, I can't speak their language."

Megan smiled and drew a metallic fingertip across her throat.

"Oh," Padric said. She turned away and looked again over the void.

"What are you thinking about?" he asked after a silence, and she smiled again.

"Nosy Paddy, always asking questions. Do you remember doing that when you were a kid?"

"No. I had all of that edited. My memories pretty much start at fifteen, and there's just a few vague things before them."

"Why did you do that?"

"What choice did I have? After Mom and Dad, and then you, all went twist, having the whole thing edited was the only thing I could do. It's hard enough as it is, without remembering it all firsthand. I'm always getting it from other people, anyway."

"Getting what?"

"The whole dump! Don't you even know about that? Back home, about doing an Angelo?" Megan shook her head, and he snorted with disgust. "That's typical. Make a mess for everyone else and just drop out. None of you had any sense of responsibility at all. You were all completely selfish. You could have thought about me, you know; about what you were doing to me."

"Doing to you? Listen, don't try to pull that on me, kid. You think I like looking this way?"

"You didn't have to take the job——"

"No? InterStel took me to places you'd never even imagine, they gave me the winds between the stars and the taste of novae and the way a comet sings. I felt things that we haven't even got names for. I was riding it, Paddy, riding the whole incredible universe——"

"You should have thought ahead. You should have thought about what would happen when it was over."

"It wasn't going to be over. It was going to be the beginning of something that would go on and on, open the entire universe to us. Sure, there were backups in the contract. They said they'd revert me, they said they'd pension me, they said all sorts of lies, and when they went under, they couldn't meet a one of them. So they unhooked me and kicked me out. I tried to make it, for a while. Who's going to hire a three-meter-tall purple freak, um? What the hell good was I, except in a traveling circus?"

"But——"

"And do you really think you'd have been better off growing up around me, brother to the freak?"

"Well," he said defensively, "maybe not. But you didn't have to steal all that stuff. People remembered what Mom and Dad had done, and you just made it worse for me. They figured since the rest of you had gone twist, it was only a matter of time until I went myself. You think growing up like that was easy?"

"You think living like this was easy? When I took that stuff, I figured that InterStel owed me. The value of what I took wasn't half what they'd promised me, Paddy. And I couldn't stay put. I couldn't live that way."

They sat in silence for a moment, then she said, "Do you know about painted birds, Paddy?"

"What?"

"Painted birds. You take a bird out of a wild flock and paint it different colors, then let it back into the flock. And the other birds will peck it to death, every time. Painting a bird's not something the Taebish would ever think up—only Terrans come up with sadistic trips like that. Well, I wasn't going to be the painted bird, and I don't want to be the painted bird now."

"So what are you planning to do?"

"I'm not going to tell them I'm a Terran," she said quietly. "I'm going to tell the Taebish that I'm of a different race than you are."

Padric shook his head. "Won't work," he said. "I think Abrams, the chief, the ethnologist, knows enough about my background to guess who you are. Even if we don't even talk to each other, he'd guess."

"Okay, so be it. You people have finally found this planet, and I don't want to have anything to do with you. So if I can't manage to disassociate myself from you that way, I think I'll just go back home."

"But you can't do that! We're supposed to go into the city tomorrow!"

"So go without me."

"No, listen, Megan. I'm sorry, I didn't mean to argue. I apologize. If you want me not to tell anybody, I won't. I'll stay away from you. I'll tell Abrams I don't know what you are. But you've got to come into the city with us—we need you."

"I wasn't planning to come for your sake. I'd come because Tebye-Mother asked me to. I'd come for the Taebish."

"I don't care if you're coming for the great god Peanuts," Padric said. "But if you don't make some sense out of all of this, Abrams is going to get us all butchered, and he'll probably take your precious Taebish with us."

"Tell me about Abrams," she commanded.

Padric described the short ethnologist: his background, his personality, his pretensions. "He's only got this job because all of the company's good chiefs quit last year, when it looked like the company was going down the tubes for good. We lost a lot of people. I guess that's why we're running a seven-crew ship with five of us. And if we don't get something out of this business, it's the end for the whole thing. Abrams knows that he won't be picked up by any other company because he's incompetent, and it's the first job I've ever had. If I don't do well here, Megan, I'll never get another chance. Listen, you've got to come. You've got to help us out. I swear it—this is really important."

"How important? What would you be willing to do to get what you want?"

"I think Abrams would be willing to do anything."

Megan frowned, and a web of vertical lines creased her high forehead. "What sort of ship do you have?"

"Just a shuttle module down here, but the base ship's

topside. Full factory conversion modules, processing modules, protectives—"

"Protectives?"

"Sure, every ship's got them. Just in case, you know. We've got meteor shields and high-impact cannon and light-beamers and the whole bit."

"And you'll use them?"

"Well, we're not supposed to. But if Abrams thought he could get away with it—if he thought he'd get a big enough haul so that the company'd have to forgive him—" Padric shrugged eloquently.

"And you'd fry the Taebish?"

"Look, we only want to mine a little bit. It's not like we want to dig up the whole damned planet."

"Not yet, at any rate."

He glanced up, surprised at the hatred and bitterness in her voice. "Whose side are you on, Megan? You're a Terran too, you know."

"Am I?" She pushed herself away from the edge, stood atop the boulder and tensed her shoulders. Padric scrambled up to stand beside her.

"You keep your mouth shut about our kinship," she said. "If it comes out by itself, or by accident, so be it. But don't go advertising it, understand?"

"Okay."

"Fine. I'll go into the city. But remember, little brother, it's not for you. No way is it for you."

She stalked back toward the camp, the glow of her skin illuminating the trees as she went.

While Tebye-Mother watched, Megan stripped quickly and plunged into the chill mountain stream to scrub the dirt of the journey from her skin. Then, using a clean cloth, she polished the faces of her meters and dials until they gleamed. She draped her long body in a thin white fisher's robe, leaving her arms, legs, and one meter-decked shoulder bare.

"You will be cold, up there in the city," Tebye-Mother observed.

"No, cold doesn't affect me."

She wound a ceremonial fisher headband about her forehead, so that the transducer couplings in her scalp were hidden, and lastly she settled a billowing white cloak over her shoulders.

"Aren't you going to clean up?" Megan asked Tebye. "We're entering the city in another hour."

"No, I'm an old woman and there's no need to impress them. But I don't understand all of that." The Taebish waved her hand at Megan's clothes. "You will either send them running terrified, or worshiping at your feet."

"I'm a fisher, aren't I?" Megan countered. "And proud of it."

"A fisher. Perhaps. You are perhaps any number of things."

"I would rather be perhaps Taebish than perhaps Terran."

Tebye shook her head. "Be careful of your thoughts, Megan. You mustn't gift us with virtues we don't have. We go to meet a crafty priest and a soft king, a suspicious adviser and a conniving ambassador, and some perhaps-godlings of whom we know less than nothing. Every unfounded assumption you carry with you is a potential liability."

"You left out a hothead fisher," Megan said.

"Krispeh. Very well. I too carry assumptions, although I try not to. Yet I find it difficult to deal objectively with my own daughter."

Megan looked down at the gray Taebish and smiled. "You keep an eye on my assumptions, and I'll keep an eye on yours."

"So be it." Tebye-Mother rose briskly, and together they rejoined the waiting fishers.

Six

HAN-TOR STOOD calmly by the broad staircase, his robes tight around him against the sharp evening wind. Occasional gusts lifted the pale material from his fingers and spread it winglike against the black of the open temple gate behind him. The broad steps of the temple fell before him to the wide avenue leading to the main eastern gate, and both steps and avenue were lined with Taebish in court finery, gathered here at Han-Tor's direction to welcome the return of Tebye-Mother and her perhaps-mythical river-dwelling alien. Only Agin King was missing, and he, ever conscious of his own position, would appear at the last possible moment, stay to receive the homage of the visitors, and depart, cloaked in royal dignity, to his rooms again.

The crowd stirred as a large banner was raised over the eastern gate, the signal that the fisherfolk had entered the far outskirts of Apantha the City and were now proceeding toward the walled and gated temple and palace complex. Korvan, standing to Han-Tor's right and one step down, snorted and, folding his arms, stared with great boredom toward the mountain, his contempt for the proceedings and the people honored obvious in his every twitch. Only slightly less intense was his contempt for Han-Tor himself—a contempt so masked that, to all but the most discerning, it easily passed as nothing more than a rather cold and formal deference to the high priest of Tayteklosh and brother to the king. Han-Tor, noting Korvan's posturing, allowed himself a moment of amusement. He had carried his argument, his victory displayed in the broad, brightly decked ranks of courtiers positioned below him, and the high priest could afford a secret smile at Korvan's disdain. But not too broad a smile, nor too easy an amusement—Korvan might, at times, come close to the ridiculous, but he was nonetheless a dangerous enemy.

Even the western ambassador, elegantly attired, had appeared, and stood one step below Korvan, calmly surveying the crowd and banners. Han-Tor's secret smile was replaced by an equally secret frown. He suspected that the ambassador regarded the Apanthese in the same spirit that Agin regarded the fishers—as a rude peasant folk, unworthy of serious aesthetic thought but, nonetheless, capable of being troublesome and unpleasant if not dealt with properly. And the ambassador represented a ruler both stronger and more perceptive than Agin.

More troublesome and potentially more dangerous than either adviser or ambassador, though, were the Terrans, ranged below and to the left, and unobtrusively guarded by the sanctuary's warrior-priests. The Terrans had been treated ceremoniously and politely, as befitted guests of indeterminate but probably lofty rank, during the fourteen days since Tebye-Mother's departure. However, Krispeh had managed to insinuate herself with them and had spent many long hours conferring with their leader. Even now she shared their position on the steps, although by tradition she was entitled to a place four steps higher. Han-Tor knew her personally only slightly, but knew her reputation

somewhat more. She had a name as a troublemaker, an
agitator, firmly set against the dominion of the Apanthese
and their city, their culture, and their gods. She had, as
Tebye-Mother's daughter, accompanied the river delegation for five years now, and had attended many of the
feasts and entertainments under the watchful eye of her
mother, as though the old one hoped to temper Krispeh's
radicalism with the tolerance of knowledge. As far as
Han-Tor could see, this policy had done little good, and
now Krispeh stood whispering and gesturing among the
Terrans, and the high priest doubted whether what she discussed was aimed in the direction of peace and responsibility.

Krispeh, though, was only the most visible of those
whose interest in the Terrans was deep and concerned.
Han-Tor knew of his own activities, and suspected that
Korvan and the western ambassador were as hard at work
as he, but each to his own end. The Terrans, he decided,
might be more a cause of trouble as what they symbolized,
than as what they might actually do.

The harsh noise of a gong sounded as the fisherfolk approached the eastern gate, and at that moment Agin appeared to take his place four steps above his brother.
Han-Tor noted that, for all the king's complaints of the
needlessness of welcome, Agin had arrayed himself in his
newest and finest robes and most resplendent jewels; the
king stood flashing and billowing upon his step like some
bedecked pleasure god newly descended from the peaks.
Han-Tor thanked Tayteklosh silently for the king's occasionally convenient vanity, and turned to face the gate
again.

The eastern gate creaked open, great wooden beams
swinging ponderously along their tracks, and the motley
group of fisherfolk entered. Though they were still too far
away to be seen clearly, the Taebish and the Terrans on
the temple steps tensed and stared down the avenue. Han-
Tor squinted, seeing the Taebish lining the far end of the
avenue move suddenly, seeming to step back and forward
again as though some pressure pushed against them and
released them with its passing. The crowds continued to
sway, the tension on the steps increased, then the fishers
reached the foot of the staircase and a sudden silence descended over Apantha the City. In that deep quiet, three
figures took the lead and climbed toward the priest.

Tebye-Mother climbed easily, her back straight and her head held high. She knew exactly what honor was given to her, and she was going to take every advantage of it—her ascent was a thing of ceremonial dignity. Han-Tor approved. Beside her the Terran Padric climbed sullenly, his fists thrust into his pockets, eyes down. He halted when he reached his fellow Terrans, and they moved aside to make room for him. Abrams began speaking, but Padric abruptly and with ill humor waved the little man to silence.

The third figure, though, left Han-Tor stunned. Immensely tall and immensely thin, lavender-skinned, and absolutely alien—bright gleams flashed from her shoulders, and the ritual headband of the fishers rode above stubborn, pulsing, multicolored eyes. A walk of grace, of precision, of absolute arrogance, and the wind, alternately billowing and smoothing her simple white robe and cloak, only enhanced her dignity. She seemed something of infinite aspect and infinite power, for whom an awed silence was the only appropriate greeting.

She stopped by the Terrans and looked down on them without changing expression, then continued up the stairs, ignoring the lesser court functionaries, until she stood a step below the high priest and bent her neck to look at him.

Han-Tor was torn between the urge to kneel and the urge to applaud, so perfect, so arrogant had been her ascent of the temple.

She turned to the stunned and staring king, bowed briefly, and said in the accents of the river folk, "I am Megan. I have come at the request of my chieftain to aid your negotiations with the aliens."

But the king, wide-eyed, detached the glittering snow stone from his brow and, his hand shaking, bound it against her forehead. A great sigh issued from the Taebish, and in the gust of that multisouled emotion, Han-Tor was delivered of revelation.

"I will show you what the Terrans have done," Korvan said. Megan and Tebye followed him to one of the palace's enclosed courtyards, a place of greenery and fountains. Here the king's adviser waved a hand toward a pile of slag in the center of the area.

"They arranged a display of their power, melted this stone fountain, picked flyers from the air with invisible

beams and brought them to hand, slaughtered three live
food-grets brought up from the kitchen, and induced
noises from the air which they claimed originated with
their far ship, although such soft sounds could not possibly
have traveled that great distance by themselves. They then
caused the waters in all other fountains to burst into
flame, and they retired."

"Did they threaten you?" Megan asked.

"Did they have to?" Korvan replied. "We have not kept
them from receiving visitors. Krispeh the fisher is often
with them, and I am told that the western ambassador has
also paid them a number of visits. The high priest, too,
spends some time with them."

"Are these significant, beyond simple curiosity?"

But Korvan evaded the question. As he escorted them
through the maze of palace corridors toward the entrance,
he pointed out various highlights of architecture and, finally, asked whether their accommodations in the temple
were adequate.

"They are pleasant," Megan replied.

He glanced at her with a peculiar combination of awe
and dislike. "And have you seen the high priest yet?"

"Aside from yesterday's greeting, no."

"Ah," the adviser said. "Ah." After a moment of
silence, he said, "We are not pleased with all of this, you
know."

"It's a tense matter."

"We seem to be invaded by progressions of the yet more
foreign."

"So I see."

"Caution is always the best course."

"I understand."

Again he glanced at her, this time with speculation, and
gestured her to wait while Tebye strode ahead. Then, rising as high as he could, he whispered, "Be careful of the
western ambassador. He is not trustworthy. Watch out for
Krispeh. And Han-Tor, the priest—"

"Yes?"

But he made an eloquent motion with his head, and
they followed after the striding fisher.

"How the hell should I know what she is?" Padric lied
in desperation. "They dragged me off to her place, she
came out, took a look at me, and the next thing I knew

we were all on the way back up. And that's all I know, I swear it."

"You're useless," Abrams fumed. "Do I have to figure everything out by myself? She speaks Standard, she must have said something about where she comes from, who she is."

Padric shrugged and returned to his dinner. He was thankful that his sister's reputation had, over the years, centered almost entirely on her thefts and flights, and the story of her transformation from human to bizarre was almost forgotten. Now, if Abrams would only quit pestering him—

"She's got to be Terran," Abrams said. "No one else has space flight, and she sure as hell wasn't born here. And anything as ugly as that we'd have to know about, someone would have to know about. Can't you think of anything at all?"

The pilot and technicians shook their heads.

Abrams pushed his plate away and stood up from the table. "I've got to talk with her before these stupid 'negotiations' start. She may be a freak, but she's got to be a Terran, and she's *got* to be on our side."

"I wouldn't count on it," Padric said bitterly. "She seems to think we're about on the level of maggots."

"Nonsense. You know her—you go over to the temple and tell her that I want to see her. And make sure she comes."

"What makes you think I can get her over here? What makes you think that she'd be willing to come with me?"

"Listen, Angelo, that is an order. You go get the freak and bring her over here, and that's that."

Padric slammed his palms against the table and rose, grabbed his jacket, and strode from the room.

"At least have something to eat, Han. You haven't sat to a meal since last night."

Han-Tor automatically shook his head. Kiv-An put her hand across his forearm and said, "Please." He stopped, smiled, and nodded.

"Good. I've some fruit, a little wine, some bread. That will be enough for now, and I can get you more—"

"No, don't bother. Just a little fruit."

She watched him as he ate. "You've been in the sanctuary for hours," she said finally.

"Yes."

"Has the god helped?"

He picked up another piece of fruit and balanced it in his hand. "I don't know, Kiv. There's so much at stake here, so many questions, that I can't even begin to find my way out. And I have to, soon, or everything will collapse."

"Surely you're overdramatizing. Obviously the Terrans can't have High Valley. It's unthinkable. They'll just have to be told to leave."

"No, they won't simply go because we tell them to."

"But what can they do to us? They can't possibly destroy Apantha."

"No? Remember that demonstration they gave at the palace? Remember what they did to that fountain?"

"They would do that to us?" she said in shock.

"I don't doubt it."

"But—but Tayteklosh would not allow it! That's what you were in sanctuary for, wasn't it, Han? To ask the god for protection?"

"Do you really think Tayteklosh can shelter us?"

"What other hope do we have?" she asked, and the high priest shook his head.

"I think we can be honest with each other," said the western ambassador. "We seem, after all, to be the only ones involved in this business who can afford to look at it with clear minds."

Megan raised her brows in inquiry; then, realizing that the ambassador could not interpret her expressions, she said, "I'm not sure I completely understand."

"Quite simple. We are dealing with barbarians on the one hand, and advanced technology on the other. Civilization, and the Apanthese are not prepared to cope with it. I doubt even that Han-Tor, who seems the brightest of the bunch, yet realizes what's been placed within their grasp."

"Which is?"

"The stars, my friend." The ambassador leaned forward, cradling his wineglass in his hands. "Just think of it—trade routes out to the stars, an influx of advanced learning, of advanced methods, that could lift this planet by its scruff, could mean untold wealth. And we, in turn, could benefit the Federation—is that a negative?"

"Yes. Do you know what would happen to this planet if the Federation did decide to move in? Unless something radical has changed, you wouldn't be granted any part of the Federation at all. Instead, your world would be colonized, you would be put under a Terran ruler, you would cease to have any say whatsoever about the destiny of your people or your planet. The Federation simply isn't geared to accepting alien members."

"But your information, surely, is out of date? You have spent twelve years on this planet, out of contact with the Federation. Twelve years is a long time. Things may have changed."

"I doubt it. Things move slowly at Central."

The ambassador waved a hand negligently. "Possibly. Nonetheless, even should this planet become a colony for the Terrans, the kingdom of contact would wield the most power, would automatically become the most important culture. Instead, the entire venture is threatened by the superstitions of the Apanthese. It's a pity that the Terrans didn't set down further to the west."

"As it is, though, Apantha is not a part of the western kingdom," Megan said carefully, but the ambassador only smiled.

"You're not a Terran, though, are you?" he asked.

"I didn't come to speak of myself," Megan said.

"The subject is inevitable. You are—distinctive, you know."

Megan shrugged and did not bother to interpret the gesture. "I thank you for your hospitality," she said formally, preparing to rise, but whatever response the ambassador had prepared was interrupted by a crash from the antechamber, and a bedraggled Taebish rushed through the hangings toward the ambassador, a tapering dagger clutched in his hand. Megan moved with a speed she thought she'd lost—'ported herself directly in front of the assassin, splintered his weapon, locked him, and had him dangling in shock a meter from the ground before the ambassador could finish his scream of warning. The guards rushed into the room and stared, openmouthed, while she lowered her right arm, gently setting the assassin on the floor.

"You'd best find out who sent him," Megan said evenly.

"Korvan. It has to be Korvan."

"Not necessarily," Megan began.

"Of course it is. My government shall hear of this." He gestured at the guards, and they approached cautiously, took the limp man and retreated, their eyes still fastened on Megan. The ambassador turned to his worktable, stopped, and turned back slowly.

"I owe you my life," he said.

"No, there is no debt."

"And I did not even see you move."

"My reflexes are fast," she said, turning to leave.

"Are the other Terrans as fast?" he asked quickly, but she made no answer.

Seven

"ECONOMIC REALITIES," ABRAMS pontificated, "dictate that our position on mining High Valley be uncompromised. We are prepared to be more than generous to the—er—Apanthese, but we are not prepared to withdraw our claims completely."

"What claims? What sort of claim can you possibly have on High Valley, if not the illegal claim of piracy and robbery? The valley is not a piece of loose rock, after all, to be seized by the first vagrant to pass by. Until you cease this nonsense about 'claims,' we cannot even begin to negotiate." Korvan, heavy with the dignity of his robes of office, sat once more. Tāebish and Terran, each in the manner of his kind, glowered at each other.

Megan shook her head and reached out for a beaker of water. The session had lasted seven hours so far, and showed no sign of reaching any conclusion whatsoever. The argument over claims was only the latest in a series of semantic acrobatics, each side apparently assuming that, given the proper sequence of noises, the other side would give in without further contest. And neither side worked for an acceptable settlement, or even gave any sign of realizing the complexity of the other's position.

Or positions, she thought wryly. The Taebish certainly had enough different elements among them to complicate any discussion. Megan's treatment of the would-be assassin had so terrified him that he was still catatonic, and it was impossible to determine who had sent him to kill the western ambassador. Korvan, therefore, kept his position as chief representative of Agin King, but not, perhaps, as representative of Agin's desires. The adviser's wishes were quite simple—he wanted the Terrans out of Apantha and out of the entire kingdom; he wanted the fishers completely subservient to the Apanthese; he wanted the western ambassador to disappear and, with luck, take the western kingdom with him. The western ambassador, however, was not at all likely to vanish. As far as Megan could see, the ambassador wanted the Terrans for his own kingdom, and if the Terrans insisted on having High Valley and only High Valley, well, this was a surmountable problem—if the valley could not be moved, the borders of the kingdom could. Since a nation in chaos is most easily conquered, the ambassador watched and plotted and, Megan was sure, occasionally added to the confusion himself. Here, Megan's suspicions and Korvan's jibed perfectly, but Agin King was too fond of the goods from the west to listen to any counsel against his ideals.

The Apanthese themselves were disturbed as they watched royalty and foreigners dickering over the fate of their god's home, while the high priest seemed lost in convolutions which no one else could follow, but which seemed far removed from the protection of High Valley.

And, lastly, Krispeh made her silent ways about the palace and temple, wishing only for the destruction of Apantha, the west, the Terrans, and all too willing to use each element against the others.

The Terran position was equally intricate, and whatever impressions of it Megan had picked up before had been confirmed by her conversation with Abrams earlier that morning. The decision to land on this particular planet, in that particular valley, had not been dictated merely by whim—Abrams' insistence on his "rights" reflected a bitter economic and political reality which was nonetheless strong for being centered light-years away. Padric had said that the mining company would go under if this particular venture did not bring in a great enough return, and Abrams had emphasized this point. The ship had been scouting for ten months Terran before happening on this planet—her fuel supplies were almost exhausted, and with each week that she remained empty and spacebound, the company's position worsened. Megan had also gleaned bits of information concerning a probable, and life-saving, merger with a larger combine in GalCentral. The merger, according to Abrams, would not be effected until the company showed its ability to make a profit, and the option time was fast running out. In addition Megan suspected more hidden, and stronger, political factors at work, factors that dictated that the Terrans not simply belly into the valley and take what they desired by force. Padric had mentioned something about a Relinquishment Movement at work in the Federation. The bills sponsored by the movement would, supposedly, return control of colony worlds to their own native sapients, but would legislate and oversee acceptable Terran behavior among alien sapients, and might eventually lead to the acceptance of non-Terrans into the Federation itself. Abrams, therefore, found himself caught between two equally impelling demands—on the one hand, that he bring in a large and valuable cargo in the near future, on the other, that he avoid the traditional violence that would serve only to fuel the Relinquishment Movement and therefore serve to stifle even more the company's future activities in space. But while Megan fervently hoped that the political factors were strong enough to render Abrams' threats of violence mere bluff, she could not convince herself that, cornered, Abrams would not pick the immediate good of his company over the more distant and therefore more ambiguous hope of lenient political sanctions.

Megan put down the beaker of water, straightened her shoulders, and began to explain, yet again, to Korvan why the Terrans could not be persuaded simply to seek another planet, and to Abrams why the Taebish found it impossible to relinquish their most holy lands and the home of their god. She felt, as she spoke, as though she were caught in an eternal loop of impossible frustration, forever explaining a brick wall to a brick wall.

Abrams stopped her before she left the room at the end of the session, and Korvan, not to be left out, paused also well within hearing. But the ethnologist did not seem to care.

"I've just thought of another piece of information that you might find interesting," he said, smirking.

"What is it?" Megan said wearily.

"I know who you are," he announced.

"You what?"

"Listen, you may be able to fool the Tabbies here, but you're not fooling me, not one little bit. I know who you are and where you come from, all of it. Maybe you think you know where your interests lie, maybe you think you've got a cozy little setup going here, but just remember that I can explode the whole thing with just a few words. Understand?"

"No, I don't think I do," Megan replied uneasily.

"I see the way the Tabbies treat you, always making room for you, looking at you. The old god dodge."

"For God's sake, turn off your translator," Megan said.

Abrams grinned and complied. "Sure. I can understand. You convinced the Tabbies that we're not gods, and I don't really hold that against you. After all, we're the newcomers here, right? You've got things the way you want them. All right. But let's be realistic. Now I know something that you don't want broadcast, right? And you can help me get something I want in return. So maybe we can work something out between us."

"Did Padric—"

"Padric didn't say a word, and didn't have to." Abrams' grin widened. "And I wasn't completely sure, until you asked that. So, maybe we can work something out now."

Megan glanced around, seeing Korvan still standing by the doorway, frowning as he tried to pierce through the alien tongue. The lesser functionaries and the many observers had already filtered from the room.

"Look, Abrams, you go ahead and tell the Taebish what I am. I've never told them I was a god or anything else. So go on ahead; I don't care."

"Then why did you make me turn the translator off?"

"Frankly, because I'd rather not be associated with you, any of you."

"No? That's too bad. Because you will be, you know. And I can also tell them that you're a thief, and a freak, and—"

"Don't you understand that I'm the only hope you've got on this planet? That if you ruin their belief in me, you'll never get High Valley?"

"I'm just being a nice guy. I could take it anytime I wanted to."

"And that really is a bluff."

"Try me," Abrams said jauntily, and left the room. Korvan, his body stiff with suspicion, regarded Megan for a moment before he followed the Terran out.

"Damn it, Padric—"

"I didn't say anything, I swear it!"

"Then how the hell did Abrams know?"

"He's got the tapes, he's got my background file, and it's full of stuff about you, too. I told you that the whole thing was common knowledge. You didn't believe me."

"Common knowledge. Do you have any idea what that common knowledge is likely to do to all of us? I'm the only one that everyone in this business can deal with. Maybe they don't all trust me, but at least they think they can believe me more than any of the others. If Abrams discredits me, he might as well bust his translator, because he won't get anything from anybody."

"So don't make him do it. Arrange things so the Tabbies give us the valley, we'll mine it, away we'll go, and everything here can go back to what it was before. You can forget me, and I'll do my best to forget you."

"Paddy, it can't work that way! How would you feel if some powerful aliens landed in—in Althing Green, say, right in the middle of the Houses of Council? And wanted to turn the whole thing into a slag heap?"

"We wouldn't let them. We'd run them off."

"And if you couldn't? How would you feel if the representative from Acadia started telling everyone just to shut up and let the aliens take the Green?"

"Megan, there's no comparison. That just simply wouldn't happen."

"Use your imagination, Paddy! Use your empathy! Or did you have that blanked, too?"

"Megan—"

"No, I'm sorry. I take it back. But you've got to help me."

"How? What can I do?"

"How can I get back at Abrams? Does he have any secrets, anything he's ashamed of? Anything I can use, anything at all?"

"You really *don't* want the Tabbies to find out about you. You'd make yourself another Abrams just to prevent it."

"Paddy—"

"Besides, I don't know anything that would help. He's an ass, he's stupid, he's egotistical, but how's that going to help?"

"I don't know. Can't you think of anything else? Anything at all?"

"What are you so afraid of?"

"I don't want to be part of you, Paddy. I don't want to

have anything to do with any of you. I don't even want to be associated with Terrans. Grasping, violent, cruel, stupid—"

"You can't disavow us, Megan. No matter what you want, we're still your people. You're not going to escape that."

"Yes? Watch me."

But she couldn't tell Tebye-Mother.

She paced through the halls of the temple, past priests and acolytes and civilians who stepped back along the sides of the rooms and corridors, maintaining a respectful silence and a respectful distance. She paused in one of the gardens where a young woman was playing with two very young kitlings. The Taebish suddenly noticed her and rose quickly to leave, but Megan insisted that she and her kitlings remain, and turned away from the greenery and the splash of fountains. Two floors up and along one of the outer walls, she discovered the sanctuary being prepared for Hatama, the god of the fishers. Workmen, under the direction of the master artist, carefully applied pigments to the stone walls, depicting the River Margave in its seasonal fluctuations, the bounty of fishes, the myths of the god. Silence as she entered, and the master artist came to the doorway, wiping her hands on her apron as she approached.

"Will you inspect the work?" the artist asked respectfully. "We have taken much time, I have listened to your myth singers, and your chieftain has spent much time aiding us. Is it to your liking? Is it proper? Are you pleased?"

"Yes," Megan replied. "Hatama will like it here."

"We are pleased," the artist replied. Megan was suddenly tempted to ask the artist what she thought Megan was, but grew afraid of the answer. Instead, she bowed and left quickly, and heard the buzz of conversation rise in the unfinished sanctuary.

Eventually she found the quarters for the fisher delegation. Tebye-Mother was out, but the other fishers welcomed Megan warmly, and made room for her at the low table where they were playing fisher games.

"How goes it?" one of the fishers asked. Megan imitated the Taebish shrug.

"It's a fish speaking to a fish about birds." she replied, and the fishers laughed at the old river-folk saying.

"Typical of the mountain folk," the fisher replied, and the others nodded in agreement.

"Takes a fisher to make sense."

"Aye. Megan, remember the time the Apanthese came down the river to the coast?"

"And the cataracts?"

"And they never thought to carry the boats around, rather than go right over?"

"Lack of sense, pure and simple. They have to borrow it, because they'll never learn it by themselves."

"Pass the bones, let's start again. Megan, do you want a hand in?"

"Yes, I think I do. Are we playing simple to right, or double-over?"

"Double-over! With you? The last time you played double-over with Tebye—"

"An entire hutful of fish—"

"You're not a coward, are you?"

"Who, me? Of course not. I'm just exercising my common sense."

"Fisher!"

Two hours later, when the messenger from Han-Tor finally found her, she was slumped along the benches with the rest of the fishers, sipping from a mug of fermented juice and sharing stories.

"The high priest wishes your company at dinner," the messenger said, striving to ignore his surroundings.

"Tender my compliments to Han-Tor," Megan replied. "Tell him that I have promised this evening to my people, and will not go from them. Tell him I thank him for the honor, but I'm spending the evening at home."

The messenger bowed stiffly and moved out of the room, tail erect.

"More juice, Megan? Good. Remember the time when—"

Eight

"YOUR HEAD OUGHT to hurt," Tebye-Mother said unsympathetically. "I hadn't thought you'd be that irresponsible."

Megan sat slowly, fingering her scalp as though, if she touched it too hard, her entire head would slip from her fingers and fly out the window. "Did I insult Han-Tor?" she asked.

"Not terminally. He's invited you to dinner this evening." The old fisher lifted the invitation-string from the table. "Fairly informal, for the high priest, brother to the king and all that. What remains to be seen is whether the informality is a mark of favor or of disrespect."

Megan didn't answer immediately. She concentrated on her body, releasing with the power of her mind the implanted assists that cleared her bloodstream and her nerves of the accumulation of alcohol, and she felt the headache recede and sobriety return. Tebye followed her into the bathing chamber and sat on a ledge while Megan stripped and folded her long body into the bathing pool.

"Tebye, I don't want to have dinner with Han-Tor tonight. I don't think I want to see any of them again, except at the sessions. And maybe not even there."

"You are weary so soon? We've only been here three days."

"Long enough for almost everyone involved to take me aside and try to bend me to his way of thinking. Everyone except Han-Tor, who's going to get at me tonight, and Krispeh."

"She won't bother you. I think she thinks you're one of the enemy. Along with Agin, Han-Tor, the Terrans, the westerner, Korvan, me, and everyone else. But part of your job is to be taken aside and spoken to. Otherwise, how could you know all the sides of the argument? They speak to you because they cannot speak to each other."

"Because I am as alien to each as I am to the others?"

"Yes."

Megan slid forward until her head was under water, then sat abruptly. Her eyes peered at Tebye from beneath the transparent lids.

"I'm a Terran," she said, and slid under water again.

"So?" Tebye said when Megan emerged. "You're still more of a middle-one than anyone else."

"Don't you think it would color my sympathies?"

"No, why should it? You are rather an odd Terran, and certainly more a fisher than anything else."

"Damned fisher rationality." Megan climbed dripping from the pool and wrapped herself in a length of cloth. "It's more complicated than that. Why are you taking this so calmly? Aren't you surprised?"

"Don't be like that fool Krispeh, and assume that I'm

both old and blind. I suspected it when the Terrans were first brought to Apantha the City, and I was sure of it when I brought the young Terran down the river to you."

"It doesn't bother you? No, I can see not. But it's going to bother everyone else."

"Don't tell them."

"I think I may have to."

Megan tossed the soaked cloth over the side of the pool and stalked back to the sleeping chamber, where Tebye once again found a comfortable ledge.

"Abrams, the Terran leader, knows what I am."

"You told him?"

"No. He figured it out. Yesterday he took me aside after the session and told me to swing the negotiations his way, or he would announce my background to everyone, discredit me, and take the valley by force."

"Have you told this to anyone?"

"Just you. And I wasn't even going to do that."

"What are you going to do?"

Megan fastened the sides of the fisher kilt and shook her head. "I don't know yet. But I know what I want to do. I want to march out of here, take the eastern gate, and go home. Now."

"Cowardice."

"Is cowardice in the will, or in the action?"

Tebye conceded the point with a flick of her tail.

"So what will you do?"

"Stall for time," Megan replied, winding the headband about her forehead.

"Time's in short supply."

"Everything's in short supply, including my patience. Tebye, now that you know I'm a Terran, do I repulse you?"

"Why should you?"

"You thought I was a typical whatever I was, before they showed up. Now that you've seen them, now that you know what Terrans are supposed to look like, don't you find me unsettling?"

"You're behaving like a kitling. I think of all of you as freaks," Tebye-Mother said easily. "I always have. You look to me like Megan, who lives up the river. The session's about to begin; are you going?"

"But there are things I haven't told you," Megan cried.

"You will, eventually. You'd better go."

Megan stared at the old Taebish for a moment, then flung her white cloak over her shoulders and stalked toward the door.

"Wait, you're forgetting something," Tebye called.

Megan turned, and the fisher threw something to her. Megan caught it in her palm, opened her fist and stared down at Agin's bright snow stone.

Padric stood outside the doorway, frowning fiercely. The guards ignored him, as did the occasional Taebish who passed through the door, always intent. Runners, Padric wondered, gone to bear tales to king or priest? To gutter-sweep or minister? Everyone in Apantha seemed privy to the negotiations, except himself. The chambers were guarded, true, but the guard seemed to be ceremonial only, and did not prevent the easy access of Taebish or Terrans to the deliberations within. But Padric feared the guards, and feared the cold reception he would get from the other Terrans within the room, as he feared the smooth, undecipherable looks of the Taebish. And, of course, his sister was in there, calmly dealing with crises of misunderstanding and cross-purposes, being competent and intelligent and valued. While he was not yet ready to admit that he feared his sister, the emotion was there, only slightly clouded by ambiguities of term.

He had seen her twice since their entrance to Apantha the City—once as she walked swiftly down a corridor, debating intensely with a bedecked official of the court, and the second time when she had found him half hidden in a garden and had accused him of betraying her to Abrams. The few times he had sought out her rooms, he had been turned away by the guard-priests that stood constantly by her door. Or the old, gray Taebish would come out to him and tell him that his sister was too busy to see him, or out at some conference, or sleeping. He had shrugged, muttered, wandered the public corridors of temple or palace, brooding. And despite whatever rationalizations he made, this second abandonment seemed even more brutal, more abrupt and unwarranted, than the last.

He had been abandoned, too, by the other Terrans. Abrams had taken him aside privately and interrogated him about his relationship to his startling lavender sister, and when Padric had refused even to confirm that which Abrams had known to be true, the ethnologist had branded Padric as no longer trustworthy, and cast him adrift from the society of the other crew members, so that Padric moved aimlessly among the corridors, rooms, and hidden gardens, rebuffed by his colleagues, suspicious of the mildly contemptuous fisherfolk, awed and frightened by the tall, stern-faced mountain Taebish, and once again severed from what family he had. The constant conflict of these emotions was such that even his usual bitterness drowned under an ever-increasing confusion.

His frown deepened as the voices within the room rose, and he quickly moved away down the corridor, unwilling to be present when negotiators and spectators emerged for the midday break. Despite his speed, though, one of the spectators caught up with him and touched his shoulder. Startled, he turned around to find himself facing the younger Taebish Krispeh. She spoke a few words in her own language and gestured toward a doorway.

"It's no use," Padric replied in Standard. "I don't understand a word you're saying."

He nonetheless followed her into the room, and she produced an analog-translator from the folds of her robe and clicked it on.

"Where did you get that?" Padric demanded in a whisper.

"Your leader has about three of them, and I just borrowed one for a while. You don't mind, do you? I wanted to talk to you, and I can't while he's around."

"No, I guess I don't mind. Turn it down, though. Here, like this." He reached for the translator, but she snatched it away from his fingers.

"I'll do it," she said. "This plate? Is that better?"

"Yes. I wasn't trying to take it."

"Sit down."

For the first time, he glanced about and discovered that they were in one of the palace's many small antechambers. He picked a comfortable cushion and lowered himself onto it, keeping his eye on the young Taebish. She waited until he was seated before curling herself onto another cushion and leaning toward him.

"How would you like to rule Apantha?" she said evenly.

"What? Rule Apantha?"

"Exactly. Those idiots in there are running about shouting nonsense, and nothing is being done. The palace is in constant commotion, the temple is busy seeking coun-

sel from its false godling, the people of the city are confused. What better time to step in and take power?"

"You've got the wrong person, Krispeh. You should talk
to Abrams, or even to Megan, but not to me."

"No. Abrams is a fool, a stupid fool, and Megan is
negligible. You're the only one who could do it, the only
one who could pull it off and then handle it afterward.
I've been watching you, and you're just the one we need."

"*We* need? Who's 'we'?"

"I and others. There are many enemies of Apantha, and
the least of them live in the west. This is a kingdom of oppressors, Padric. A kingdom of thieves and murderers—
they take our goods, they take our labors, they even take
our lives when it pleases them, and they use our tears to
carpet their chambers and fill their goblets. Even this city
they stole from those who lived here before, and they too
would hail you as a savior if you would take Apantha in
your palm and free its people."

Her long brown-furred arms reached out to him, and
one hand clenched his thigh.

"Steal Abrams' control box, the one he claims can bring
the ship upon us. Steal it and blast the palace to shards,
blast the temple of their fraudulent godling back to dust.
And when the people have risen to thank you, we can take
your ship to the far places of the planet, we can have all
peoples bow to your name, bring tribute and great praise."

And Padric found himself tempted, found himself for a
moment entranced by the vision she presented, saw himself floating over a green globe and ruler of all he saw.
But, as always, his mind made its practiced flip into suspicion, and he moved away from her.

"Why me?" he demanded. "What do you want from
me?"

"We want freedom," she cried. "We want our homes
and our lives back. Is this so hard for you to understand?"

"But why me? Why not another Taebish? You don't
want the Apanthese as rulers; why pick someone who isn't
even from the same planet?"

"Because you have access to the ship," she said. "You
can command such power that even the westerners would
cringe at your name."

"No. If you want your freedom, you'll have to get it
for yourself. I'd get the control box, take over Apantha,

and at the first likely moment you'd kill me. I want no part of this."

She stood, furious, slammed the translator off, and spat words at him in Taebish until he shouted back in Standard and stormed from the room. Such was his fury that he marched straight back to the negotiating rooms, where the afternoon session was about to begin. He ignored the guards and moved straight across the room to where his sister was speaking privately to Abrams, but before he could reach her, the ethnologist spun around and came toward the door. Abrams grabbed Padric's arm, stuck his face close to Padric's own, and hissed, "Stupidity runs in your family, whelp. But she's done it this time. When I'm through with her, there won't be a Tabby on this planet who'd consent to keep her from dying."

Abrams pushed Padric away and strode through the door. But when Padric looked for his sister, she was gone.

Megan rose as Han-Tor entered the room. "I apologize for having kept you waiting," he said before she could speak. "I did not expect to see you so early."

"And I apologize for intruding on you, but I did feel that it was urgent."

"Nothing," said the priest, "is so urgent that it cannot wait for a glass of wine. Will you have some?"

"I—yes, thank you."

The high priest produced a decanter and two goblets, and set them down on a low table before sinking into one of the cushions. Megan sat opposite him and watched him pour the pale wine.

"I have heard that Terrans are fond of a benediction before drinking," Han-Tor said. "Would you care to make one?"

She put the glass down carefully and looked at him.

"How did you know?"

"In a complicated fashion," Han-Tor replied. "I do not spy upon my guests, although it may on occasion seem that way. Your bathkeeper is paid by Korvan, and I only wish he were paid by me—he's a very clever man, and generally quite cautious. He overheard your conversation with Tebye-Mother this morning and reported it to Korvan's so-called house-warden, who reported it to Korvan in deepest secrecy. Korvan's house-warden, however, is bedmate to a certain young woman who is paid by me.

And also, I suspect, by my lord the western ambassador, who is in turn spied upon by Korvan's minions, and they by Agin's spies. And all of this, mind you, is only high diplomatic spying. We are infiltrated by agents for the cities' guilds, by friends of Tebye-Mother's daughter, by those in the pay of traveling merchants—I'm surprised that the Terrans have not yet gotten into the act, although I expect their debut any day now. By noon today, your background was well known to all of us. By evening, I'm sure it will be common knowledge throughout Apantha, and by the end of this season, the western king will dine on the tidbit in the comfort of his own chambers. Do drink, the wine is quite good."

Megan sipped the wine without tasting it, and replaced the cup.

"Why didn't you stop me from being in this morning's session, if you knew?"

"Tebye-Mother said that you were mostly fisher, and I believe her. You need not worry on that count."

"Since you know it all so well, do you think of me as a freak?" she demanded. "Do I repulse you?"

"You make much too large an issue of it," Han-Tor replied. "I wondered about that, but the answer is really quite simple. Come with me a moment, and I will show you."

Megan followed the priest into an adjoining room. Here the walls were heavy with intricately woven hangings, each one tautly fastened to the wall. Han-Tor stopped before the one nearest the door and gestured.

"Family history," he said. "Not much of it, I'm afraid—certainly much less than Tebye-Mother could recite. Here is the first of our line to enter Apantha the City—a dappled Taebish known by the mark of a circle on the right brow. His oldest son, here, was ginger-colored completely, with no other marks at all. His eldest, over here, was black and tan. His child, my father, was pure black with one white irregular patch on his right arm— that's this knot here, above the generation signal. And here is the mark for my brother, dappled again. You see, we are constantly changing. While I'd imagine that any one family of Terrans displays a fairly constant set of family resemblances, skin color and hair color and eye color, am I right?"

"But I am also taller, and my limbs are of different proportions, and I have these things on my shoulders—"

"Not important. You are still unmistakably Terran, once one pauses to look."

They returned to the cushioned room in silence.

"So you see," Han-Tor continued when they were seated, "that your 'differences' make very little difference to us."

"And you don't believe that I would lean to the Terran side?"

"Will you?"

"No," she admitted with a smile. "I told Abrams so this afternoon. That's why I came here—I wanted to tell you myself, before he had a chance to. It seemed the most honorable thing to do." She paused and contemplated her goblet. "It's not just that I'm a Terran, though. I left the Federation rather abruptly. I—well, I stole a lot."

"Oh?"

She quickly outlined her story to him, leaving out nothing but her own fears and pains. "So I decided that Inter-Stel owed me these things, and I took them. And came here. Since you don't object to my being a Terran, do you object to my being a thief?"

"But what do you think we were?" Han-Tor said, smiling. "Apantha the City was not ours to begin with. We came and took it. The entire kingdom we grabbed originally from those who owned it first, from the fishers and the Apanthese and the border folk and the gatherers."

"This is approved doctrine? That you are a race of thieves?"

"No, not that we *are*, but that we *were*. As you were a thief, but are one no longer."

"That seems a dubious morality to me."

"Perhaps. But Tebye, for example, understands this. Her culture is immeasurably older than ours, and better adapted to its world. Understands better than we do what reality is like. This, I'm afraid, is something that my brother the king does not always appreciate, nor does he realize that we have much to learn from Tebye's people." The priest gestured wryly. "It is a point of contention between us."

Megan was tempted to draw the conversation back to her own problems, but sensed that Han-Tor was getting closer to what he had originally planned for their conversation.

"The river life is stable, as I've seen," Megan said. "But your own culture must still be changing at a fairly rapid rate."

"Perhaps more rapid than we care to acknowledge, and the advent of the Terrans hastens things even more. For example, take poor old Tayteklosh, over there in the corner."

Megan turned to look at the stone figure of the god, perched in a fur-covered niche.

"A warrior-god," Han-Tor continued. "A proper god for a people bent on expansion and conquest, on consolidating their holdings, on creating a place for themselves. Stealing it, if necessary. But we are no longer that people. We are now an urban culture, and our main concerns must of necessity be peace with our neighbors rather than war, understanding of our subjects rather than oppression. We need a deity who can guide us through this maze of new goals and desires, and I'm afraid that the old man here is not that deity."

Megan set down her goblet. "I wouldn't have expected you to see that," she said frankly.

"I'm not expected to see a lot," the priest said. "Or, in any event, I'm not to speak of it. But it can't be so rare, to find someone who seems to see beyond his own time. My father back five times saw ahead, saw to the drought and the migrations, and shaped his people into ones who could cope with the changes. But I am not birth-king, and must do my best. So, despite my firm knowledge that our needs are changing, the old god, the old one, hangs on, and still radiates his own power. Not just over the people themselves, although there remains a belief in him. But in High Valley, in the home of the god—a sense of presence. It's difficult to explain, without hiding in the rhetoric of religion, but it is indeed there. Yet I do believe that, if both god and people were faced with a new deity, one closer to our current concerns, Tayteklosh would take himself off to his deserved rest."

"I don't imagine, though, that it would be easy to engineer a god," Megan remarked. Despite her interest in the priest's conversation, the tensions of the day were beginning to weigh on her, and she thought longingly of the hot bathing pool, and a long sleep. But Han-Tor leaned forward, intent, and she was drawn again into his conversation.

"Gods are given to us," he said, "and they come of their own will. So say, rather, that they engineer us, they choose us, and how can one resist the choice of the god?"

"Having none myself, I couldn't begin to answer."

"No gods? No guiding powers, no encompassing responsibilities, nothing to bind the universe?"

"No. Simply a will toward peace and solitude, a desire to tend my own garden and let the world tend its without requiring my presence."

"And yet," said Han-Tor slowly, "one must make a choice. Simply to abdicate responsibility entirely, to retreat from the question, cannot be a firm basis for life."

"I've not abdicated, although I could perhaps be accused of retreat. And my choice is made, firmly and unalterably. If there is a binding of the universe, an overriding power, it is in a sprouting seed, or in the quiet of the river at evening."

"And what of others?"

"I don't ask anything of them, and am grateful when they ask nothing of me."

"Yet here you are, in Apantha, dealing with people you despise for a cause which is not your own."

Megan gestured uncomfortably, and the light caught on the dials at her shoulders. "So I am. I have never claimed to be entirely consistent in my choices."

"And neither is a god."

She raised her head and stared at him. "I don't think I understand your meaning."

"No? Listen, then. You have come to us from the river folk, and in your journey have bound Apantha the City to the lands of the river tribes. You have no gods above you. Your concerns are those of growth, fruition, resurrection, and—perhaps despite yourself—mediation. You have powers above those which we possess—"

"No—"

"Yes. Tebye-Mother told me of the time you forded the river in flood, without a canoe."

"Flotation units, they were built into me."

"And of the building of your house, which she tells me you accomplished in one afternoon, from felling the trees to finishing the roof."

"Power assists. I wasn't born with them."

"And of the time you flew."

"Antigravity packs. Not mine, not mine."

"And you saved the life of the western ambassador."

"They made my reflexes very quick. But none of these things are mine—they were all given to me, planted in me. *I* haven't these powers."

"The spear of Tayteklosh, which stirs the mountains, was a gift from the nether gods. The shield of Tayteklosh, before which the enemy is rendered harmless, was taken as battle prize from the arctic demons. His eyes, his tongue, his heels, and his ears he stole from the Seven Blind Ones. Take his gifts and thievings from him and he becomes a sorry, bedraggled, boasting kitling. But should your gift-powers go from you, you will possess something which Tayteklosh in all his glory never had."

Han-Tor stood quickly and drew back a hanging, revealing a polished sheet of metal. "Look at yourself," he said. "Is this not an aspect of the god?"

"Oh, no," Megan said, turning quickly from the mirror. "We've spoken long enough. I've been, so far, invited to go home, to become a westerner, to become a Terran, to die, and to become a god. This is nonsense, and you of all people should have the sense to know it."

"The river folk have always claimed that the altitude has rarefied our brains from us," Han-Tor said as he dropped the hanging back into place.

"The river folk—is Tebye—have you and she—"

"Tebye-Mother was invited to bring us a river god."

"You've prepared a sanctuary for Hatama. Hatama will come to fill it. Not me, high priest. Not me."

Nine

WHILE CONTEMPLATING SUICIDE, Padric discovered a garden deep within the stone maze of the palace. Sunlight, shunted through a complicated channel of tunnels and polished-metal mirrors, bathed the luxuriant growth within the large room; a stream curved through the arbors, gently waving the pallid roots of the trees, and an occasional flyer tittered in the branches. Here he felt some of his tension drain from him, felt a certain safety from Taebish and Terrans both—picking an obscure corner of the room, he settled down beneath the protective overhang of a

drooping tree and fell into a state halfway between wake-
fulness and sleep.

"Over here," a voice called softly. Padric sat up,
startled, and was about to reply when Abrams' voice answered.

"Okay, here I am. What do you want?"

"Hush. Even here we could be overheard."

Padric recognized the dull tones of the translator over-
lapping the softer Taebish. His first impulse was to call
out, but the next exchange stifled the impulse, and he
crouched lower behind his protective screen of branches.

"Well, what is it?"

"We want to tell you that you're wasting your time.
These meetings, these negotiations, are all unnecessary.
Within two days you could have the valley and everything
in it, at minimum risk, and instead you have been misled
into endless discussions that will serve only to keep you
from what you need. You must not let them do this."

Padric, moving quietly, turned around and parted the
branches, then peered at the speakers. Abrams stood with
his back to Padric's hiding place, and beyond him stood
Krispeh and another Taebish, his face hidden in the folds
of his robe.

The muffled Taebish said, "You need not fear that you
will not be supported. My government is willing to aid you
to the fullest."

"But my government has regulations," Abrams said.
"We can't simply take the valley—there would be reper-
cussions. After all, the Apanthese own the valley—"

"The mountain folk own nothing," Krispeh said. "What
they have, they stole from those who came before. They are
oppressors. They have built their cities and gained their
riches through exploitation. They made us fight in their
wars of expansion. They make us labor for their benefit,
while our own people starve."

"Certainly the Apanthese are no boon to their neighbors," the other Taebish said. "My government is constantly annoyed by border raids, by incursions, by the
constant threat of war. The Apanthese are troublemakers,
and we would be well rid of them."

"This still doesn't help me out," Abrams protested. "I
still have to justify all my actions—"

"If the mountain folk were destroyed, the river folk
would hail you as their savior. We would back you to the

last drop of our blood. We would praise you to your leaders, as a great maker of freedom."

"I see. Well—"

"And with the power you would hold, even my own government would willingly bow to you. We would be more than willing to cooperate in your concerns, in ways that the Apanthese are not."

And brief silence ensued. Then Abrams said, "But how do you suggest that we—that is, that this be—"

"Bring down your skyship and take the valley. It is that simple. The mountain folk have a bare handful of priests in High Valley, and they could be eliminated immediately. Then you can take from the valley what you wish, and be gone before the Apanthese can even muster a defense."

"And we will not fight for them, not this time."

"And how will this help your people?"

"With High Valley gone, the morale of the mountain folk will be gone. They are superstitious, they invest the total of their dignity in their god, and when they see that Tayteklosh is powerless even to defend his own home, their will will crumble and we will be able to free ourselves."

"I see. And then we will have our cargo, and you will have your freedom. And you will back us up, should there ever be an inquiry, right?"

"Yes, and more than that. I can tell you confidentially that my government has positioned troops along the border. Take your cargo, and when you return to us, my government will be only too willing to come to a trade agreement with you."

"Yes, yes, but you must act immediately, before the mountain folk have a chance to prepare themselves, while you still hold the element of surprise. If you summon the skyship now, the valley will be yours within the hour, and the mountain folk will be too stunned to present opposition."

"But I have to consult with the others—"

"Aren't you the leader? Don't you have the power of decision? Are you now going to tell me that you're not the proper authority?"

"No, no, that's not the case at all. Of course I'm the leader of this expedition, naturally—"

"Every minute that passes lessens the surprise, every hour moves you farther from your goal."

"All right! Look, here's my communicator, my control box. I've simply got to, like this, and then like that, and it's automatic, the computer knows what to do—ah! There!"

"The skyship is now coming down?"

"Yes, immediately. It should reach High Valley within the hour."

"An hour. And the temples of Tayteklosh will crumble, the mountain folk will fall. It is a great thing you have done for the people of this world, Terran. Your memory will stand high in our regard for as long as there are river folk to keep your name alive."

"And your welcome is ensured when you return from your great cities in the sky. But come, quickly, we must leave. You and your crew must be out of Apantha within the hour, for the news will travel fast, perhaps the blast will be visible from the turrets. Come, this way, good, yes . . ."

Voices and rapid footsteps faded into the distance. Padric stood, shivered once, then turned and sprinted out of the garden and through the long corridors toward his sister's rooms.

In the midst of the shouting, he heard the old gray Taebish say something like the name of the high priest, and he grabbed her by the arm.

"Take me," he shouted in Standard. "Megan, Han-Tor, take me there."

She stood still for a moment, then jerked her arm away, grabbed her cloak, and ran from the room. He sped after her, through the winding corridors of the temple, past startled Taebish. She sped through a doorway, gestured toward the far hangings, and barked something at the Taebish guards as Padric ran through the hangings and collided with his sister.

"Abrams," he shouted. "Ship . . . in the valley . . . wiping out . . . on the control box—"

Megan hoisted him to a chair and held a wineglass to his lips while the priest muttered something and delved into the folds of his robe. He came out holding yet another translator, which he flipped on with an expert twist of the thumb.

"We're all thieves," his machine-translated voice said. "What did you say? What is it?"

"I overheard Abrams talking with that river woman, Krispeh, and another Taebish, all wrapped up in his cloak. He seemed to be from somewhere else—he talked about 'his government.' They talked Abrams into bringing down the ship. He's set the computer to destroy the temple in High Valley. It should be done in less than an hour. Abrams and the crew are trying to get away."

"The ambassador," Han-Tor said immediately. "I should have expected this."

"Find Abrams," Megan ordered. "Separate him from the Taebish and from his crew, and lock them all up. Surround him. Threaten him with death if the ship harms the valley. Tebye, call the river folk. They're quartered not far from the ambassador's suite. Tell them to find him and hold him. And you'll have to find Krispeh."

Tebye gestured and ran from the room.

"Han-Tor, you'd better send someone to alert Agin and Korvan, and bring them both back here. Don't let the word leak out—we have to avoid a panic. I want to know as soon as you've caught Abrams. I have to get to him immediately. I'll want him brought back here if there's time. I want to speak to everyone together."

Han-Tor paused, his hand on the bell rope. "And from what stance will you speak?"

Megan straightened. "I speak for the Taebish. Do I have a choice?"

"You had one. And you just made it." Triumphantly, the priest pulled on the rope. Padric chose that moment to leap from the chair and through the doorway.

"Paddy! Come back here! You'll be killed," Megan shouted after him. If he'd had the breath or time to do it, he would have grinned.

The high hill in the middle of Apantha the City seethed and glowed in the failing light of the sun, but the gates to the outer city were closed tight, and guards kept a strict watch to make sure that neither rumors nor citizens passed through them. Yet the commotion was not so easily hidden, and the citizens of the city gathered beneath the closed portals, murmuring and shifting, calling questions up to the close-lipped guards. Wild rumors moved through the crowd: the palace had caught fire, the king was in danger, the temple had fallen. Some of the more enterprising citizens mounted to the roofs of tall buildings near the walls and called down news to their fellows, but such was the confusion on the hill that no sense could be made of it, and the reports from the watchers only added to the nervousness of the people. Within fifteen minutes, plans were afoot to break the gates.

Well before that time, the fishers had found and caught the western ambassador as he made ready to flee the city. He now sat, bound and declaring innocence, in a corner of the high priest's room. His river-folk captors guarded him in silence. The three Terran crew members had also been captured and brought to the chamber—they now stood about in mute terror, unable to comprehend the questions the Taebish shouted at them. Megan had long since left to pursue her own course about the temple and palace, moving so quickly that she blurred before the running Taebish, and her instructions lingered in the air long after she herself had disappeared. Agin King, proceeding to his brother's chambers, saw her as a pale flash in a dimly lighted room, and her command to hurry seemed to follow her appearance as thunder follows lightning. The king made an uneasy gesture of reverence and passed onward.

Tebye-Mother, searching through her daughter's rooms, was startled to find Megan suddenly at her side.

"Where is she?"

"Fled," Tebye replied. "With the Terran—one of the guards saw them a while ago, moving west through the temple."

"Good," Megan said and was gone again before the old fisher could speak again. Tebye-Mother dropped the cloths she was holding and slowly sat in her daughter's room, her head bowed.

Padric, too, moved west through the temple, choosing his course by instinct as much as knowledge. Abrams would not attempt to flee the city on foot—rather, he would seek the highest point of the temple and, when the ship had finished with the valley, would have it pick him up. The Apanthese, unused to thinking in terms of flight, would concentrate their search on the lower floors of the temple, and at the city's gates. So Padric ran, constantly moving upward and westward, guessing at each maze-like intersection, doubling back when he had chosen wrongly, taking each upward-leading flight he found. Abrams would be moving more slowly, burdened with equipment—Padric soon heard the ethnologist's labored breathing. He doubled his speed and arrived at the temple's roof just behind Abrams and Krispeh.

A shadow show, as the three figures were set against the slanting rays of the sun—the pacing, the gestures, the sudden lunges and sudden parries. Tebye-Mother ran out to a high ledge of the temple and joined her voice to the cries of the Apanthese as she saw her daughter high above. King, priest, and adviser were all drawn outside by the cries and silences.

The two Terrans struggled at the building's edge, and Padric wrenched Abrams' control box from him. Holding it high above his head, he turned away from the roof's edge just as Krispeh threw herself on him. The box arched from his fingers and fell toward the distant courtyard, and Megan suddenly rose from one of the lower ledges, soaring with outstretched fingers toward the falling box. As her fingers touched it, the sky was bathed with light—the entire top of Apantha the Mountain leaped out of darkness, etched in flickering red. The Apanthese, after one initial scream, fell into an absolute silence, and in that silence Padric and Krispeh teetered over the brink of the temple roof. Reaching desperately for support, Padric's hand closed over Abrams' shoulder—the three figures described lazy curves in the scarlet sky as they fell.

Megan, still airborn, threw the box from her and raced toward them. She caught Krispeh and Padric, but Abrams' body slipped from her and plummeted to the earth. The weight of the two bodies in her arms bore her downward, until at the last possible moment the assists broke her fall, and she rose slowly.

Silence still, as she came down gently before Tebye-Mother and laid her burden on the stone ledge. Krispeh's neck was broken, and her sharp knife protruded from Padric's side.

"My brother," Megan whispered. "Padric my brother."

A deep and urgent sound welled up from the gathered Taebish. Megan stood in the light of the burning valley, gazed out over the city of kneeling people, and finally understood that they were shouting her name.

SCREWTOP

Vonda N. McIntyre

Vonda McIntyre, who lives in the Pacific Northwest, was trained as a geneticist, but succumbed early to the literary bug. One of the first alumnae of the Clarion Science Fiction Writers' Workshop—and eventually West Coast administrator of Clarion—she began selling fiction professionally in 1971, and was quickly recognized as a promising beginner. That promise was fulfilled a few years later with her story "Of Mist, and Grass, and Sand," which made her in 1973 one of the youngest of all Nebula winners. Since then she has published her first novel, edited an anthology, and written a good many impressive short stories—and now this novella of prisoners on a remote, hopeless planet.

HOT AND WET from the fine, steamy rain, Kylis sat on her heels at the top of the drilling pit and waited for the second-duty shift to end. She rubbed at a streak of the thick red mud that had spattered her legs and her white boots when she walked across the compound. Redsun's huge dim star altered colors; white became a sort of pinkish gray. But among the forest's black foliage and against the Pit's clay, white uniforms stood out and made prisoners easier for the guards to see.

A few other people waited with Kylis at the south end of the deep slash in the earth. Like them, she crouched unsheltered from the rain, strands of wet hair plastered to her cheeks, watching for friends she had not seen in forty days.

Below lay two completed generator domes; above them rose the immense delicate cooling towers, and the antenna beaming power along the relay system to North Continent. Fences and guards protected the finished installations from the prisoners. Kylis and the rest worked only on clearing the fern forest, extending the Pit, drilling a third steam well—the dirty, dangerous jobs.

Paralleling the distant wall of volcanoes in the east, the drill pit extended northward. Its far end was invisible, obscured by the rain and by clouds of acrid smoke that billowed from the trash piles. The Pit was being lengthened again to follow the fault line where drilling was most efficient. Another strip of frond forest had been destroyed, and its huge primitive ferns now lay in blackened heaps. The stalks never burned completely. but until the coals died a bank of irritating smoke and sticky ash would hang

138

over the prison camp. The fine rain sizzled into steam when it fell on glowing embers.

Kylis started at the long shrill siren that ended the second shift. For an instant she was afraid the hallucinations had returned, but the normal sounds of the prison responded to the signal. The faraway roar of bulldozers ceased; the high whine of the drill slipped down in pitch and finally stopped. People left their machines, threw down their tools, and straggled toward the trail. They passed beneath the guards' towers, watched and counted by the Lizard's crew. One by one and in occasional pairs they started up the steep slope of clay and debris and volcanic ash, picking their way around gullies and across muddy rivulets. Screwtop seemed very quiet now, almost peaceful, with no noise but the hum of turbines in the two geothermal power plants, and the rhythmic clatter of the pumps that kept the drill pit unflooded.

Kylis could not yet see Jason. She frowned. He and Gryf, who was on the third shift, had both been all right when she got off duty. She was sure of that, for news of accidents traveled instantaneously between working crews. But Kylis had been alone, sleeping much of the time, in the nine hours since the end of her shift. Anything could happen in nine hours. She tried to reassure herself about her friends' safety, because the pattern and rhythm of the work just ended had been too normal to follow a really bad accident.

She could not put aside her anxiety, and knew she would not until she had seen and spoken to and touched both Gryf and Jason. She still found herself surprised that she could care so much about two other human beings. Her past life had depended on complete independence and self-sufficiency.

Below, Gryf would be standing in the group of prisoners near the drilling rig. She tried to make him out, but the only person she could distinguish at this distance was the guard captain, called by everyone—when he was out of earshot—the Lizard, for his clean-shaven face and head gave him a smoothly impervious reptilian appearance. He was standing alone, facing the prisoners, giving orders. He wore black, as if in defiance of the heat, as a symbol of his superiority over everyone else in the camp. Even so, he was conspicuous now only because he was separated from the others. Gryf was conspicuous in any crowd, but the rig was too far away for Kylis to identify even Gryf's astonishing ebony and tan calico-patterned skin. The first time she had seen him, his first day at Screwtop, she had stared at him so long that he noticed and laughed at her. It was not a ridiculing laugh, but an understanding one. Gryf laughed at himself, too, sometimes, and often at the people who had made him what he was.

Gryf was the first tetraparental Kylis had ever seen or heard of, and even among tetras Gryf was unusual. Of his four biological parents, it happened that two of them were dark, and two fair. Gryf had been planned to be a uniform light brown, only his hair, perhaps, varicolored. Genes for hair color did not blend like those for skin. But the sets of sperm and ova had been matched wrong, so the mixture of two embryos forming Gryf made him his strange paisley pattern. He still had all the selectable intellectual gifts of his various parents. Those qualities, not his skin, were important.

New tetraparentals were special; the life of each was fully planned. Gryf was part of a team, and it was inconceivable to the government of Redsun and to the other tetras that after all the work of making him, after all the training and preparation, he would refuse his duty. When he did, he was sent for punishment to Redsun's strictest prison. If he changed his mind, he could at a word return to the tetra's secluded retreat. He had been at Screwtop half a year and he had not said that word.

Kylis was no Redsun native; she was oblivious to the others' awe of Gryf. She was curious about him. Neither because of nor in spite of the pattern of his skin, he was beautiful. Kylis wondered how his hair would feel, the locks half black and wiry, half blond and fine.

He was assigned to a nearby crew. Kylis saw immediately that he had been given hard and dirty jobs, not the most dangerous ones but those most tiring. The guards' task was not to kill him but to make life so unpleasant that he would return to the tetras.

Kylis waited to speak to him until she would not risk discipline for either of them. Without seeming to, the Lizard was watching Gryf closely, padding by every so often in his stealthy, silent way, his close-set eyes heavy-lidded, the direction of his gaze impossible to determine. But eventually his duties took him to another part of the camp, and Kylis left her own work to tell Gryf the tricks experience had taught her to make the labor a little easier.

Their first night together was Gryf's first night at Screwtop. When the shift ended, it seemed natural to walk back to the prisoners' shelters together. They were too tired to do much more than sleep, but the companionship was a comfort and the potential for more existed. They lay facing each other in the darkness. Starlight shone through a break in the clouds and glinted from the blond locks of Gryf's hair.

"I may never be let out of here," Gryf said. He was not asking for sympathy, but telling her his future as best he knew it. He had a pleasant, musical voice. Kylis realized these were the first words she heard him say. But she remembered his thanking her for her advice—and recalled that he had thanked her with his smile and a nod and the look in his eyes.

"I'm in for a long time," Kylis said. "I don't think there's that much difference between us." Screwtop could kill either of them the next day or the day before release.

Kylis reached up and touched Gryf's hair. It was stiff and matted with sweat. He took her hand and kissed her grimy palm. From then on they stayed together, growing closer but never speaking of a future outside the prison.

Several sets later Jason arrived and changed everything.

Kylis brought herself back to the present. She knew Gryf was below somewhere, though she could not make him out in the blotch of dirty white. She had been on the last shift during a previous set and she knew the schedule. The prisoners still working would not be exposed to much more danger today. Instead, they would have the dullest and most exhausting job of the period. During the last shift before the free day, once every forty days, all the equipment was cleaned and inspected. Anything done wrong was done over; the shift could drag on long past its normal end. Kylis hoped that would not happen this time.

At the bottom of the slope, Jason emerged from the bright cancer of machinery. He was muddy and grease-spattered, gold-flecked with bleached hair. He was very large and very fair, and even on Redsun where the light had little ultraviolet he sunburned easily. Though he had been working from dusk to midmorning his legs were horizontally striped with sunburn, darkest at the top of his thighs and lightest just below his knees, marking the different levels to which he had pulled the cuffs of his boots. Right now they were folded all the way down.

He glanced up and saw Kylis. His carriage changed; he straightened and waved. His blond beard was bristly and uncombed and his hair was plastered down with sweat. The waistband of his shorts was red with mud spattered onto his body and washed down by perspiration and rain. As he came closer she saw that he was thinner, and that the lines around his eyes had deepened. They had been lines of thought and laughter; now they were of fatigue and exposure. He hurried toward her, slipping on the clay, and she realized he, too, had been worried.

He heard I was in sensory deprivation, she thought, and he was afraid for me. She stood motionless for a few seconds. She was not quite used to him yet; his easy acceptance of her and his concern seemed innocent and admirable compared to the persistent distrust Kylis had felt toward him for so long. She started forward to meet him.

He stopped and held out his hands. She touched him, and he came forward, almost trembling, holding himself taut against exhaustion. His pose collapsed. Bending down, he rested his forehead on her shoulder. She put her hands on his back, very gently.

"Was it bad?" His voice was naturally low but now it was rough and hoarse. He had probably been directing his crew, shouting above the roar of machinery for eighteen hours.

"Bad enough," Kylis said. "I've been glad of the work since."

Still leaning against her, he shook his head.

"I'm okay now. I've quit hallucinating," she said, hoping it was true. "And you? Are you all right?" She could feel his breath on her damp shoulder.

"Yes. Now. Thanks to Gryf."

Jason had started this set on first day shift, which began at midnight and ended in the afternoon. Its members worked through the hottest part of the day when they were most tired. Halfway through his third work period Jason had collapsed. He was delirious and dehydrated, sunburned even through his shirt. The sun drained him. Gryf, just getting off when Jason fell, had worked through his own sleep period to finish Jason's shift. For them to switch shifts, Gryf had worked almost two of Redsun's days straight. When Kylis heard about that, she could not see how anyone could do it, even Gryf.

Gryf had broken the rules, but no one had made Jason go back to his original shift. The Lizard must never have said anything about it. Kylis could imagine him standing in shadow, watching, while Gryf waited for a confrontation that never came. It was something the Lizard would do.

Jason's shoulders were scarred where blisters had formed in the sun, but Kylis saw that they had healed cleanly. She put her arm around Jason's waist to support him. "Come on. I found a place to sleep." They were both sticky with sweat and the heat.

"Okay." They crossed the barren mud where all the vegetation had been stripped away so the machines could pass. Before they turned off the path they drew rations from the mechanical dispenser near the prisoners' quarters. The tasteless bars dropped through a slot, two each. There were times in Kylis' life when she had not eaten well, but she had seldom eaten anything as boring as prison rations. Jason put one of his bars into his belt pouch.

"When are you going to give that up?"

Jason nibbled a corner of his second ration bar. "I'm not." His grin made the statement almost a joke. He saved part of his food against what Kylis thought ludicrous plans of escape. When he had saved enough supplies, he was going to hike out through the marsh.

"You don't have to save anything today." She slipped her tag back into the slot and kept reinserting it until the extra points were used and a small pile of ration bars lay in the hopper.

"They forgot to void my card for the time I was in the deprivation box," Kylis said. In sensory deprivation, one of the prison's punishments for mistakes, she had been fed intravenously. She gave Jason the extra food. He thanked her and put it in his belt pouch. Together they crossed the bare clay and entered the forest.

Jason had been at Screwtop only three sets. He was losing weight quickly here, for he was a big-boned man with little fat to burn. Kylis hoped his family would discover where he was and ransom him soon. And she hoped they would find him before he tried to run away, though she had stopped trying to argue him out of the dream. The marsh was impassable except by hovercraft. There were no solid paths through it, and people claimed it held undiscovered animals that would crush a boat or raft. Kylis neither believed nor disbelieved in the animals; she was certain only that a few prisoners had tried to escape during her time at Screwtop, and the guards had not even bothered to look for them. Redsun was not a place where the authorities allowed escape toward freedom, only toward death. The naked volcanoes cut off escape to the north and east with their barren lava escarpments and billowing clouds of poison gas; the marsh barred west and south. Screwtop was an economical prison, requiring fences only to protect the guards' quarters and the power domes, not to enclose the captives. And even if Jason could escape alive, he could never get off Redsun. He did not have Kylis' experience at traveling undetected.

The fern forest's shadows closed in around them, and they walked between the towering blackish-red stalks and lacy fronds. The foliage was heavy with huge droplets formed slowly by the misty rain. Kylis brushed past a leaf and the water cascaded down her side, making a faint track in the ashes and mud on her skin. She had washed herself when she got off duty, but staying clean was impossible at Screwtop.

They reached the sleeping place she had discovered. Several clumps of ferns had grown together and died, the stems falling over to make a conical shelter. Kylis pulled aside a handful of withered fronds and showed Jason in. Outside it looked like nothing but a pile of dead plants.

"It isn't even damp," he said, surprised. "And it's almost cool in here." He sat down on the carpet of dead moss and ferns and leaned back smiling. "I don't see how you found it. I never would have looked in here."

Kylis sat beside him. A few hours ago she had slept the soundest sleep she had had in Screwtop. The shade alleviated the heat, and the fronds kept the misty rain from drifting inside and collecting. Best of all, it was quiet.

"I thought you and Gryf would like it."

"Have you seen him?"

"Only across the compound. He looked all right."

Jason said aloud what Kylis feared. "The Lizard must have had a reason for letting him take my shift. To make it harder on him." He too was worried, and Kylis could see he felt guilty. "I shouldn't have let him do it," he said.

"Have you ever tried to stop him from doing something he thinks he should?"

Jason smiled. "No. I don't think I want to." He let himself sink further down in the moss. "Gods," he said, drawing out the word. "It's good to see you."

"It's been lonely," Kylis said, with the quiet sort of wonder she felt every time she realized that she did care enough to miss someone. Loneliness was more painful now, but she was not lonely all the time. She did not know how to feel about her newly discovered pleasure in the company of Gryf and Jason. Sometimes it frightened her. They had broached her defenses of solitude and suspicion, and at times she felt exposed and vulnerable. She trusted them, but there were even more betrayers at Screwtop than there were outside.

"I didn't give you those extra rations so you could save them all," she said. "I gave them to you so you'd stop starving yourself for one day at least."

"We could all get out of here," he said, "if we saved just a little more food." Even at midmorning, beneath the ferns, it was almost too dark to make out his features, but Kylis knew he was not joking. She said nothing. Jason thought the prisoners who fled into the marsh were still alive there; he thought he could join them and be helped. Kylis thought they were all dead. Jason believed escape on foot possible, and Kylis believed it death. Jason was an optimist, and Kylis was experienced.

"All right," Jason said. "I'll eat one more. In a while." He lay down flat and put his hands behind his head.

"How was your shift?" Kylis asked.

"Too much fresh meat."

Kylis grinned. Jason was talking like a veteran, hardened and disdainful of new prisoners, the fresh meat, who had not yet learned the ways of Screwtop.

"We only got a couple new people," she said. "You must have had almost the whole bunch."

"It would have been tolerable if three of them hadn't been assigned to the drilling rig."

"Did you lose any?"

"No. By some miracle."

"We were fresh once too. Gryf's the only one I ever saw who didn't start out doing really stupid things."

"Was I really that fresh?"

She did not want to hurt his feelings or even tease him.

"I was, wasn't I?"

"Jason . . . I'm sorry, but you were the freshest I ever

saw. I didn't think you had any chance at all. Only Gryf did."

"I hardly remember anything about the first set, except how much time he spent helping me."

"I know," Kylis said. Jason had needed a great deal of help. Kylis had forgiven him for being the cause of her first real taste of loneliness, but she could not quite forget it.

"Gods—this last set," Jason said. "I didn't know how bad it was alone." Then he smiled. "I used to think I was a solitary person." Where Kylis was contemptuous of her discovered weaknesses, Jason was amused at and interested in his. "What did you do before Gryf came?"

"Before Gryf came, I didn't know how bad it was alone, either," she said rather roughly. "You'd better get some sleep."

He smiled. "You're right. Good morning." He fell asleep instantly.

Relaxed, he looked tireder. His hair had grown long enough to tie back, but it had escaped from its knot and curled in tangled, dirty tendrils around his face. Jason hated being dirty, but working with the drill left little energy for extras, like bathing. He would never really adjust to Screwtop as Gryf and Kylis had. His first day here, Gryf had kept him from being killed or crippled at least twice. Kylis had been working on the same shift but a different crew, driving one of the bulldozers and clearing another section of forest. The drill could not be set up among the giant ferns, because the ground itself would not stand much stress. Beneath a layer of humus was clay, so wet that in response to pressure it turned semiliquid, almost like quicksand. The crews had to strip off the vegetation and the layers of clay and volcanic ash until bedrock lay exposed. Kylis drove the dozer back and forth, cutting through ferns in a much wider path than the power plants themselves would have required. She had to make room for the excavated earth, which was piled well back from the Pit's edges. Even so the slopes sometimes collapsed in mudslides.

At the end of the day of Jason's arrival, the siren went off and Kylis drove the dozer to the old end of the Pit and into the recharging stall. Gryf was waiting for her, and a big fair man was with him, sitting slumped on the ground with his head between his knees and his hands limp on the ground. Kylis hardly noticed him. She took Gryf's hand, to walk with him back to the shelters, but he quietly stopped her and helped the other man to his feet. The new prisoner's expression was blank with exhaustion; in the dawn light he looked deathly pale. Hardly anyone on Redsun was as fair as he, even in the north. Kylis supposed he was from off-world, but he did not have the shoulder tattoo that would have made her trust him instantly. But Gryf was half carrying the big clumsy man, so she supported him on the other side. Together she and Gryf got him to their shelter. He neither ate nor drank nor even spoke, but collapsed on the hard lumpy platform and fell asleep. Gryf watched him with a troubled expression.

"Who is that?" Kylis did not bother to hide the note of contempt in her voice.

Gryf told her the man's name, which was long and complicated and contained a lot of double vowels. She never remembered it all, even now. "He says to call him Jason."

"Did you know him before?" She was willing to help Gryf save an old friend, though she did not quite see how they would do it. In one day he had spent himself completely.

"No," Gryf said. "But I read his work. I never thought I'd get to meet him."

The undisguised awe in Gryf's voice hurt Kylis, not so much because she was jealous as because it reminded her how limited her own skills were. The admiration in the faces of drunks and children in spaceport bazaars, which Kylis had experienced, was nothing compared to Gryf's feeling for the accomplishments of this man.

"Is he in here for writing a book?"

"No, thank gods—they don't know who he is. They think he's a transient. He travels under his personal name instead of his family name. They are making him work for his passage home."

"How long?"

"Six sets."

"Oh, Gryf."

"He must live and be released."

"If he's important, why hasn't anybody ransomed him?"

"His family doesn't know where he is. They would have to be contacted in secret. If the government finds out who he is, they will never let him go. His books are smuggled in."

Kylis shook her head.

"He affected my life, Kylis. He helped me understand the idea of freedom. And personal responsibility. The things you have known all your life from your own experience."

"You mean you wouldn't be here except for him."

"I never thought of it that way, but you are right."

"Look at him, Gryf. This place will grind him up."

Gryf stared somberly at Jason, who slept so heavily he hardly seemed to breathe. "He should not be here. He's a person who should not be hurt."

"We should?"

"He's different."

Kylis did not say Jason would be hurt at Screwtop. Gryf knew that well enough.

Jason had been hurt, and he had changed. What Gryf had responded to in his work was a pure idealism and innocence that could not exist in captivity. Kylis had been afraid Jason would fight the prison by arming himself with its qualities; she was afraid of what that would do to Gryf. But Jason had survived by growing more mature, by retaining his humor, not by becoming brutal. Kylis had never read a word he had written, but the longer she knew him, the more she liked and admired him.

Now she left him sleeping among the ferns. She had slept as much as she wanted to for the moment. She knew from experience that she had to time her sleeping carefully on the day off. In the timeless environment of space, where she had spent most of her life, Kylis' natural circadian rhythm was about twenty-three hours. A standard day of twenty-four did not bother her, but Redsun's twenty-seven hour rotation made her uncomfortable. She could not afford to sleep too much or too little and return to work exhausted and inattentive. At Screwtop inattention was worth punishment at best, and at worst, death.

She was no longer tired, but she was hungry for anything besides the tasteless prison rations. The vegetation on Redsun, afflicted with a low mutation rate, had not evolved very far. The plants were not yet complex enough to produce fruiting bodies. Some of the stalks and roots, though, were edible.

On Redsun, there were no flowers.

Kylis headed deeper into the shadows of the rain forest. Away from the clearings people had made, the primitive plants reached great heights. Kylis wandered among them, her feet sinking into the soft moist humus. Her footprints remained distinct. She turned and looked back. Only a few paces behind her, seeping water had already formed small pools in the deeper marks of her bootheels.

She wished she and Gryf and Jason had been on the same shift. As it was, half of their precious free time would be spent sleeping and readjusting their time schedules. When Gryf finally got off, they would have less than one day together, even before he rested. Sometimes Kylis felt that the single free day in every forty was more a punishment than if the prisoners had been forced to work their sentences straight through. The brief respite allowed them to remember just how much they hated Screwtop, and just how impossible it was to escape.

Since she could not be with both her friends, she preferred complete solitude. For Kylis it was almost instinctive to make certain no one could follow her. Unfolding the cuffs of her boots, she protected her legs to halfway up her thighs. She did not seal the boots to her shorts because of the heat.

The floor of the forest dipped and rose gently, forming wide hollows where the rain collected. Kylis stepped into one of the huge shallow pools and waded across it, walking slowly, feeling ahead with her toe before she put her foot down firmly. The mist and shadows, the reddish sunlight, and the glassy surface created illusions that concealed occasional deep pits. Where the water lay still and calm, microscopic parasites crawled out of the earth and swarmed. They normally reproduced inside small fishes and primitive amphibians, but they were not particular about their host. They would invade a human body through a cut or abrasion, causing agonizing muscle lesions. Sometimes they traveled slowly to the brain. The forest was no place to fall into a water hole.

Avoiding one deep spot, Kylis reached the far bank and stepped out onto a slick outcropping of rock where her footprints would not show. Where the stone ended and she reentered the frond forest, the ground was higher and less sodden, although the misty rain still fell continuously.

The ferns thinned, the ground rose steeply, and Kylis began to climb. At the top of the hill the air stirred, and the vegetation was not so thick. Kylis found some edible shoots, picked them, and peeled them carefully. The pulp was spicy and crunchy. The juice, pungent and sour, trickled down her throat. She picked a few more stalks and tied the small bundle to her belt. Those that were sporing she was careful not to disturb. Edible plants no longer grew near camp; in fact, nothing edible grew close enough to Screwtop to reach on any but the free day.

Redsun traveled upright in its circular orbit; it had no seasons. The plants had no sun-determined clock by which to synchronize their reproduction, so a few branches of any one plant or a few plants of any one species would spore while the rest remained asexual. A few days later a different random set would begin. It was not a very efficient method of spreading traits through the gene pool, but it had sufficed until people came along and destroyed fertile plants as well as spored-out ones. Kylis, who had noticed in her wanderings that evolution ceased at the point when human beings arrived and began to make their changes, tried not to cause that kind of damage.

A flash of white, a movement, caught the edge of her vision. She froze, wishing the hallucinations away but certain they had come back. White was not a natural color in the frond forest, not even the muddy pink that passed for white under Redsun's enormous star. But no strange fantasy creatures paraded around her; she heard no furious imaginary sounds. Her feet remained firmly on the ground, the warm fine rain hung around her, the ferns drooped with their burden of droplets. Slowly Kylis turned until she faced the direction of the motion. She was not alone.

She moved quietly forward until she could look through the black foliage. What she had seen was the uniform of Screwtop, white boots, white shorts, white shirt for anyone with a reason to wear it. One of the other prisoners sat on a rock, looking out across the forest, toward the swamp. Tears rolled slowly down her face, though she made no sound. Miria.

Feeling only a little guilty about invading her privacy, Kylis watched her, as she had been watching her for some time. Kylis thought Miria was a survivor, someone who would leave Screwtop without being broken. She kept to herself; she had no partners. Kylis had admired her tremendous capacity for work. She was taller than Kylis, bigger, potentially stronger, but clearly unaccustomed to great physical labor. For a while she had worn her shirt tied up under her breasts, but like most others she had discarded it because of the heat.

Miria survived in the camp without using other people or allowing herself to be used. Except when given a direct order, she acted as if the guards simply did not exist, in effect defying them without giving them a reasonable excuse to punish her. They did not always wait for reasonable excuses. Miria received somewhat more than her share of pain, but her dignity remained intact.

Kylis retreated a couple of steps, then came noisily out of the forest, giving Miria a few seconds to wipe away her tears if she wanted to. But when Kylis stopped, pretending to be surprised at finding another person so near, Miria simply turned toward her.

"Hello, Kylis."

Kylis went closer. "Is anything wrong?" That was such a silly question that she added, "I mean, is there anything I can do?"

Miria's smile erased the lines of tension in her forehead and revealed laugh lines Kylis had never noticed before. "No," Miria said. "Nothing anyone can do. But thank you."

"I guess I'd better go."

"Please don't," Miria said quickly. "I'm so tired of being alone—" She cut herself off and turned away, as if she were sorry to have revealed so much of herself. Kylis knew how she felt. She sat down nearby.

Miria looked out again over the forest. The fronds were a soft reddish black. The marsh trees were harsher, darker, interspersed with gray patches of water. Beyond the marsh, over the horizon, lay an ocean that covered all of Redsun except the large inhabited North Continent and the tiny South Continent where the prison camp lay.

Kylis could see the ugly scar of the pits where the crews were still drilling, but Miria had her back half turned and she gazed only at unspoiled forest.

"It could all be so beautiful," Miria said.

"Do you really think so?" Kylis thought it ugly—the black foliage, the dim light, the day too long, the heat, no animals except insects that did not swim or crawl. Redsun was the most nearly intolerable planet she had ever been on.

"Yes. Don't you?"

"No. I don't see any way I ever could."

"It's sometimes hard, I know," Miria said. "Sometimes, when I'm tiredest, I even feel the same. But the world's so rich and so strange—don't you see the challenge?"

"I only want to leave it," Kylis said.

Miria looked at her for a moment, then nodded. "You're not from Redsun, are you?"

Kylis shook her head.

"No, there's no reason for you to have the same feelings as someone born here."

This was a side of Miria that Kylis had never seen, one of quiet but intense dedication to a world whose rulers had imprisoned her. Despite her liking for Miria, Kylis was confused. "How can you feel that way when they've sent you here? I hate them, I hate this place—"

"Were you wrongly arrested?" Miria asked with sympathy.

"They could have just deported me. That's what usually happens."

"Sometimes injustice is done," Miria said sadly. "I know that. I wish it wouldn't happen. But I deserve to be here, and I know that too. When my sentence is completed, I'll be forgiven."

More than once Kylis had thought of staying on some world and trying to live the way other people did, even of accepting punishment, if necessary, but what had always stopped her was the doubt that forgiveness was often, or ever, fully given. Redsun seemed an unlikely place to find amnesty.

"What did you do?"

Kylis felt Miria tense and wished she had not asked. Not asking questions about the past was one of the few tacit rules among the prisoners.

"I'm sorry . . . it's not that I wouldn't tell you, but I just cannot talk about it."

Kylis sat in silence for a few minutes, scuffing the toe of her boot along the rock like an anxious child and rubbing the silver tattoo on the point of her left shoulder. The pigment caused irritation and slight scarring. The intricate design had not hurt for a long time, nor even itched, but she could feel the delicate lines. Rubbing them was a habit. Even though the tattoo represented a life to which she would probably never return, it was soothing.

"What's that?" Miria asked. Abruptly she grimaced. "I'm sorry, I'm doing just what I asked you not to do."

"It doesn't matter," Kylis said. "I don't mind. It's a spaceport rat tattoo. You get it when the other rats accept you." Despite everything, she was proud of the mark.

"What's a spaceport rat?"

That Miria was unfamiliar with the rats did not surprise Kylis. Few Redsun people had heard of them. On almost every other world Kylis ever visited, the rats were, if not exactly esteemed, at least admired. Some places she had been actively worshiped. Even where she was officially unwelcome, the popular regard was high enough to prevent the kind of entrapment Redsun had started.

"I used to be one. It's what everybody calls people who sneak on board starships and live in them and in spaceports. We travel all over."

"That sounds . . . interesting," Miria said. "But didn't it bother you to steal like that?"

A year before, Kylis would have laughed at the question, even knowing, as she did, that Miria was quite sincere. But recently Kylis had begun to wonder: Might something be more important than outwitting spaceport security guards? While she was wondering she came to Redsun, so she never had a chance to find out.

"I started when I was ten," Kylis said to Miria. "So I didn't think of it like that."

"You sneaked onto a starship when you were only ten?"

"Yes."

"All by yourself?"

"Until the others start to recognize you, no one will help you much. It's possible. And I thought it was my only chance to get away from where I was."

"You must have been in a terrible place."

"It's hard to remember if it was really as bad as I think. I can remember my parents, but never smiling, only yelling at each other and hitting me."

Miria shook her head. "That's terrible, to be driven away by your own people—to have nowhere to grow up. . . . Did you ever go back?"

"I don't think so."

"What?"

"I can't remember much about where I was born. I always thought I'd recognize the spaceport, but there might have been more than one, so maybe I have been back and maybe I haven't. The thing is, I can't remember what they called the planet. Maybe I never knew."

"I cannot imagine it—not to know who you are or where you come from or even who your parents were."

"I know *that*," Kylis said.

"You could find out about the world. Fingerprints or ship records or regression—"

"I guess I could. If I ever wanted to. Sometime I might even do it, if I ever get out of here."

"I'm sorry we stopped you. Really. It's just that we feel that everyone who can should contribute a fair share."

Kylis still found it hard to believe that after being sent to Screwtop Miria would include herself in Redsun's collective conscience, but she had said "we." Kylis only thought of authorities as "they."

She shrugged. "Spaceport rats know they can get caught. It doesn't happen too often and usually you hear that you should avoid the place."

"I wish you had."

"We take the chance." She touched the silver tattoo again. "You don't get one of these until you've proved you can be trusted. So when places use informers against us, we usually know who they are."

"But on Redsun you were betrayed?"

"I never expected them to use a child," Kylis said bitterly.

"A child!"

"This little kid sneaked on my ship. He did a decent job of it, and he reminded me of me. He was only ten or eleven, and he was all beat up. I guess we aren't so suspicious of kids because most of us started at the same age." Kylis glanced at Miria and saw that she was staring at her, horrified.

"They used a child? And injured him, just to catch you?"

"Does that really surprise you?"

"Yes," Miria said.

"Miria, half the people who were killed during the last set weren't more than five or six years older than the boy who turned me in. Most of the people being sent here now are that age. What could they possibly have done terrible enough to get them sent here?"

"I don't know," Miria said softly without looking up. "We need the power generators. Someone has to drill the steam wells. Some of us will die in the work. But you're right about the young people. I've been thinking about ... other things. I had not noticed." She said that as if she had committed a crime, or more exactly a sin, by not noticing. "And the child ..." Her voice trailed off and she smiled sadly at Kylis. "How old are you?"

"I don't know. Maybe twenty."

Miria raised one eyebrow. "Twenty? Older in experience, but not that old in time. You should not be here."

"But I am. I'll survive it."

"I think you will. And what then?"

"Gryf and Jason and I have plans."

"On Redsun?"

"Gods, no."

"Kylis," Miria said carefully, "you do not know much about tetraparentals, do you?"

"How much do I need to know?"

"I was born here. I used to ... to work for them. Their whole purpose is their intelligence. Normal people like you and me bore them. They cannot tolerate us for long."

"Miria, stop it!"

"Your friend will only cause you pain. Give him up. Put him away from you. Urge him to go home."

"No! He knows I'm an ordinary person. We know what we're going to do."

"It makes no difference," Miria said with abrupt coldness. "He will not be allowed to leave Redsun."

Kylis felt the blood drain from her face. No one had ever said that so directly and brutally before. "They can't keep him. How long will they make him stay here before they realize they can't break him?"

"He is important. He owes Redsun his existence."

"But he's a person with his own dreams. They can't make him a slave!"

"His research team is worthless without him."

"I don't care," Kylis said.

"*You*—" Miria cut herself off. Her voice became much gentler. "They will try to persuade him to follow their plans. He may decide to do as they ask."

"I wouldn't feel any obligation to the people who run things on Redsun even if I lived here. Why should he be loyal to them? Why should you? What did they ever do but send you here? What will they let you do when you get out? Anything decent or just more dirty, murderous jobs like this one?" She realized she was shouting, and Miria looked stunned.

"I don't know," Miria said. "I don't know, Kylis. Please stop saying such dangerous things." She was terrified and shaken, much more upset than when she had been crying.

Kylis moved nearer and took her hand. "I'm sorry, Miria, I didn't mean to hurt you or say anything that could get you in trouble." She paused, wondering how far Miria's fear of Redsun's government might take her from her loyalty.

"Miria," she said on impulse, "have you ever thought of partnering with anybody?"

Miria hesitated so long that Kylis thought she would not answer. Kylis wondered if she had intruded on Miria's past again.

"No," Miria finally said. "Never."

"Would you?"

"Think about it? Or do it?"

"Both. Partner with me and Gryf and Jason. Not just here, but when we get out."

"No," Miria said. "No, I couldn't." She sounded frightened again.

"Because we want to leave Redsun?"

"Other reasons."

"Would you just think about it?"

Miria shook her head.

"I know you don't usually live in groups on Redsun," Kylis said. "But where I was born, a lot of people did, even though my parents were alone. I remember, before I ran away, my friends were never afraid to go home like I was. Jason spent all his life in a group family, and he says it's a lot easier to get along." She was skipping over her own occasional doubts that any world could be as pleasant as the one Jason described. Whatever it was like, it had to be better than her own former existence of constant hiding and constant uncertainty; it had to be better than what Gryf told her of Redsun, with its emphasis on loyalty to the government at the expense of any family structure too big to move instantly at the whim or order of the rulers.

Miria did not respond.

"Anyway, three people aren't enough—we thought we'd find others after we got out. But I think——"

"Gryf doesn't——" Miria interrupted Kylis, then stopped

herself and started over. "They don't know you were going to ask me?"

"Not exactly, but they both know you," Kylis said defensively. She thought Miria might be afraid Kylis' partners would refuse her. Kylis knew they would not but could not put how she knew into proper words.

The rain had blurred away the marks of tears on Miria's cheeks, and now she smiled and squeezed Kylis' hand. "Thank you, Kylis," she said. "I wish I could accept. I can't, but not for the reasons you think. You'll find someone better." She started up, but Kylis stopped her.

"No, you stay here. This is your place." Kylis stood. "If you change your mind, just say. All right?"

"I won't change my mind."

"I wish you wouldn't be so sure." Reluctantly, she started away.

"Kylis?"

"Yes?"

"Please don't tell anyone you asked me this."

"Not even Gryf and Jason?"

"No one. Please."

"All right," Kylis said unwillingly.

Kylis left Miria on the stony hillside. She glanced back once before entering the forest. Miria was sitting on the stone again, hunched forward, her forearms on her knees. Now she was looking down at the huge slash of clay and trash heaps, the complicated delicate cooling towers that condensed the generators' steam, the high impervious antenna beaming power north toward the cities.

When Kylis reached the sleeping place, the sun was high. Beneath the dead fern trees it was still almost cool. She crept in quietly and sat down near Jason without waking him. He lay sprawled in dry moss, breathing deeply, solid and real. As if he could feel her watching him, he half opened his eyes.

Kylis lay down and drew her hand up his side, feeling bones that had become more prominent, dry and flaking sunburned skin, and the scabs of cuts and scratches. He was bruised as though the guards had beaten him, perhaps because of his occasional amusement at things so odd that his reaction seemed insolence. But for now, she would not notice his new scars, and he would not notice hers.

"Are you awake?"

He laughed softly. "I think so."

"Do you want to go back to sleep?"

He reached out and touched her face. "I'm not that tired."

Kylis smiled and leaned over to kiss him. The hairs of his short beard were soft and stiff against her lips and tongue. For a while she and Jason could ignore the heat.

Lying beside Jason, not quite touching because the afternoon was growing hot, Kylis only dozed while Jason again slept soundly. She sat up and pulled on her shorts and boots, brushed a lock of Jason's sunstreaked hair from his damp forehead, and slipped outside. A couple of hours of Gryf's work shift remained, so Kylis headed toward the guards' enclosure and the hovercraft dock.

Beyond the drill-pit clearing, the forest extended for a short distance westward. The ground continued to fall, growing wetter and wetter, changing perceptibly into marsh. The enclosure, a hemispherical electrified fence completely covering the guards' residence domes, was built at the juncture of relatively solid land and shallow, standing water. It protected the hovercraft ramp, and it was invulnerable. She had tried to get through it. She had even tried to dig beneath it. Digging under a fence or cutting through one was something no spaceport rat would do, short of desperation. After her first few days at Screwtop, Kylis had been desperate. She had not believed she could survive her sentence in the prison. So, late that night, she crept over to the electrified fence and began to dig. At dawn she had not reached the bottom of the fence supports, and the ground was wet enough to start carrying electricity to her in small warning tingles.

Her shift would begin soon; guards would be coming in and going out, and she would be caught if she did not stop. She planned to cover over the hole she had dug and hope it was not discovered.

She was lying flat on the ground, digging a narrow deep hole with a flat rock and both hands, smeared all over with the red clay, her fingernails ripped past the quick. She reached down for one last handful of dirt, and grabbed a trap wire.

The current swept through her, contracting every muscle in her body. It lasted only an instant. She lay quivering, almost insensible, conscious enough to be glad the wire had been set to stun, not kill. She tried to get up and run, but she could not move properly. She began to shudder again. Her muscles were overstimulated, incapable of distinguishing a real signal. She ached all over, so badly that she could not even guess if the sudden clench of muscles had broken any bones.

A light shone toward her. She heard footsteps as the guards approached to investigate the alarm the trap wire had set off. The sound thundered through her ears, as though the electric current had heightened all her senses, toward pain. The footsteps stopped; the light beam blinded her, then left her face. Her dazzled vision blurred the figure standing over her, but she knew it was the Lizard. It occurred to her, in a vague, slow-motion thought, that she did not know his real name. (She learned later that no one else did either.) He dragged Kylis to her feet and held her upright, glaring at her, his face taut with anger and his eyes narrow.

"Now you know we're not as easy to cheat as starship owners," he said. His voice was low and raspy, softly hoarse. He let her go, and she collapsed again. "You're on probation. Don't make any more mistakes. And don't be late for duty."

The other guards followed him away. They did not even bother to fill in the hole she had dug.

Kylis had staggered through that workday; she survived it, and the next, and the next, until she knew that the work itself would not kill her. She did not try to dig beneath the fence again, but she still watched the hovercraft when it arrived.

By the time she reached her place of concealment on the bank above the fence, the hovercraft had already climbed the ramp and settled. The gate was locked behind it. Kylis watched the new prisoners being unloaded. The cargo bay door swung open. The people staggered out on deck and down the gangway, disoriented by the long journey in heat and darkness. One of the prisoners stumbled and fell to his knees, retching.

Kylis remembered how she had felt after so many hours in the pitch-dark hold. Even talking was impossible, for the engines were on the other side of the hold's interior bulkhead and the fans were immediately below. She was too keyed up to go into a trance, and a trance would be dangerous while she was crowded in with so many people.

The noise was what Kylis remembered most about coming to Screwtop—incessant, penetrating noise, the high whine of the engines and the roar of the fans. She had been half deaf for days afterward. The compartment was small. Despite the heat the prisoners could not avoid sitting and leaning against each other, and as soon as the engines started the temperature began to rise. By the time the hovercraft reached the prison, the hold was thick with the stench of human misery. Kylis hardly noticed when the craft's sickening swaying ceased. When the hatch opened and red light spilled in, faintly dissipating the blackness, Kylis looked up with all the others, and, like all the others, blinked like a frightened animal.

The guards had no sympathy for cramped muscles or nausea. Their shouted commands faded like faraway echoes through Kylis' abused hearing. She pushed herself up, using the wall as support. Her legs and feet were asleep. They began regaining sensation, and she felt as if she were walking on tiny knives. She hobbled out, but at the bottom of the gangway she, too, had stumbled. A guard's curse and the prod of his club brought her to her feet in a fury, fists clenched, but she quelled her violent temper instantly. The guard watched with a smile, waiting. But Kylis had been to Earth, where one of the few animals left outside the game preserves and zoos was the possum. She had learned its lesson well.

Now she crouched on the bank and watched the new prisoners realize, as she had, that the end of the trip did not end the terrible heat. Screwtop was almost on the equator of Redsun, and the heat and humidity never lessened. Even the rain was lukewarm.

The guards prodded the captives into a compact group and turned hoses on them, spraying off filth and sweat. Afterward the new people plodded through the mud to the processing dome. Kylis watched each one pass through the doorway. She had never defined what she looked for when she watched the new arrivals, but whatever it was, she did not find it today. Even more of them were terribly young, and they all had the look of hopelessness that would make them nothing more than fresh meat, new bodies for the work to use up. Screwtop would grind them down and throw them away. They would die of disease or exhaustion or carelessness. Kylis did not see in one of them the spark of defiance that might get them through their sentences intact in body or spirit. But sometimes the spark only came out later, exposed by the real adversity of the work.

The hatch swung shut and the hovercraft's engines roared to full power. No one at all had been taken on board for release on North Continent.

The boat quivered on its skirts and floated back down the ramp, through the entrance, onto the glassy gray surface of the water. The gate sparked shut. Kylis was vaguely disappointed, for the landing was no different from any she had seen since she was brought to Screwtop herself. There was no way to get on board the boat. The familiar admission still annoyed her. For a spaceport rat, admitting defeat to the safeguards of an earthbound vehicle was humiliating. She could not even think of a way to get herself out of Screwtop, much less herself and Gryf and Jason. She was afraid that if she did not find some chance of escape, Jason might really try to flee through the swamp.

She ran her fingers through her short black hair and shook her head, flinging out the misty rain that gathered in huge drops and slipped down her face and neck and back. The heat and the rain—she hated both.

In an hour or two the evening rain would fall in solid sheets, washing the mist away. But an hour after that the faint infuriating droplets would begin again. They did not seem to fall, but hung in the air and collected on skin, on hair, beneath trees, inside shelters.

Kylis grabbed an overhanging plant and stripped off a few of its red-black fronds, flinging them to the ground in anger.

She stood up, but suddenly crouched down in hiding again. Below, Miria walked up to the fence, placed her hand against the palm lock, and waited, glancing over her shoulder as if making certain she was alone. As the gate swung open and Miria, a prisoner, walked alone and free into the guards' enclosure, Kylis felt her knees grow weak. Miria stopped at a dome, and the door opened for her. Kylis thought she could see the Lizard in the dimness beyond.

Almost the only thing this could mean was that Miria was a spy. Kylis began to tremble in fear and anger, fear of what Miria could tell the Lizard that would help him increase the pressure on Gryf, anger at herself for trusting Miria. She had made another mistake in judgment like the one that had imprisoned her, and this time the consequences could be much worse.

She sat in the mud and the rain trying to think, until she realized that Gryf would be off work in only a few minutes. She did not even have time to wake Jason.

When Kylis turned her back on the guards' domes, Miria had not yet come out.

Kylis was a few minutes late reaching the drill pit. The third shift had already ended; all the prisoners were out and drifting away. Gryf was nowhere around, and he was nothing if not conspicuous. She began to worry, because Gryf was frequently first out, never last—he did not seem to tire. Certainly he would wait for her.

She stood indecisively, worried, thinking, He might have wanted something in the shelter.

She did not believe that for a moment. She glanced back toward the bottom of the Pit.

Everything happened at once. She forgot about Miria, Lizard, the prison. She cried out for Jason, knowing her voice would not carry that far. She ran downhill, fighting the clay that sucked at her feet. Two people she knew slightly trudged up the hill—Troi, skeletal, sharp-featured, sardonic, and Chuzo, squarely built and withdrawn. Both were very young; both were aging quickly here.

They supported Gryf between them.

Ash and grease disguised the pattern of his paisley skin. Kylis knew he was alive only because no one at Screwtop would spend any energy on someone who was dead. When she was closer, she could see the ends of deep slashes made by the whip where it had curled around his body. Blood had dried in narrow steaks on his sides. His wrists were abraded where he had been tied for the punishment.

"Oh, Gryf—"

Hearing her, Gryf raised his head. She felt great relief. Troi and Chuzo stopped when Kylis reached them.

"The Lizard ordered it himself," Troi said bitterly. Screwtop held few amenities, but people were seldom flogged on the last day of the shift.

"Why?"

"I don't know. I was too far away. Anything. Nothing. What reason do they ever have?"

Kylis quieted her anger for the moment. She took over for Chuzo. "Thank you," she said, quite formally.

Troi stayed where he was. "Get him to the top, anyway," he said in his gruff manner.

"Gryf? Can you make it?"

He tightened his hand on her shoulder. They started up the steep path. When they finally reached the top, the immense sun had set. The sky was pink and scarlet in the west, and the volcanoes eastward glowed blood red.

"Thanks," Kylis said again. Chuzo hesitated, but Troi nodded and left. After a moment Chuzo followed him.

Gryf leaned heavily on her, but she could support him. She tried to turn toward the shelters and their meager stock of medical supplies, but he resisted weakly and guided her toward the waterfall. If he wanted to go there first, he must think his wounds had been contaminated.

"Gods," Kylis whispered. Clumsily, they hurried. She wished Jason had heard her, for with him they could have gone faster. It was her fault he was not there. She could not hold Gryf up alone without hurting his back.

Gryf managed a smile, just perceptible, telling her, I hurt but I am strong.

Yes, Kylis thought, stronger than Jason, stronger than me. We'll survive.

They continued.

"Kylis! Gryf!"

Gryf stopped. Kylis let him, with relief. Jason splashed toward them.

Gryf's knees buckled. Kylis strained to keep him out of the mud, away from more parasites. Jason reached them and picked Gryf up.

"Could you hear me?" Kylis asked.

"No," Jason said. "I woke up and came looking. Where are you taking him?"

"To the overflow pipe."

Jason needed no explanation of the dangers of infection. He carried Gryf toward the waterfall, swearing softly.

The cooling towers from the steam wells produced the only safe water the prisoners had for bathing. It spewed from a pipe to a concrete platform and spilled from there to the ground, forming a muddy pool that spread into the forest. The water was too hot for anyone to go directly beneath the cascade. Jason stopped in knee-deep hot water. They were all standing in heavy spray.

Jason held Gryf against his chest while Kylis splashed water on Gryf's back from her cupped hands. She washed him as gently as she could and still be safe. She found no parasites and none of their eggs. The water swept away mud and sweat, turning Jason bright pink and Kylis auburn and Gryf all shades of dark brown and tan.

Kylis cursed the Lizard. He knew he would look bad in the eyes of the tetra committee if Gryf were crushed or bled to death or went home with everything but his brain. But he would look worse if he could not force Gryf to go home at all.

Gryf's eyelids flickered. His eyes were bright blue, flecked irregularly with black.

"How do you feel?"

He smiled, but he had been hurt—she could see the memory of pain. They had touched his spirit. He looked away from her and made Jason let him turn. He staggered. His knees would not support him, which seemed to surprise him. Jason held him up, and Gryf took the last thin flake of antiseptic soap from Kylis' hand.

"What's the matter?" she asked.

Gryf turned her around. For a moment his touch was painful, then she felt the sharp sting of soap on raw flesh. Gryf showed her his hand, which glittered with a mass of tiny, fragile eggs like mica flakes. Gryf used up her soap scrubbing her side, and Jason got out what soap he had left.

"This cut's pretty deep but it's clean now. You must have fallen and smashed a nest."

"I don't remember—" She had a kinesthetic memory, from running down into the Pit. "Yes, I do . . ." It hit her then, a quick shock of the fear of what might have been—paralysis, senility, agony—if Gryf had not noticed, if the eggs had healed beneath her skin and hatched. Kylis shuddered.

They returned to the compound, supporting Gryf between them. The wall-less, stilt-legged shelters were almost deserted.

Jason climbed the slanted ladder to their shelter backward, leaning against it for stability while he helped Gryf. The steps were slick with yellow lichen. Kylis chinned herself onto the platform. In their floor locker she had to paw through little stacks of Jason's crumbling ration bars before she found their mold poultice and the web box. She had been very hungry, but she had never eaten any of her friend's hoarded food. She would not have had such restraint a year ago.

Jason put Gryf down between the makeshift partitions

that marked their section of the shelter. Gryf was pale beneath the pattern of tan and pigment. Kylis almost wished Troi and Chuzo had left him in the Pit. The Lizard might then have been forced to put him in the hospital. She wondered if Troi or Chuzo might be helping the Lizard make Screwtop as hard on Gryf as they could. She did not want to believe that, but she did not want to believe Miria was an informer, either.

Their spider—Kylis thought of it as a spider, though it was a Redsun-evolved creature—skittered up the corner post to a new web. Kylis often imagined the little brown-mottled creature hanging above them on her tiny fringed feet, hating them. Yet she was free to crawl down the stilt and into the jungle, or to spin a glider and float away, and she never did. In dreams, Kylis envied her; awake, she named her Stupid. Kylis hoped the web box held enough silk to soothe Gryf's back.

"Hey," Jason said, "this stuff is ready."

"Okay." Kylis took the bowl of greenish mold paste. "Gryf?"

He glanced up. His eyelashes and eyebrows were black and blond, narrowly striped.

"Hang on, it might hurt."

He nodded.

Jason held Gryf's hands while Kylis applied first the mold, then delicate strips of spider silk. Gryf did not move. Even now he had enough strength to put aside the pain.

When she was done, Jason stroked Gryf's forehead and gave him water. He did not want to eat, even broth, so they kissed him and sat near him, for his reassurance and their own, until he fell asleep. That did not take long. When he was breathing deeply, Jason got up and went to Kylis, carrying the bowl.

"I want to look at that cut."

"Okay," Kylis said, "but don't use all the paste."

The poultice burned coldly, and Jason's hands were cool on her skin. She sat with her forearms on her drawn-up knees, accepting the pain rather than ignoring it. When he had finished treating her, she took the bowl and daubed the mold on his cuts. She almost told Jason about Miria, but finally decided not to. Kylis had created the problem; she wanted to solve it herself if she could. And, she admitted, she was ashamed of her misjudgment. She could think of no explanation for Miria's actions that would absolve her.

Jason yawned widely.

"Give me your tag and go back to sleep," Kylis said. Since she had been the first to get off work this time, it was her turn to collect their rations. She took Gryf's tag from his belt pouch and jumped from the edge of the platform to the ground.

Kylis approached the ration dispenser cautiously. On Redsun, violent criminals were sent to rehabilitation centers, not to work camps. Kylis was glad of that, though she did not much like to remember the stories of obedient, blank-eyed people coming out of rehab.

Still, some prisoners were confident or foolish or desperate enough to try to overpower others and steal. At Screwtop it was safest to collect neither obligations nor hatreds. Vengeance was much too simple here. The underground society of spaceport rats had not been free of psychopaths; Kylis knew how to defend herself. Here she had never had to resort to more serious measures. If she did, the drill pit was a quick equalizer between a bully and a smaller person. Mistakes could be planned; machines malfunctioned.

The duty assignments were posted on the ration dispenser. Kylis read them and was astonished and overjoyed to find herself and her friends all on the same shift, the night shift. She hurried back to tell them the news, but Jason was sound asleep, and she did not have the heart to wake him. Gryf had gone.

Kylis threw the rations in the floor locker and sat on the edge of the platform. A scavenger insect crawled across the lumpy floor of fern stalks. Kylis caught it and let it go near Stupid, barricading it until the spider, stalking, left her new web and seized the insect, paralyzed it, wrapped it in silk to store it, and dragged it away. Kylis wondered if their spider ever slept, or if spiders even needed sleep. Then she stole the web.

She grew worried. She knew Gryf could take care of himself. He always did. He had probably never really reached his limits, but Gryf might overestimate even his strength and endurance. He had rested barely an hour.

Kylis fidgeted for a little while longer. Finally she slid down into the mud again.

Water seeped quickly into new footprints in the battered earth around the shelters; Gryf had left no trail that she could distinguish from the other marks in the clay. She went into the forest, with some knowledge and some intuition of where he might be. Above her, huge insects flitted past, barely brushing clawed wingtips against the ferns. It was dark, and the star path, streaked across the sky like the half-circular support of a globe, gave a dim yellow light through broken clouds.

Kylis was startled and frightened by a tickling of the short hair at the back of her neck. She flinched and turned. Gryf looked down at her, smiling, amused.

"Kylis, my friend, you really needn't worry about me all the time." She was always surprised, when he spoke, to remember how pleasant and calming his voice was.

His eyes were dilated so the iris was only a narrow circle of light and dark striations.

Every few sets, someone died from sucking slime. It grew in the forest, in small patches like purple jellyfish. It was hallucinogenic, and it was poisonous. Kylis had argued with Gryf about his using it, before her sentence in the sensory deprivation chamber showed her what Screwtop was like for Gryf all the time.

"Gryf—"

"Don't reproach me!"

"I won't," Kylis said. "Not anymore."

Her response startled him only for a moment; that it startled him at all revealed how completely drained he really was. He nodded and put his arms around her.

"Now you know," he said, with sympathy and understanding. "How long did they make you stay in the box?"

"Eight days. That's what they said, anyway."

He passed his hand across her hair, just touching it. "My poor friend. It seems so much longer."

"It doesn't matter. It's over for me." She almost believed the hallucinations had stopped, but she wondered if she would ever be certain they would never return.

"Do you think the Lizard sentenced you because of me?"

"I don't know. I guess he'd use anything he could if he thought it'd work. Never mind. I'm all right."

"I would have done what they want, but I could not. Can you believe I tried?"

"Do you think I wanted you to?" She touched his face, tracing bone structure with her fingers like someone blind. She could feel the difference between the blond and black hair in his striped eyebrows, but the texture of his skin was smooth. She drew her fingers from his temples to the corners of his jaw, to the tendons of his neck and the tension-knotted muscles of his shoulders. "No one should make friends here," she said.

He smiled, closing his eyes, understanding her irony. "We would lose our souls if we did not."

He turned away abruptly and sat down on a large rock with his head between his knees, struggling against nausea. The new scars did not seem to hurt him. He breathed deeply for some time, then sat up slowly.

"How is Jason?"

"Fine. Recovered. You didn't have to take his shift. Lizard couldn't let him die like that."

"I think the Lizard collects methods of death."

Kylis remembered Miria with a quick shock of returning fear. "Oh, gods, Gryf, what's the use of fighting them?"

Gryf drew her closer. "The use is that you and Jason will not let them destroy you and I believe I am stronger than those who wish to keep me here, and justified in wishing to make my own mistakes rather than theirs." He held out his hand, pale-swirled in the darkness. It was long and fine. Kylis reached out and rubbed it, his wrist, his tense forearm. Gryf relaxed slightly, but Kylis was still afraid. She had never felt frightened before, not like this. But Miria, uncertainty, seeing Gryf hurt, had all combined to make her doubt the possibility of a future.

Gryf was caught and shaken by another spasm of retching. This time he could not suppress it, and it was more severe because he had not eaten. Kylis stood by, unable to do anything but hold his shoulders and hope he would survive the drug this time, as he had all the times before. The dry vomiting was replaced by a fit of coughing. Sweat dripped from his face and down his sides. When the pitch of his coughing rose and his breath grew more ragged, Kylis realized he was sobbing. On her knees beside him, she tried to soothe him. She did not know if he was crying from the sickness, from some vision she would never see, or from despair. She held him until, gradually, he was able to stop.

Sparkles of starlight passed between the clouds, mottling Gryf with a third color. He lay face down on the smooth stone, hands flat against it, cheek pressed to the rock. Kylis knew how he felt, drained, removed, heavy.

"Kylis . . . I never slept before like this . . ."

"I won't go far."

She hoped he heard her. She sat cross-legged on the wide rock beside him, watching slow movements of muscle as he breathed. His roan eyelashes were very long and touched with sweat droplets. The deep welts in his back would leave scars. Kylis' back had similar scars, but she felt that the marks she carried were a brand of shame, while Gryf's meant defiance and pride. She reached toward him, but drew back when her hand's vague shadow touched his face.

When she was certain he was sleeping easily, she left him and went to look nearby for patches of the green antibiotic mold. Their supply was exhausted. It was real medicine, not a superstition. Its active factor was synthesized back north and exported.

Being allowed to walk away from Screwtop, however briefly, made remaining almost endurable, but the privilege had a more important purpose. It was a constant reminder of freedom. The short moment of respite only strengthened the need to get out, and, more important, the need never to come back. Redsun knew how to reinforce obedience.

Kylis wandered, never going very far from Gryf, looking for green mold and finding the rarer purple hallucinogenic slime instead. She tried to deny that it tempted her. She could have taken some to Gryf—she almost did—but in the end she left it under the rocks where it belonged.

"I want to talk to you."

She spun, startled, recognizing the rough voice, fearing it, concealing her fear badly. She did not answer, only looked toward the Lizard.

"Come sit with me," he said. Starlight glinted on his clean fingernails as he gestured to the other end of an immense uprooted fern tree. It sagged but held when he sat on it.

As always, his black protective boots were pulled up and sealed to his black shorts. He was even bigger than Jason, taller, heavier, and though he had allowed his body to go slightly to fat, his face had remained narrow and hard. His clean-shaven scalp and face never tanned or burned, but somehow remained pale, in contrast to his deep-set black eyes. He licked his thin lips quickly with the tip of his tongue.

"What do you want?" She did not approach him.

He leaned forward and leaned his forearms on his knees. "I've been watching you."

She had no answer. He watched everyone. Standing there before him, Kylis was uneasy for reasons that somehow had nothing to do with his capacity for brutality. The Lizard never acted this way. He was direct and abrupt.

"I made a decision when sensory deprivation didn't break you," he said. "That was the last test."

The breeze shifted slightly. Kylis smelled a sharp odor as the Lizard lifted a small pipe to his lips and drew on it deeply. He held his breath and offered the pipe to her.

She wanted some. It was good stuff. She and Gryf and Jason had used the last of theirs at the end of the previous set, the night before they went on different shifts. Kylis was surprised that the Lizard used it at all. She would never have expected him to pare off the corners of his aggression out here. She shook her head.

"No?" He shrugged and put the pipe down, letting it waste, burning unattended. "All right."

She let the silence stretch on, hoping he would forget her and whatever he wanted to say, wander off or get hungry or go to sleep.

"You've got a long time left to stay here," he said.

Again, Kylis had no answer.

"I could make it easier for you."

"You could make it easier for most of us."

"That's not my job." He ignored the contradiction.

"What are you trying to say?"

"I've been looking for someone like you for a long time. You're strong, and you're stubborn." He got up and came toward her, hesitated to glance back at his pipe but left it where he was. He took a deep breath. He was trying so hard to look sincere that Kylis had an almost overwhelming urge to laugh. She did not, but if she had, it would have been equally a laugh of nervous fear. She realized suddenly, with wonder: The Lizard's as scared as I am.

"Open for me, Kylis."

Incredulity was her first reaction. He would not joke, he could not, but he might mock her. Or was he asking her an impossibility, knowing she would refuse, so he could offer to let her alone if Gryf would return to the tetras. She kept her voice very calm.

"I can't do that."

"Don't you think I'm serious?"

"How could you be?"

He forced away his scowl, like an inexperienced mime changing expressions. The muscles of his jaw were set. He moved closer, so she had to look up to see his eyes.

"I am."

"But that's not something you ask for," Kylis said. "That's something a family all wants and decides on." She realized he would not understand what she meant.

"*I've* decided. There's only me now." His voice was only a bit too loud.

"Aren't you lonely?" She heard her words, not knowing why she had said them. If the Lizard had been hurt, she would revel in his pain. She could not imagine people who would live with him, unless something terrible had changed him.

"I had a kid—" He cut himself off, scowling, angry for revealing so much.

"Ah," she said involuntarily. She had seen his manner of superficial control over badly suppressed violence before. Screwtop gave the Lizard justifiable opportunities to use his rage. Anywhere else it would burst out whenever he felt safe, against anyone who was defenseless and vulnerable. This was the kind of person who was asking her for a child.

"The board had no right to give him to her instead of me."

He would think that, of course. No right to protect the child? She did not say it.

"Well?"

To comply would be easy. She would probably be allowed to live in the comfort and coolness of the domes, and of course she would get good food. She could forget the dangerous machines and the Lizard's whip. She imagined what it would be like to feel a child quickening within her, and she imagined waiting to give birth to a human being, knowing she must hand it over to the Lizard to raise, all alone, with no other model, no other teacher, only this dreadful, crippled person.

"No," she said.

"You could if you wanted to."

So many things she had discovered about herself here had mocked her; now it was a claim she had once made to Gryf: I would do anything to get out of here.

"Leave it at that," she said quietly. "I don't want to." She backed away.

"I thought you were stubborn and strong. Maybe I made a mistake. Maybe you're just stupid, or crazy like the rest of them."

She tried to think of words he would understand, but always came up against the irreconcilable differences between her perception of the Lizard and what he thought of himself. He would not recognize her description.

"Or you want something more from me. What is it?"

She started to say there was nothing, but hesitated. "All right," she said, afraid her voice would be too shrill. Somehow it sounded perfectly normal. "Tell Gryf's people to set him free. Get Jason a parole and a ticket off-world." For a moment she almost allowed herself to hope he had believed her offer was sincere. She was a very good liar.

The Lizard's expression changed. "No. I need them around so you'll do what I say."

"I won't."

"Pick something else."

For an instant's flash Kylis remembered being taunted like this before, when she was very small. Anything but that. Anything but what you really want. She pushed the recollection away.

"There isn't anything else," she said.

"Don't hold out. You can't bribe me to let them go. I'm not a fool."

He needed no officially acceptable reason to hurt her. She knew that. Fear of his kind of power was almost an instinctive reaction for Kylis. But she whispered, "Yes, Lizard, you are," and, half blind, she turned and fled.

She almost outran him, but he lunged, grabbed her shoulder, pulled her around. "Kylis—"

Standing stiffly, coldly, she looked at his hand. "If that's what you want—"

Even the Lizard was not that twisted. Slowly, he let his hand fall to his side.

"I could force you," he said.

Her gaze met his and did not waver. "Could you?"

"I could drug you."

"For seven sets?" She realized, with a jog of alienness,

that she had unconsciously translated the time from standard months to sets of forty days.

"Long enough to mess up your control. Long enough to
make you pregnant."

"You couldn't keep me alive that long, drugged down
that far. If the drugs didn't kill it, I would. I wouldn't
even need to be conscious. I could abort it."

"I don't think you're that good."

"I am. You can't live like I did and not be that good."

"I can put you in the deprivation box until you swear
to—"

She laughed bitterly. "And expect me to honor that
oath?"

"You'd have children with Gryf and Jason."

This was real, much more than a game for the Lizard to
play against Gryf. He wanted her compliance desperately.
Kylis was certain of that, as certain as she was that he
would use his own dreams to help fulfill his duty to
Redsun. Still she could not understand why he felt he had
some right to accuse her.

"Not like this," she said. "*With* them—but not *for* one
of them. And they wouldn't make themselves fertile, either, if you were a woman and asked one of them to give
you a child."

"I'm quitting. I'd take him out of here. I'd give him a
good home. Am I asking that much? I'm offering a lot for
a little of your time and one ovulation." His voice held the
roughness of rising temper.

"You're asking for a human being."

She waited for some reaction, any reaction, but he just
stood there, accepting what she said as a simple statement
of fact without emotional meaning or moral resonance.

"I'd kill a child before I'd give it to you," she said. "I'd
kill myself." She felt herself trembling, though it did not
show in her hands or in her voice. She was trembling because what she had said was true.

He reacted not at all. She turned and ran into the
darkness, and this time the Lizard did not follow.

When she was sure she was not being watched, she returned to Gryf's rock in the forest. Gryf still slept. He had
not moved from the time he fell asleep, but the gray rock
around him gleamed with his sweat. Kylis sat down beside
him, drew up her knees and wrapped her arms around
them, put her head down. She had never felt as she felt

now—unclean by implication, ashamed, diminished—and she could not explain the feeling to herself. She felt a tear slide down her cheek and clenched her teeth in anger. He will not make me cry, she thought. She breathed deeply, slowly, thinking, Control. Slow the heartbeat, turn off the adrenaline, you don't need it now. Relax. Her body, at least, responded. Kylis sat motionless for a long time.

The heavy, moist wind began to blow, bringing low black clouds to cut off the stars. Soon it would be too dark to see.

"Gryf?" Kylis touched his shoulder. He did not move until she shook him gently; then he woke with a start.

"Storm's coming," Kylis said.

In the dimming starlight, a blond lock of Gryf's hair glinted as he rose. Kylis helped him up. Dead ferns rustled at their feet, and the sleeping insects wrapped themselves more closely in their wings.

At the edge of the forest Kylis and Gryf picked their way across a slag heap and reached the trail to the prisoners' area. A faint blue glow emanated from their shelter, where Jason sat hunched over a cold light reading a book he had managed to scrounge. He did not hear them until they climbed the stairs.

"I was beginning to get worried," he said mildly, squinting to see them past the light.

"Gryf was sick."

"You okay now?" Jason asked.

Gryf nodded, and he and Kylis sat down in the circle of bioluminescence that did not waver in the wind. Jason put his book away and got their rations and water bottles from the locker. The stalks Kylis had picked were by now a bit wilted, but she gave them to Gryf anyway. He shared them out. The meal was slightly better and slightly more pleasant than most at Screwtop, but Kylis was not hungry. She was ashamed to tell her friends what had happened.

"What's the matter?" Jason asked suddenly.

"What?" Kylis glanced up at him, then at Gryf. Both were watching her with concern.

"You look upset."

"I'm okay." She leaned back gradually as she spoke, so her face was no longer in the light. "I'm tired, I guess." She searched for words to put into the silence. "I'm so tired I almost forgot to tell you we're all on night shift."

That was good enough news to change the subject and

take her friends' attention from her. It was even good
enough news to cheer her.

Later they returned to the hiding place in the forest and
slept, lying close with Gryf in the middle. In the distance
the sky flashed bright, then darkened. Only a faint mutter
reached them, but the lightning revealed heavy clouds and
the wind carried the sound closer. Kylis touched Gryf
gently, taking comfort in his deep and regular breathing.
Lightning scarred the sky again, and seconds later thunder
rumbled softly. The wind rustled dry fronds.

Gryf stroked Kylis' tattooed shoulder. He touched her
hand and their fingers intertwined.

"I wish you could get out," she whispered. "I wish you
would." The lightning flashed again, vivid and close, its
thunder simultaneous. Jason started in his sleep. During
the brief flare Gryf looked at Kylis, frowning.

It began to rain.

In the morning Kylis woke by reflex, despite the ab-
sence of the siren. The whole day was free, but she and
her friends had to rest, for the night shift was first on
duty.

Gryf was already sitting up. He smiled in his it's-all-
right way.

"Let's see," Kylis said.

He turned. The welts were silver-gray down their
lengths, even where they crossed. They were uninfected
and the ends had begun to heal. Gryf stretched his arms
and looked over his shoulder. Kylis watched his face, the
fine lines at the corners of his eyes, but he did not flinch.
Biocontrol was one thing Kylis had proper training in, and
she knew Gryf could not stretch human limits indefinitely.
This time, though, he had succeeded.

"How much better are you?" she asked.

He grinned and Kylis laughed in spite of herself. She
forced away the thought and worry of the Lizard. Together she and Gryf woke Jason.

But all the rest of the day her apprehension grew. She
was certain the Lizard would not accept her refusal easily.
Now Kylis had to look twice at the little movements in her
peripheral vision, once to make sure they were not hallucinations and again to make sure they were not the Lizard.
By evening she was taut with acting out a pose of normal-
ity and maintaining an artificial calm, and she was affect-
ing Jason and Gryf with her agitation. She would not

speak of the reason. She could be nearly as stubborn as Gryf.

Kylis was almost relieved when the siren shrieked and they had to return to the installation to gather their rations and the set's allowance of medicinal soap. She had tried being angry, and sullen, and heedless, but under it all she was frightened.

They walked past the guard stations, across the lengthening shadows of afternoon. At the top of the Pit they stopped, looking down. But they could not delay; they descended.

The heat from the unworked day seemed to pool in the center of Screwtop. The sides of the Pit reflected heat; the metal of the machinery radiated it. The effects of temperature and noise combined synergistically.

Kylis and Gryf and Jason were all assigned to the probe crew. Across the Pit, Kylis saw the Lizard watching her with no expression at all. She looked away. Miria was on this shift, too, but Kylis did not see her.

They dragged out the new drill bit and raised it; it hung suspended above the shaft, taller than a person, narrow and dangerous. It frequently seemed to recognize the absurdity of its domestication by weak human beings, and rebelled. At Screwtop it was all too easy to ascribe personality and malevolent intentions to inanimate objects.

Shaft sections lay in racks like giant petals around the stem of the drill, fanning out in rays opposite the bubble-covered works of the first two generators. The hum of turbines spread across the floor of the Pit, through bootsoles, reaching flesh and blood and bone. To Kylis, the vibration seemed to be the anger of the wounded earth, unwillingly giving up the secrets and the energy of its interior, helpless in its resentment.

When this shaft was finished, the temperature at its bottom would approach 800 degrees C. When the crew broke through the caprock and released the pressure, that temperature was enough to turn the water below into super-heated steam. It was enough to drive another generator. It was enough, if they did not seal the caprock properly, to kill them all instantly. They would seal it, tap it, and build an air-conditioned bubble over it. Then engineers, heavily protected, would move in and build the machinery. The prisoners, who were not trusted anywhere near the generators, would move farther on to drill another well.

This was a clean way of generating power, and cheap in all but human terms. The wells eventually ran dry and power needs for North Continent grew greater. Redsun had no fossil fuel, few radioactive elements, too many clouds to use the energy of its dim star.

Gryf's job was to guide the shaft sections to the drill. Some concession was made to his value; he was not put on the most dangerous jobs. The command to begin was given, and the small contrived delays and grumblings ceased.

The work turned the prisoners almost into automata. It was monotonous, but not monotonous enough. Complete boredom would have allowed daydreams, but danger hung too close for fantasizing. Sweat slid into Kylis' eyes when she was too busy to wipe it away. The world sparkled and stung around her. The night passed slowly. The Lizard watched from a distance, a shade like any other shadow. While he was near, Kylis felt alone and, somehow, obscenely naked.

At midnight the prisoners were allowed to stop for a few minutes to eat. Gryf eased himself down the control tower ladder. At the bottom, Kylis and Jason waited for him. They sat together to eat and swallow salt tablets. The break gave them time to rest against the morning.

Kylis sat on the ground, her back against metal, half asleep, waiting for the bell. The floor of the pit was wet and muddy and littered with broken rock and ash, so she did not lie down. The Lizard had kept his distance all evening. Kylis thought he was unlikely to do anything direct while she was among so many people, though they could do nothing against him.

"Get up."

She started, frightened out of a light doze by the Lizard's voice. He and his people had their backs to her; they moved between her and Gryf and encircled him. He rose, emerging from the shadows like a tortoiseshell cat.

The Lizard looked at him, then at Kylis. "Take him," he said to his people.

"What are you going to do?" Hearing the note of panic in her own voice, Kylis clenched her fists.

"The tetras want him back. They need him. They're getting impatient."

"You're sending him home?" Kylis asked in disbelief.

"Of course," the Lizard said. He looked away from Kylis, at Gryf. "As soon as he's had enough of the deprivation box."

Beside Gryf, Jason stood up. Gryf put his hand on Jason's arm. The Lizard's people were moving nearer, closing in, should the Lizard need aid. A few of the prisoners came closer to see what was happening. Miria was among them. Kylis watched her from shadows, unseen. As the guards led Gryf away, Miria half smiled. Kylis wanted to scream with rage.

"How will they like it if you kill him?" Jason shouted.

"They take that chance," the Lizard said.

"It won't work," Kylis said. The deprivation box would never make Gryf go back to the tetras, and it could not force Kylis to do what the Lizard wanted. Even for Gryf she could not do that.

"Won't it?" The Lizard's voice was heavy and angry.

"Don't do this to him," Kylis said. "Gryf is—just being here is like being in the box. If you put him in a real one—" She was pleading for Gryf; she had never begged for anything in her life. The worst of it was she knew it was useless. She hoped bitterly that Miria was still human enough to understand what her spying had done.

"Shall I take you instead of him?" Without waiting for an answer, laughing at her, the Lizard turned away.

"Yes," Kylis said.

He swung around, astonished.

"You can put me in the box instead of him."

The Lizard sneered at her. "And send the tetras you instead of him? What use do you think you'd be to any of *them*? You could be a pet—you could be a host mother for another little speckled baby!"

Leaning down, scooping up a handful of mud, Kylis took one step toward the Lizard and threw the sticky clay. It caught him in the chest, spattering his black uniform and pale skin. Kylis turned, bending down again. This time the clay was heavy and rocky.

"Kylis!" Jason cried.

"And *you*!" Kylis shouted. She flung the mud and stones at Miria.

As the Lizard's people grabbed her, Kylis saw Miria fall. Under the spotlights the clay was red, but not as red as the blood spurting from Miria's forehead.

The Lizard, scowling, wiping clay from his chin, barely glanced at Miria's unmoving form. He gestured to Kylis.

"Put her where she can't hurt anyone else."

They marched her away, leaving Jason behind, alone.

They put Kylis in a bare cell with one glass wall and a ledge without corners and ventilation that did not temper the heat. They stripped her and locked her in. The room passively prevented self-injury; even the walls and the window yielded softly to blows.

From inside, she could see the deprivation box. It was the correct shape for a coffin, but larger, and it stood on supports that eliminated the vibration of the generator.

The guards led Gryf into the deprivation room. He, too, was naked, and the guards had hosed him down. He looked around quickly, like a hunted animal alarmed from two sides at once. There was no help, only Kylis, pressed against the window with her fists clenched. Gryf tried to smile, but she could see he was afraid.

As they blindfolded him and worked to prepare him, Kylis remembered the feel of the soft padding packed in around her body, restraining head and arms and legs, preventing all movement and all sensation. First it had been pleasant; the box was dark and silent and gave no sensation of either heat or cold. Tubes and painless needles carried wastes from her body and nourishment in. Kylis had slept for what seemed a very long time, until her body became saturated with sleep. Without any tactile stimulation she grew remote from the physical world, and shrank down as a being to a small spot of consciousness behind the place her eyes had been. She then tried to put herself in a trance, but they had expected that. They prevented it with drugs. Her thoughts had become knit with fantasies, at first such gentle ones that she did not notice. Later they separated themselves from reality and became bizarre and identifiable. Finally they were indistinguishable from a reality too remote to believe in. She remembered the encompassing certainty of madness.

Kylis watched them lock Gryf into the same fate. They turned on the monitors. If he tried to ask to be let out, the subvocalization would be detected and his wish would be granted.

After that no one came near them. Kylis' sentence in the box had been eight days, but the sensory deprivation had overcome her time sense and stretched the time to weeks, months, years. She spent her time now waiting, almost as isolated. At intervals she fell asleep without meaning to, but when she awoke, everything was always the same. She was afraid to think of Gryf, afraid to think what might be happening to Jason alone outside, afraid to think about herself. The hallucinations crept back to haunt her. The glass turned to ice and melted in puddles, and the walls turned to snow clouds and drifted away. Her body would begin to shiver, and then she would realize that the walls were still there, quite real, and she would feel the heat again. She would feel Gryf's touch, and turn to embrace him, but he was never there. She felt herself slipping into a pit of confusion and visions and she could not gather strength or will to pull herself out. Sometimes she cried.

She lay in the cell and felt herself change, felt her courage dissolve in the sterile whiteness. The floor of the cell cradled her, softly, like a soothing voice telling her she could do what was easiest, anything that would ensure her own survival.

She sat up abruptly, digging her nails into her palms.

If she believed all that, she should yell and beat her fists on the glass until the guards came, beg them to take her to the Lizard, and do what he had asked. If she did that, everything Gryf was going through and everything she had endured would be betrayed. If she decided now to let another person make her decisions for her, or if she lost herself so completely that she could not make them herself, then she had only trivial reasons for what she had done.

Her reasons were not trivial; she could not force herself to believe they were, not for Gryf's sake or Jason's or her own. Gryf had found the strength to gamble coming to Screwtop on the chance of his own freedom; Jason had found the strength to stay alive where by all rights he should have died. Kylis knew she would have to find the same kind of strength to keep her sanity and her control.

She wiped the back of her hand across her eyes, put her right hand on the point of her left shoulder, leaned against the wall, and very slowly relaxed, concentrating on the reality of each individual muscle, the touch of plastic beneath her, the drop of sweat sliding down between her breasts.

When a cool draft of air brushed her legs, she opened her eyes. The Lizard stood in the doorway, looking down at her, a black shape surrounded by concentric rings of color. She had never seen him with such a gentle expression, but she did not return his expectant smile.

"Have you decided?"

Kylis blinked and all the bright colors dispersed, leaving a stark black-clothed figure. His expression hardened as Kylis gradually returned to Redsun's hell and made the connections she needed to answer him. Her fingers were half curled. She turned her hands over and flattened them on the floor.

"You haven't changed . . . you haven't changed me."

The Lizard glared at her, his expression changing to disbelief. Kylis said nothing more. She did not move. The Lizard made a sound of disgust and slammed the door. The cool air stopped.

He did not return, but Kylis did not try to convince herself she had beaten him.

She stared through the window and willed the tetras to come and free her friend. They must keep track of what was done to him. She could not believe they did not realize what such isolation would do to one of their own kind.

She had been staring at the same scene for so long that it took her a moment to realize it had changed. Four guards came in and began to open the sensory deprivation chamber. Kylis leaped up and pressed her hands to the glass. The deprivation chamber swung open. Kylis remembered her own first glimpse of light as the guards had pulled the padding from her eyes and disconnected tubes and needles. Gryf would be trying to focus his black-flecked blue eyes, blinking; his roan eyelashes would brush his cheeks.

The guards lifted him out, and he did not move. His long limbs dangled limp and lifeless. They carried him away.

Kylis sank to the floor and hugged her knees, hiding her face. When the guards came, they had to pull her to her feet and shake and slap her to force her to stand. They led her through their compound and pushed her through the exit, locking the gate behind her. They did not speak.

Kylis stood in the harsh illumination of spotlights for a few blank moments, then walked slowly toward the comforting shadows of night. She had needed darkness for a long time. Everything seemed more than real, with the absurd clarity of shock.

She saw Jason before he heard her; he was a pale patch

on the edge of the light, sitting with his knees drawn up and his head down. Kylis was afraid to go to him.

"Kylis?"

She stopped. Jason's voice was rough, almost controlled but breaking. She turned around and saw him peering at her over his folded arms. His eyes were very bright. He pushed himself to his feet.

"I was afraid," he said. "I was afraid they'd take you both, and I didn't want to stay here alone."

"Go away."

"What? Kylis, why?"

"Gryf's dead." Desperation made her cruel. She wanted to go to him, and mourn with him, but she was afraid she would cause his destruction too. "And Gryf's the only thing that kept us together."

Stunned, Jason said nothing.

"Stay away from me," Kylis said, and walked past him.

"If Gryf is dead, we've got to—"

"No!"

"Are you sure he's dead? What happened?"

"I'm sure." She did not face him.

He put his hands on her shoulders. "We've got to get out of here before they kill us too. We've got to get north and tell people what's going on."

"Crazy!" She pulled free.

"Don't do this to me, Kylis."

His plea sliced through her grief and guilt, and even through her fear for him. She could not stand to hurt him. There was no fault in Jason, and no blame to assign to him. His only flaw was a loyalty she hardly deserved. Kylis looked around her, at the bare earth and the distant machines and the soft black ferns, all so alien. She turned back.

"I'm sorry," she said.

They held each other, but it was not enough comfort. Jason's tears fell cool on her shoulder, but she could not cry.

"There's something more than Gryf and the tetras," Jason said. "Please let me help. Tell me why all this is happening."

She shook her head. "It's dangerous for you to stay with me."

Suddenly he clenched his fingers around her arm. She pulled back, startled, and when she looked up, he scared her. She had never seen cruelty in Jason, but that was how he looked, cruel and filled with hatred.

"Jason—"

"I won't kill him," he said. "I won't . . . let me go—" He looked down and realized he was gripping Kylis' arm. "Oh, gods." He let her go and turned and walked into the forest.

Rubbing the bruise he had left, Kylis slowly looked behind her. What Jason had seen was the Lizard watching them from the gateway of the guards' enclosure. He did not move. Kylis ran.

The thick band of multicolored stars, shining through breaks in the clouds, lighted the way only where the ferns did not close in overhead. Kylis stumbled through the darkness, not even slowing for pools of rainwater. Her legs ached from fighting the suction of wet clay. Suddenly her shoulder rammed a rough stalk and her momentum spun her, flinging her against another. She stopped, gasping for breath, the air burning her throat.

Kylis straightened and looked around, getting her bearings. The stars glittered like sparks in the surface of standing water. She walked more carefully among the ferns. Her footsteps spread ripples out around her and the water sloshed gently from her boots. Only when she reached the shelter of dead ferns did she realize how silly and unnecessary it had been for her to be careful not to fall.

Inside the cool nest she lay down and composed herself. When she finally caught her breath, she began breathing slowly and regularly, counting her heartbeats. Gradually she extended the number of beats for each inhalation, for each exhalation, then she slowed her heart as well. She thought about Gryf, dying deliberately rather than giving his life to those he hated. And she thought about Jason, who would never kill even in vengeance. She was certain of that. If she were gone, he at least would be safe.

She felt the gasp reflex growing stronger and set her perception of it aside. Her breathing had ceased now, and her heartbeat would stop soon. Her thoughts slowed, her memory drifted to more pleasant times. She found herself with Gryf again, kissing him, standing in the clean hot lake, touched by spray from the overflow pipe. She smiled. A bright yellow star glittered through a gap between the ferns. Kylis let her eyes close, shutting out the last light.

Insistent hands shook her. She was dimly aware of them

and of a voice calling her name. She concentrated more strongly on dying. A fist pounded her chest and she gasped involuntarily. Someone leaned down and breathed into her mouth, holding her chin up and her head back, forcing air into her lungs. Her heart pounded. Pushing the person away, Kylis sat up angrily and almost fainted.

Miria caught her and made her lie down again. "Thank gods, I found you. I could hear you but then you disappeared."

Kylis did not answer, but only blinked her eyes against the light Miria carried. She tried to be angry at her, but it seemed too futile.

"Kylis!" Miria's voice rose in panic. "Are you there? Can you hear me?"

"Of course I'm here," she said. She felt dizzy. She wondered why Miria had asked such a silly question. "What do you mean, am I here?"

Miria relaxed and brightened her lantern. "I was afraid I'd come too late." She had a bad scar, pink and new, on her forehead.

"Get away from me. Why couldn't you let us alone?" Kylis knew she would not be able to try to kill herself again for quite a while; she had used up too much strength.

"Gryf's all right," Miria said.

Kylis stared at her. "But I saw— How do you know? You're lying!"

"He's all right, Kylis. I know. Please trust me."

"Trust you! You told the Lizard about Gryf and Jason and me! He never knew before how much he could hurt us! And now he'll go after Jason, too, so I'll—" She stopped.

"The Lizard knew you were together, but I never told him your plans. You honored me with a request to join your family. Do you think your judgment of me was so wrong?"

Kylis sighed. "It wasn't very good about the kid who turned me in." She had to rest and breathe a moment. "I saw you go inside the fence without any guards. And after that, the Lizard—"

"What was he trying to make you do?"

"Have a child and give it to him."

Miria sat back on her heels. "To *Lizard*? Gods." She shook her head in disbelief, in sympathy for Kylis, for anyone, particularly a child who would come under the Lizard's control. The yellow lantern glow glinted from the dark and lighter brown strands of Miria's hair. Kylis suddenly saw the two distinct colors for the first time. The lighter brown was not sun-streaked—it grew that way naturally.

"You're a tetra, aren't you?"

Miria looked up, and Kylis knew she would not lie. "Yes. Anyway," she said sadly, "I used to be."

"They let you go?"

"No!" She ran her hand across her hair and spoke more calmly. "No. I was never like Gryf. I never understood what he wanted, at least until a few days ago. After you and I talked . . ." She drew in a long breath. "I was in an accident. I was foolish. I took chances I had no right to take, and I nearly drowned. I died for several minutes. No oxygen could get to my brain." She looked away, fiddling with the control on the lantern. "I can remember who I used to be, but I'm not her any more. I cannot do the work I was meant for. I feel so *stupid*. . . . I was afraid you'd done that to yourself, damaged your brain."

"I'm all right, Miria." Kylis pushed herself up on her elbow, suspicion and anger forgotten for a moment. "They sent you here because you had an accident? I think that's awful."

"They could have—they should have, for what I did. But I'm here to watch Gryf."

"To protect him? And you let them put him in the box?"

"You know enough about Gryf to know . . ." Miria's voice faltered. "I was not here only to be sure he lived. I wanted to force him to go back to his team. I wanted him . . . to make up for my failure."

"Why should he be responsible?"

"Because we're the same."

"Miria, I don't understand."

"He had the same place I did, on a different team. For important projects we make two groups and keep them separate, so they will confirm each other's research or develop alternate lines. Gryf is my trans-brother. That is what we call tetras with the same parents in opposite couples." She rubbed her tawny forearm. "He was never meant to be a trans, of course, but it made no difference for the work. I crippled my team—I felt I had to keep Gryf from crippling his. I felt responsible."

"What's going to happen now?"

"Now . . ." Miria grasped Kylis' hands. "I'm not a tetra any more, Kylis. I have no vote. But I have a say, and I will do my best to persuade them to set him free."

"Miria, if you can—"

"I may do no better than keep them from sending him back here."

"Why did you change your mind?"

"Because of what you told me. I thought about it all the time Gryf was in deprivation. What I was doing to him to force him to share my loyalties—I almost killed him! I allowed the Lizard to torture him. You knew better than I what that could mean."

"But he's all right—you said he's all right."

"He is," Miria said quickly. "He will be. He overcame the drugs and put himself in a deep trance. I haven't lied. But I had nothing to do with freeing him before he died. I understand now what happened. After two days I realized Gryf must be let go, but the Lizard would not come out and he would not reply to my messages. He hoped to break you to his will and Gryf to mine. When he could not—finally he was afraid to keep Gryf in there any longer." Her voice was strained. "I've caused you so much pain. I hope some day you will all be together, and happy, and will be able to forgive me."

"Miria, I wish—"

The roar of a plane drowned out her words. Kylis glanced up reflexively. In all the time she had been at Screwtop, she had never heard or seen a plane. The North Continent was too far away, and here there was no place to land.

"I've got to go. I shouldn't have left Gryf, but I had to talk to you." Miria helped Kylis to her feet and out of the shelter. Kylis accepted the help gratefully. She felt wobbly.

They waded through shimmering shadows as Miria's light swung on her hip.

"Kylis," Miria said slowly, "I don't know what will happen. I hope I can free Gryf. I will try to help you. And Jason. But the Lizard serves the government well. They may decide he was right and I wrong. Whatever happens will take time, and I may not be able to do anything at all. I don't want to deceive you."

"I understand." Jason was in no less danger now, nor was she. But at least Gryf was safe. For a few moments Kylis could set aside her fear in the joy that he was alive.

They entered the compound's long clearing and reached the path that led toward the prisoners' shelter. Kylis saw the vertical takeoff plane hanging in midair. It slowly lowered itself, straight down, until it was out of sight behind the bank. Its engines slowed, idling.

"I can't take you to your shelter," Miria said. "I'm sorry—"

"Can I come the rest of the way—just to be sure—?"

"Gryf will already be on the plane, Kylis. You wouldn't be allowed to see him."

"All right," she said reluctantly. "I can get back myself from here."

"Are you sure? Will you be all right?"

Kylis nodded. "For now."

"Yes . . ." Miria shifted her weight back and forth, reluctant to leave her alone but anxious to meet the plane.

"Go on," Kylis said.

"Yes. I must . . ." She hesitated a moment more, then leaned quickly forward and embraced Kylis. "This is such a terrible place," she whispered. "Somehow I'll change it." She turned abruptly and hurried away.

Miria walked silhouetted against the lights and lantern. Kylis watched her go. At least she could hope now. She realized she must find Jason and tell him everything, but most particularly that Gryf was alive and out of the prison. Perhaps to be free. Then he could contact Jason's family—

"Oh, gods," Kylis groaned. "Miria! Miria, wait!" She ran toward the enclosure, stumbling from exhaustion.

She reached the bank above the fence just as Miria put her palm against the lock. The gate swung open.

"Miria!" Kylis cried. She was afraid Miria would not hear her over the engines of the plane, now inside the enclosure. But she cried out once more, sliding down the hill, and Miria turned.

She met Kylis between the bank and the fence, taking her elbow to support her as she struggled for breath.

"Jason's family," Kylis said. "Redsun thinks he's just a transient but he's not. If his people knew he was here, they'd ransom him." She remembered most of Jason's name, his family name, and told it to Miria. "Can you tell them? Just send a message?"

Miria's eyes widened. "Is that who he is?"

Kylis nodded.

"It will have to be done carefully, to keep his identity a secret, but I can do that, Kylis, yes." Then she sobered. "You'll be alone—"

"I'm all right alone. I've always been alone before. I can protect myself, but I can't protect Jason from the Lizard. Will you do it? Will you promise?"

"I promise."

Kylis clasped Miria's hands for an instant and let her go. Miria went inside the enclosure and boarded the plane. The engines screamed, and the aircraft rose, sliding forward like a hovercraft through the gateway. Clear of the fence, it rose higher until it had cleared the height of the marsh plants. It accelerated straight north.

Kylis watched it until it was out of sight. She wished she had seen Gryf, but now she believed Miria; she could believe he was alive.

In the eerie gentle light of dawn, as Kylis started away, the harsh spotlights dimmed one by one.

SCIENCE FICTION MASTERPIECES